What

The Crimson Rose

"It had bit of everything. Romance, intrigue and action, there is something for everyone." *(four stars) - Sime~Gen*

"I wept, laughed, and fell in love. The Crimson Rose is certainly not a novel to be missed." *- In the Library*

"Having never been wild over men who wrote romance, I had prepared to deliver a crushing blow of one or two roses. I found that I was wrong in my assumption... a wonderful story of love, loss and triumph." *(four roses) - A Romance Review*

Texas Thunder

"...will have you on the edge of your seat." (Highly recommended) *- Word Weaving*

"...extra spicy, yet beautiful written with passion and tenderness...has heart and soul woven into the mix." *- The Word on Romance*

"...a teasing romance for those who enjoy a speedy read laced with silky sex scenes and a thick fleshy plot." *- The Best Reviews*

Taneika: Daughter of the Wolf

"...sex, mystery and a unique plot combine for a steamy love story." *(four stars)* - *Romantic Times*

"I had thought Leigh Greenwood was the only man who wrote wonderful romance...I was wrong...R. Casteel is right there too. Not a book to be missed by any romance/paranormal reader." - *The Best Reviews*

".... exceptional, complicated, suspenseful, and highly sensual novel that you don't want to miss. Expect to be surprised. Expect to gasp in wonder and to shake your head at this writer's daring imagination." - *The Best Reviews*

"If you like shapeshifters and wolves, Taneika is a story you won't want to miss." - *The Best Reviews*

Discover for yourself why readers can't get enough of the multiple-award-winning publisher Ellora's Cave. Whether you prefer e-books or paperbacks, be sure to visit EC on the web at www.ellorascave.com for an erotic reading experience that will leave you breathless.

www.ellorascave.com

Ellora's Cave Publishing, Inc.
PO Box 787
Hudson, OH 44236-0787

ISBN # 1-84360-571-6

Mistress of Table Rock, 2003.
ALL RIGHTS RESERVED
Ellora's Cave Publishing, Inc.
© Mistress of Table Rock, R. Casteel, 2003.

This book may not be reproduced in whole or in part without author and publisher permission.

Mistress of Table Rock edited by Martha Punches.
Cover art by R. Casteel and Scott Carpenter

Warning: The following material contains strong sexual content meant for mature readers. *MISTRESS OF TABLE ROCK* has been rated Hard R/Borderline NC-17, erotic, by a minimum of three independent reviewers. We strongly suggest storing this book in a place where young readers not meant to view it are unlikely to happen upon it. That said, enjoy…

MISTRESS OF TABLE ROCK

Written by

R. CASTEEL

Chapter 1

August, 2006

His life, up until the morning of September 11, 2001, had been normal. A good career, a lovely wife and daughter with a secure future. He had put them on an airplane that morning, kissed his family goodbye, and gone to work. Now, all that remained were memories and a memorial marker in a Pennsylvania field.

He hated long drives. They gave him too much time to think about the past. He made the last turn in the road and started across Table Rock Dam.

The hot August sun cast shimmering reflections and shadows across the wide expanse of choppy water. Boats of every description sped across the surface. Powerful boats pulled large inner tubes and skiers. Wave Runners bounced across the wakes, lifting their riders into the air and crashing down again.

Scott Mathis pulled his motor home into the visitor's center parking lot and looked out over the water of Table Rock Lake.

Scott sighed wearily. Everything looked so clean. From the visitor center with its wide expanse of thick green grass and shade trees, to the small beach area located down the steep bank at the water's edge, not a sign of trash. Spotless, to the human eye, but what couldn't be seen was the reason he was here.

Scott opened the door, stepped out of his motor home, and stretched. The lean sculptured body of a swimmer showed through the thin shirt pulled tight across his chest. He checked his appearance in the side mirror. His sun-bleached brown hair hung heavy on his neck. Finger combing some errant strands, he finally gave up. Maybe it was time to get it trimmed.

Turning, he looked up at the sign painted on the vehicle's side, 'Clean Lakes'. He thought back over the last five years and all the lakes he had worked in. Diving everyday, he had removed tons of trash thrown into the water by careless and uncaring people.

Walking across the parking lot, Scott entered the Army Corps of Engineering office. Racks of lake maps and brochures local attractions filled one wall. A giant detailed map of Table Rock Lake covered another wall.

Scott approached a young woman dressed in the gray summer uniform of the park employees. He noticed the telltale washed-out reddish brown hair of a fellow water lover. His eyes were drawn to her uniform shirt.

"Excuse me, I'm Scott Mathis of Clean Lakes." He reached across the counter and shook her hand. "I called last week and was told to check in here before going to the marina."

She smiled and seemed to hold his hand longer than necessary.

"Welcome to Branson, Missouri, and Table Rock Lake, Mr. Mathis. I'm Aleecia Fields. I'm happy to meet you, even if you are early. How was your trip?"

"Long, and tiring. I've been on the road all night." Scott stifled a yawn. "As far as being early, I always show up at a new lake at least a week in advance. It gives me a chance to get the feel of things, familiarize myself with the lake and the community."

"Well," Aleecia smiled, "your reputation preceded you here. The local dive shops have been putting a list together of buddy divers who have shown an interest in helping you."

"Thanks," he gave her a practiced smile. "If I can help raise public awareness to the problems the trash causes, then all the time and effort will be well spent."

"Because of you being here, this year's 'Project Aware' weekend in September is all ready shaping up to be the biggest lake clean-up ever attempted."

Aleecia showed the same curiosity towards him that he had seen displayed countless times. They tried to figure out why he gave up his plush office in Boston and his summerhouse on the ocean, to spend his life cleaning trash from the bottom of cold, dark lakes.

"We're all set up and ready. Several local businesses have pitched in. A local car dealership has provided a vehicle for you. If you like, as soon as you get your motor home parked, I can run you over to pick up the keys. The Table Rock Inn is furnishing the RV parking and hookup."

Aleecia slipped off the barstool and walked from behind the counter. The bottom half was as nice as the top. Her uniform shorts showed a lovely set of tanned legs. Standing, she was several inches shorter than his five foot ten. She removed her dark glasses, and he stood transfixed, looking into the palest green eyes he had ever seen.

"If you're ready, I'll show you where to launch your boat." Aleecia looked up slightly and smiled. "I'll be your tour guide and point of contact while you're here. Anything you need, let me know, and I'll do my best to make your stay as pleasant as possible."

Scott nodded and stretched his hand toward the door. "Lead the way."

Stepping outside, the heat slapped him in the face. The humidity was so high it made breathing difficult.

Aleecia slipped her glasses back on against the blinding glare, turned her head towards Scott, and flashed him a beaming smile. "Follow me."

Or was it the sensuous heat, which radiated from her smile? His eyes followed her as she moved towards the white government four-wheel-drive Chevy parked in the parking lot. The view, as he watched her hips sashay and wiggle with each step, was stimulating. *Whoever has you on the hook,* he thought to himself, *sure landed one nice catch.*

Heat waves shimmered over the asphalt as he walked to his RV. He hit the remote, unlocked the door, and climbed in. He was thankful he'd left the air-conditioning on. The stark difference inside with the air-conditioning was a blessed relief. Scott pulled out onto Highway 165 and followed Aleecia the short distance down the road to the Table Rock Marina.

Scott backed his twenty-four-foot Proline Sportsman down the concrete ramp and into the water. Before he could get out, Aleecia was behind the vehicle and preparing to launch the boat. He climbed on board, and as the boat slid into deeper water, he started the engine. Blue smoke drifted over the water and the low rumble of the engine filled the marina.

"Pull around to slip number six or nine," she raised her voice over the noise.

"Did you say sixty-nine?" he yelled teasingly.

At twenty-seven Aleecia, although it had been a long time since she had been a virgin, still had one embarrassing quality. She blushed easily. The heat rose from her neck and face. His chuckle over her flustered state did little to help.

"No! I said six *or* nine." She turned abruptly and headed toward the parking slips.

Scott idled toward the slip and watched her as he kept an eye out for other traffic. This was a no-wake zone but inexperienced operators had a tendency to forget, especially on Wave Runners. He eased the boat around the dock and into the open slip. She was standing there waiting.

Turning off the ignition, he tossed Aleecia a line and watched as she expertly tied off the stern. "Thanks for the help."

"My pleasure. Like I said, I'm supposed to help you get set up and going."

"Well then, how about lunch as soon as I park the RV?" He raised an eyebrow in question. "I'm starved."

"Sure, we can stop on the way to get your car. Anything special you had in mind?" She regretted asking as soon as the words slipped from her mouth. His eyes traveled with excruciating slowness over her body.

"If you're going to keep blushing like that, we should probably make it someplace with dim lighting. I was thinking of a thick juicy steak." Scott tossed her the bow rope. Going to the low stern, he stepped onto the floating dock.

"Great, we have several places to choose from on the way." She tied off the line and fell in beside him as they walked back to their vehicles.

About a mile from the marina, Scott turned on the left signal and followed Aleecia into the parking lot of the Table Rock Inn. She bounced out of the truck and ran lightly across the gravel to the office door.

He started to get out of the seat when she reappeared and waved him around to the other side of the motel. He pulled around and backed up next to a motor home that looked permanent. "Probably the hired help," he mumbled to himself.

Scott turned off the key and stepped out. A tall, thin man, with long gray hair tied into a ponytail, stepped out of the other motor home.

"Electric hook up's on the pole behind mine. Need any help?"

"No, thanks. Just going to get the power turned on, and then go eat," Scott replied as he pulled the long black electric cord from its side storage bin.

The guy waved and started towards the restaurant with a long leisurely gait.

With the electric cord plugged in, Scott went inside to switch to external power. The door opened, and Aleecia looked hesitantly inside.

"Mind if I come in?"

"Help yourself. Give me a few minutes to change, and we can go."

Aleecia looked around the interior of the RV and noticed things were different from a normal camper. The front living space was cramped to the point of being almost non-existent. Along one wall, built-in storage cabinets took up most of the space. The kitchen was small but efficiently equipped.

Her eyes continued to roam about Scott's home on wheels.

The door to the bedroom was slightly ajar, and Aleecia's pulse quickly accelerated as she caught an unobstructed rear view of his nude body. He wrapped a towel around his waist and opened the door.

Aleecia quickly averted her gaze to focus on anything except the front of his towel.

"I know this is a resort town and dress is casual, but I've been driving most of the night."

"Take your time." She turned her head towards him, forcing her eyes to remain on his.

Despite the air-conditioning, her body temperature rose and her palms became damp as she heard the shower running.

Curiosity got the better of her, and she opened one of the storage cabinets. Wetsuits of different types and liners hung on special hangers. There was even a dry suit for cold water diving. The next door she opened revealed several drawers with an assortment of flashlights, gloves, boots, and hoods, all laid out in a disciplined and orderly manner. There were three masks in hard plastic cases, repair kits, extra straps, and equipment attachment clips.

Behind the last door, she found four buoyancy compensation vests; two of them were set up for single tanks, the other two for double air tanks with their regulators stored on the overhead shelf. His fins were held to the wall with straps.

Aleecia heard the shower stop, and quickly closed the cabinet doors.

Scott opened the bathroom door and stepped out. His wet hair hung to his shoulders and beads of water glistened on his chest, suspended in place by a thin covering of light brown hair.

Mistress of Table Rock

She swallowed nervously and allowed her gaze to drop even lower. The towel tied around his waist revealed a strip of white skin where the two ends didn't quite meet. A small part of her mind admonished her body for wanting Scott. The rest of her was drooling over what she could see and speculating on what she couldn't.

He felt the heat of her eyes on him, studying his body closely. The stirring of his loins as he hardened was automatic. What was it about her? Why was she so different, or had he been so long without female companionship that any woman would do?

"Almost ready." He turned away from her red face and closed the bedroom door behind him.

As he dressed, he thought about Aleecia. She appeared to be in her mid-twenties, surely no older. The fact that she still blushed like a schoolgirl was amusing, and he figured she took a lot of ribbing over it.

Normally his work, his passion for diving, didn't leave much time for personal involvement. It had never mattered before, but maybe at Table Rock he would make the time.

He finished dressing and found the living room empty. A thoughtful grin creased his face. The heat outside was still as oppressive as before. Aleecia had started her truck to allow the inside to cool down. Walking over to the passenger door, he climbed in. "Ready whenever you are."

Aleecia pulled out and headed back towards the dam. Table Rock was the biggest and deepest lake he had worked in. Some of this lake would not be cleaned, not when in places was two hundred feet deep.

On the other side of the dam, The Chateau by the Lake rose majestically from atop a large bluff giving it a commanding view. As they drew closer to Country Boulevard and the majority of the shows, traffic picked up considerably.

Aleecia turned off onto a side road. "Avoid the strip whenever possible—Highway 76 is bumper-to-bumper traffic from early morning until around midnight. This is a shortcut around most of the congestion."

"Thanks. What time does the restaurant open where I'm staying?"

Aleecia thought for a minute, and then answered. "I think at seven."

She caught his frown as she glanced quickly at him. "Is that a problem?"

"I guess not. Normally I'm leaving for the marina by seven."

Scott watched the road she traveled and began to get his bearings. He smiled with approval as she pulled into Applebee's, one of his favorite restaurants.

Waiting for their order, Scott sipped his beer and watched her over the rim of his mug. In the dim light, she had removed her dark glasses, and her eyes seemed to almost glow with their own light.

"Have I grown two heads or something?"

"Sorry, I'm fascinated by your eyes." Scott smiled as she turned her head and started to put her glasses back on.

"Please, leave 'em off." He placed his hand on her arm halting further movement. "They're too beautiful to hide."

Scott let out a soft chuckle as rose dust tinted her cheeks.

"What's so funny?"

"I bet you catch hell at work, as easy as you blush."

She lowered her lashes, and he watched the soft pink turn darker.

* * * * *

Scott sat at the kitchen table trying to concentrate on the lake map spread out in front of him. Instead of seeing lake bottom contours and water depths, he saw auburn hair and pale

Mistress of Table Rock

green eyes. Even after spending the afternoon together, he still knew very little about her.

Thinking back over the conversation, Scott realized he had been shrewdly manipulated. Aleecia had bewitched him into revealing everything about his life, while he knew very little about hers.

He turned his thoughts back to the map and the series of red circles that had been drawn on it. They represented areas of the lake that had been cleaned over the last several years. It was an impressive accomplishment, but for a lake this size, there was still a lot of work to be done. The yearly clean-up had been concentrated primarily around public beaches and popular dive sites.

Scott began marking several areas of the map with a blue highlighter. He had to start somewhere. Tomorrow, he would briefly check out the selected areas and plan his dive schedule around his findings.

From past experience with other lakes, he knew the media would be there to watch him pull out. He liked the publicity for the support it brought and the awareness to the community. Personally, he would have rather gone quietly out on the water without all the hoopla.

Picking up the list of divers that had been provided for him, he looked over each person's experience level. As usual, there was a wide range listed, and he could tell the new divers at a glance. They always listed the number of dives they had been on. The seasoned divers listed years, or special qualifications.

Some of the volunteers had specific dates they could dive. Most were from out of the area, and he suspected were taking vacation days from work to spend time diving. Many of them would log more dive time in the few days they were volunteering on the project than they would in a normal year.

Scott felt a pang of regret as he scanned the list. Aleecia's name was nowhere to be found, other than as a point of contact with a number where she could be reached. He had assumed, by the interest shown and the questions she had asked, that she was a diver.

Picking up his cell phone, he punched in Aleecia's number. He paused, his finger hovered over the send button. He had almost asked her to follow him home from the car dealer, but had hesitated to the point of feeling awkward. Regrettably, he had let her drive away.

In the last five years, he had never felt drawn towards any woman the way he was to Aleecia. Would she be receptive to a call? Was he moving too fast? Would it be better to play the wait-and-see game? Scott cleared the number and slowly put the phone down.

Chapter 2

Scott woke with the sun peeking over the tree-covered hills of Branson. Swinging his legs from the bed, he stood and stretched. He walked into the kitchen and stopped abruptly.

"Good morning," Aleecia knew her face had flushed beyond the point of red but she couldn't pull her eyes away from Scott. She had caught him literally with his pants down and he was good to look at. He seemed more surprised than embarrassed.

"I, ah, thought you might need some help this morning getting everything ready. Your door was unlocked."

"Morning," Scott reached for the coffeepot and filled it with water. *I'll be damned if I'm going to be embarrassed about walking around naked in my own house.*

"Help yourself, when it's done." Scott turned, giving her another full frontal view and watched her eyes travel up and down his length. Without waiting for further comment, he retreated to the small bathroom and stepped into the shower.

Remembering her scrutiny of his body, he grew hard and turned the hot water off. The cold water pelted his body but did little to cool the desire flowing through his veins.

Turning off the water, Scott reached for a towel and stepped out of the shower. The bathroom door swung open and Aleecia stood beside him with a cup of coffee in her hand.

"I thought you might want this." She held out the steaming cup.

Without bothering to cover himself, he reached over and took the cup from her. "Thanks." He took a sip and set the cup down on the counter.

As she started to walk away, his hand darted out to take hold of her arm. Scott pulled her against him and took her mouth in a hungry, bruising kiss. She pushed against his chest breaking the contact.

"I...I didn't come here for this." Her heart pounded wildly in her chest as she struggled to regain her normal breathing. She had resisted his kiss, knowing it came from the sexual frustration evident by his firm, erect penis pressed so intimately against her navel. His kiss left her weak-kneed, and without his arms around her, she would have been on the floor.

"I'm not so sure. You've gone out of your way this morning to demonstrate just the opposite."

She squirmed, trying to get loose. They were joined at the hip, separated only by the material of her uniform shorts.

Scott let her go, and she backed up against the sink. Her shirt buttons strained against the fabric with each deep, ragged breath she took. His eyes never left her as he picked up his dive watch and fastened the rubber strap around his wrist.

He closed the short distance between them, placed a finger under her chin and tilted her head up until her eyes met his. "I'm going to give you some advice, Aleecia. I suggest you listen very carefully.

"You show up, sitting in my living room again at the break of day, and I won't stop with a kiss. I sleep in the nude and I'm not going to change my habits just in case you might show up here again. Now, before I change my mind, I think you should wait out front."

With as much dignity as she could muster, Aleecia walked out of the bathroom and waited in the kitchen. She allowed a slight smile to play at the corner of her mouth. Little did he know, one more kiss and *she* would have been dragging *him* to the bed. Scott's kiss had been everything she had hoped for, and more. She felt his hunger, his desire, and although she wouldn't admit it out loud, she was thrilled.

She would have to deal with her lack of complete nudity later. That was something she must never allow.

The bathroom door opened, and Scott walked out wearing a pair of black Speedo trunks. Without looking in her direction, he stepped into his room and pulled on a pair of shorts and a tank top with the Clean Lakes logo on the back and a dive flag on the front. The white shirt contrasted wonderfully with his dark tanned skin.

Scott's voice came from the bedroom. "If you're serious about helping, there are a couple dive bags in the first cabinet."

"Okay." Aleecia found the heavy canvas bags and began filling one of them. She made a mental check off as she packed each item. Suit liner, wetsuit, mask, and buoyancy compensator vest. She picked up the booties, hood, and gloves, stuffing them in whatever space was left. The fins went into the long side pockets of the bag, and she zipped those shut. Picking up a flashlight, she flipped the switch making sure it worked before adding it to the bag.

Zipping the bag closed, Aleecia removed a regulator from the cabinet and coiled the long hoses into the small front storage compartment of the bag.

"You appear to have packed a bag before." Scott poured his cup full of coffee and leaned against the small counter.

"I've seen enough divers pack to know where it all goes."

"So, you don't dive." Scott watched her face.

"No...I don't."

Some gut instinct told him Aleecia was lying, but for now, he let it go. "Pity. You should try it."

Scott walked over to the third cabinet and took out extra batteries, marker buoys, and lights, placing them in a small backpack. "I'll get these loaded, then we can go eat."

Aleecia reached down and picked up the heavy dive bag with one hand. Carrying it duffle bag style by her side, she opened the door and stepped down. Scott's eyes narrowed as she effortlessly lifted his gear over the tailgate.

Thoughtfully, he swallowed the last of the coffee in his cup, picked up the smaller duffle bag, and stepped out into the morning sunlight. Distant clouds filled the sky with the threat of an afternoon storm.

"It's not supposed to rain 'til late in the afternoon." Aleecia stood beside him.

Her hair moved slightly in the soft breeze, and he resisted the urge to run his fingers through it. "Shall we eat?"

They walked around to the front of the motel. Scott held the front door open for Aleecia, and the mouthwatering aroma of fresh bacon and sausage floated out to greet him.

Scott sat down beside her at the table. It felt more intimate than last night's dinner. She tried to imagine what it would be like, there beside him in the murky cold depths, sharing their experiences together instead of being alone in the dark, shifting shadows.

The waitress arrived and took their order.

The pressure of his leg against hers increased, and she turned her head slightly to look at him. The air between them crackled with tension as she looked into his heated gaze. Aleecia saw his lips move, but his leg against hers blocked out the sound of his voice.

"I almost called you last night. I was hoping you might join me today."

The slow rhythmic motion of his leg aroused her. Aleecia forced her thoughts away from the scene in his bathroom, away from his leg touching sensuously against her. Afraid he would see the effect his nearness was having on her, she looked away and stared out the window.

"Did I say something wrong?" Scott frowned. "You seem distracted."

"No. I'm fine, thank you," she avoided looking at Scott. "My mind was on something...pressing."

Scott visualized pressing Aleecia into his mattress and turned his head towards her. "Which reminds me, why we are up so early and not still in bed?"

He was close enough to her face that she could feel the breath of his words gently caress her cheek. She turned her face away from the window. All she needed to do was lean over and their lips would touch.

What would it be like to wake up in his bed? The thought caused a flash of heat across her skin.

Scott's eyes were bright with passion.

Their waitress arrived, diverting further talk. Scott attacked his food, as if he couldn't wait to get away. His eyes never left hers, devouring her even as he shoveled food from his plate. Would his lovemaking be the same, wild and dominating, or would it be like their slow leisurely meal yesterday? Aleecia turned her face away lest he see the direction of her thoughts in her eyes.

"If I'm going to get any diving in before the rain," he abruptly pushed his chair back and stood, "I need to get moving."

Scott rushed back to his RV with Aleecia clinging to his hand. Flinging open the door, he pushed her inside. Following her through the door, he backed her up against the cabinets. His lips covered hers with a demanding hunger, which he knew wouldn't be satisfied with a single kiss.

Sliding a hand up her side, Scott cupped the fullness of her breast. Aleecia moaned and arched her back, urging him to continue. She whimpered as he broke the kiss. Releasing her, he stepped back.

His head spun from the intoxicating wine of her lips. Scott braced his arms against the wooden cabinet door, one on each side of her head.

"I'm too old to start playing games, Aleecia. If more of this isn't what you want, now is the time to say so."

Aleecia's breasts rose with each ragged breath. Her lips, swollen from his kiss, parted, and the tip of her sensuous tongue teasingly traced their fullness.

"If you had kissed me like that in the bathroom, you'd have been late for breakfast."

His hand curled around her neck, pulling her closer. Gently, he lowered his lips and kissed her. "We both have to be somewhere this morning."

"Then..." she was interrupted by another kiss, "we should be going."

They left the privacy of the RV, and Scott locked the door. "Will I see you after work?" He held out the spare key in his hand.

With trembling fingers, she took the key from him. Scott climbed into his truck, and she gave him a quick wave goodbye. Wanting Scott and not having him could be heartbreaking. *If he knows what I am, it could be dangerous for both of us. There is still time to back out. He won't understand, and I can't explain why, but it would be for the best.*

Clutching his key firmly in her hand, she shook off the despairing thoughts and climbed into her vehicle.

Aleecia pulled into the marina and noticed Scott's dive boat surrounded by reporters and a camera crew. *So much for an early start.* Walking past the group, she caught his eye and flashed him a smile. She laughed at his pleading 'rescue me' look as he talked with the reporters.

Going into the office, she glanced at the board. Yesterday when Scott arrived, her name had been removed from the normal duty schedule. In some ways, this was good. Whenever she wanted or needed to, she could leave. It was also bad, because now, when Scott didn't need her help, she was at the mercy of her supervisor.

"I see Wonder Boy is having his name glorified in the news again."

Gary Tillman, her supervisor, stood at the office window watching the commotion outside. His smile was more of a sneer as his jealousy of Scott reared its head. Gary had been a nice enough person at first. That is, until she rejected his sexual advances and had threatened him with a report. She had learned to tolerate him, but only from a distance.

"Aren't you supposed to be chaperoning the big celebrity?" He jerked his head in the direction of Scott's boat. "If he doesn't need you, I can always find a boat that needs to be cleaned."

"Mind if I pee first?" she headed to the restroom.

She heard a motor start, changed direction, and went outside. Scott was backing his boat out. The news team was filming his leaving. A reporter walked up to her.

"Excuse me, are you Aleecia Fields?"

Puzzled over how he would know her name she hesitated. "Yes"

"Hey guys, here she is!" he shouted to the others.

"What's going on?"

The reporters surrounded her. "Mr. Mathis said if we had any further questions, you would be happy to answer them."

She whipped her head around, and Scott gave her a big smile as he waved goodbye.

She gave the reporters a sassy smile. "I think you've just been given the slip. My only job is to make sure Mr. Mathis has everything he needs to do his work while here at Table Rock. I'm afraid I can't answer any of your questions about him or his work as I only met him yesterday when he arrived. Now if you will excuse me, I have work to do."

Aleecia grabbed the key to one of the lake patrol boats, untied it from the mooring cleats, and jumped aboard.

"Where do you think you're going?" Gary stood with his arms crossed, giving her a disapproving glare.

"I'm going out and make sure no one bothers the boat or gets too close to where he's diving." She started the engine and backed out. "Damn! Gary, who the hell used this boat last?"

"I did. Why?"

Aleecia closed her eyes against the anger, which had been building towards her boss and now threatened to explode.

Bastard, you sorry piece of shit...damn your worthless ass. She eased the boat around to the gas pump and turned the key. The deep rumble of the engine stopped. Tying up the boat, she began filling the empty tank.

"Is there a problem?" Gary asked tongue-in-cheek.

"You know *damn* good and well there's a problem. Policy is, when you use a boat, you clean it and top-off the tank. You did this deliberately." She turned her back on Gary and looked out over the lake.

One of these days, I'm going to wipe that smirk off your face and say to hell with this job.

Gary chuckled, "I could be persuaded to make it a little easier for you. Maybe even work out a few changes to the schedule."

When she ignored him and continued filling the fuel tank, he walked up and stood by the boat. It rocked with the weight of his foot on the railing.

"Suit yourself. Oh! Make sure the boat is clean before you leave today."

She listened to the sound of his footsteps as he walked away. "Screw you."

"Did you say something, Aleecia?"

Putting the cap back on the tank, she hung up the gas hose. "Yeah, I said, "See you."" Aleecia jumped back in the boat and started the engine. Removing the lanyard, she idled away from the pier.

At the edge of the no-wake area, she pushed the control to full throttle. Wind whipped at her hair as she sped over the surface of the lake. Each bounce sent spray flying over the bow. Within minutes of starting out, she was soaked.

About two miles from the marina, she spotted Scott's boat at anchor and the dive flag fluttering in the breeze. Pulling within two hundred feet of his marker buoy, she idled back and let the boat drift. Aleecia tracked his air bubbles breaking across the surface towards her boat. Scott's head broke the surface, and she saw the laughter in his eyes. He floated on his back and let the regulator drop from his mouth.

"If I had known you were coming out, I'd have waited." His grin told her he would have done no such thing.

"I noticed how quick you were to get away. You owe me one for that stunt with the reporters."

Scott smiled. "How about dinner tonight?"

"Sure, if you don't think you will be too tired after diving all day." Aleecia sat on the side of the boat and looked with longing at the greenish-blue water.

"I'm never too tired to take an attractive lady to dinner. Besides, I'm just checking out different sites today, getting the feel of the lake, and setting priorities to the areas. Pull up to my boat and check out the locations I plan to check. I would appreciate your input." Scott slipped off his gear.

She reached down, took his fins and tank, and lowered the ladder for him. Scott climbed aboard, and she idled over next to his boat. Scott placed the fender guards over the side as she pulled alongside. With a quick flip of his wrist, he had the two boats secured.

Aleecia handed his dive gear over to him and stepped onto his boat.

Scott pulled out a waterproof cylinder and shook the map from inside. "These are the initial sites I'm going to check. If you know of a particular area that I have missed, mark it on the map."

As she looked at the map, apprehension welled up inside her and lodged at the back of her throat. Her mouth suddenly dry, she swallowed with forced effort. "Why did you pick this spot?"

Scott looked were her finger pointed, pressed hard against the surface of the map. "It's a good fishing location with the shallow ledge and deep drop-off. Past dives have taught me fisherman lose things over the side quite often." He was puzzled over her nervousness. She had paled slightly, her eyes locked in on that one spot.

His interest was heightened as she added several marks on the map, all of them a great distance from the spot that still carried the imprint of her finger. Scott gave a cursory glance at the new dive sites. "These look good, I'll check them out today if I have time."

"Well, I'd better be going. You're not getting any bottom time standing here. Give me a call when you get in."

Aleecia hopped across to her boat and untied it. Starting the engine, she gave Scott a brief wave and sped off.

He watched her until she was a small speck on the horizon, lost amid all the other boats that crisscrossed the lake. Thoughtfully, Scott tapped the pen on the map, sliding his fingers slowly along the smooth surface only to flip the pen and start the process over. Tap, slide, flip, tap, slide, and flip, he looked down at the map to find the pen landed on the spot of Aleecia's interest.

Hauling in the anchor, Scott started the engine. Headed towards the next site, he spun the wheel around and pushed the control to full throttle. Slammed against the seat by the acceleration, he glanced ahead keeping a sharp lookout for other lake traffic. Most of the other boats were going in the opposite direction, back to shore.

Scott glanced over his shoulder and watched the black clouds rolling in from the east. The wind picked up as he sped away from the wooded shoreline. The waves were building, their white foamed crests' gave warning that the storm was moving in quickly. He hoped Aleecia was headed for the marina, but he wasn't going to bet on it.

He found Aleecia's boat anchored a mile from the Coombs Ferry area. It was pulled into a little cove, almost hidden from view by the branches of an old oak tree. If he hadn't been expecting to find her here, he might have easily missed it.

Idling the boat forward, he watched the depth gauge on the console. The readout jumped from a hundred and eighty feet to fifty feet in a matter of yards. Scott pulled back on the power, flipped the switch, and reached for his binoculars. The motor died, leaving only the sound of the wind and the waves smacking the side of the boat and the rocky shore.

Her clothes were lying on the console.

His breathing increased as panic began to build. Forcing himself to take slow, deep breaths, Scott dropped the anchor and reached for his tank. Sitting on the edge of the railing, he slipped on his fins and mask. Placing the regulator in his mouth, Scott rolled backward into the water.

Alarm bells sounded in his head as he began searching the area near the shore for Aleecia. Time was the enemy if something had happened to her. Each time he was forced to expand the search parameter distance from her boat, the greater his fear became. He came to the surface and gazed expectantly towards the shore, hoping to see her.

Scott held the inflation tube of his buoyancy vest over his head and released the air. He sank back into the depths, equalizing the pressure in his ears. If only there was some way to ease sorrow's tendrils as they tightened around his heart. His feet landed on the edge of the drop-off.

He entered the dark realm where daylight was reduced to near nothing, and switched on his lantern. The cold seeped through his wetsuit and sent its death chill ever deeper into his body.

The sloping rock wall he followed was surprisingly free of cans and beer bottles. He checked his depth gage and air supply. A hundred feet of water covered him, and his air was down to twelve hundred pounds. There was precious little time left to locate Aleecia and make his ascent back to the surface. The longer he spent at this depth, the longer his safety stop at fifteen feet would need to be.

He was breaking all the rules of diving. Alone, one small mistake would cost him his life, but that was the thrill he lived for, defying the odds, putting his life on the line. Daring God to take him, the way He had taken his wife and child.

His precious Melody, he could still hear her voice as she softly sang to their daughter, Lindsey, as she rocked her to sleep. Nothing could ever fill the emptiness inside that their dying had caused.

A flash of movement off to his left caught his attention.

He was no longer alone.

Scott turned toward the movement and kicked hard, propelling himself deeper. After what felt like only a few seconds, he stopped and looked around. Swinging the powerful flashlight in a circle around him, he searched for whomever or whatever he had seen.

He looked down at his gage. In shock, he realized he had descended another fifty feet and his air showed one hundred pounds remaining. Somehow, he had lost track of time. To surface without stopping from this depth meant the bends. Without immediate help, a slow and agonizing death would result when the nitrogen within his blood was released.

The bends were a horrible sight, and he knew deep down he didn't want his life to end that way.

But as he slowly rose through the dark waters toward the light so far away, he thought it fitting that he should die here. He had tempted God once too often, and this time, he had lost.

Slowly he began his ascent, looking around one last time upon the world that so few people actually saw, but where he felt so very much at home.

At sixty feet, Scott sucked on an empty tank. Even if he found a little air left in the tank due to expansion when he ascended higher, there wouldn't be enough. He had been down too deep, for too long. His lungs burned, screaming at him for air, his vision blurred.

Mistress of Table Rock

From somewhere in the distant depths he saw Melody coming for him, and then darkness descended over him like a heavy veil.

Aleecia watched his body go limp. She couldn't let him die, but to save his life, she exposed hers. After only a slight hesitation, she propelled her body through the water. Whatever the consequences for her, she would handle them later.

Coming from beneath Scott, she reached out and unbuckled his weight belt as she raced for his boat and another air tank. Arching her body, she sprang from the water. With one fluid motion, her hand grasped the railing and her feet swung sideways, landing on the deck.

Time was their enemy.

Counting off the seconds in her mind, she knew he was almost on the surface. Grabbing a spare regulator and fresh tank, she slipped the locking collar over the valve of the tank and secured it.

Scooping the tank up under one arm, Aleecia jumped back into the water and swam frantically towards Scott. He lay unconscious, face up in the water. She placed the regulator from the tank she carried into his mouth. Stripping off his vest, she reached around his chest and squeezed, contracting his lungs. As she loosened her hold, the positive pressure on the valve forced it open, filling his lungs with fresh air.

She twisted her body in the water and started kicking, taking Scott back to the edge of the drop-off. Aleecia felt the strain in her legs as she kicked against the buoyancy of Scott's wetsuit. Diving with her arm around him, while trying to hold onto the tank and keep air flowing in his lungs demanded more than she thought she could deliver.

Reaching the bottom, Aleecia wedged Scott's legs and the tank under an old tree limb. She felt the side of his neck and found a weak but steady pulse. *Come on, breathe! Damn you, Scott! Don't you dare quit on me.* Straddling his waist, she resumed the chest compressions using a slow steady rhythm. *Damn it breathe!*

This water world had always been her real home, and in its cold, dark depths, her mother's words came back to her.

If they find you, they will either use you or kill you. Either way, you will be dead. Anyone who knows your secret will vanish, snuffed out like a candle without thought or emotion.

Chapter 3

He was swimming in blackness, struggling to reach the surface, but he couldn't move. *Is this what it's like to be dead? If I'm dead, why do I feel the cold water?*

Breathing! I'm breathing! A steady stream of air came from his regulator. He opened his eyes. The shadowy figure of a woman swam away from him towards the surface. This had to be a dream. She wasn't wearing any dive gear.

His vest was missing and his weight belt lay across his chest. What was happening? Where was he? The questions came, swirling through his mind.

Scott checked his depth and pressure gauge. He had a full tank, which further confused him. Removing some of the weight on his belt, he picked up the air tank and began crawling up the slope towards the surface. Using the rocks to anchor himself at fifteen feet, he began the decompression stage of his dive.

Waiting as the clock slowly ticked by the minutes, he tried to again piece together what had happened. Could the woman who rescued him be a free-diver? Was it Aleecia? Why hadn't she stayed and used some air from his tank?

Scott searched the water around and above him. Would she come back?

He checked the dive computer in his watch and knew it was safe to ascend to the surface. Dropping the weight belt, he floated upward into the choppy waters and pelting rain of the storm.

His boat bounced and bobbed around like a cork. Scott grabbed a rung of the ladder only to have it ripped out of his hand. Forced to let go of the tank, he watched it sink. Reaching the safety of the deck, Scott staggered to a seat and held on as the waves once again tried to throw him back into the lake.

If the lake was this rough here in the narrow, protected cove, then trying to make it back to the marina now was going to be next to impossible.

"Aleecia!" Frantically, Scott looked to the place where her boat had been. *"Damn it!"*

She was gone. Her smaller boat didn't stand a chance in the rough waves that he knew were being kicked up on the open water. He started the motor and raised the anchor.

Grabbing a life vest, Scott applied power and left the shelter of the cove. Hugging the eastern side of the channel, he searched the shoreline and the open water around him. She was a smart woman. Why would she try to handle her boat in this chop? His boat was twice the size of hers, and he was already having difficulty.

Reaching the opening of the large cove, the waves increased, and his boat rocked wildly with each swell. Swinging the wheel to starboard, Scott headed into the crests of the waves, his eyes searching for any sign of her boat.

Thunder rolled across the water, and lightning lit up the darkened sky. A jagged fork of death streaked overhead and a tree burst into flames on the opposite bank. The acrid smell of brimstone and scorched timber drifted across the water.

Aleecia's boat was beached in a shallow, wind-protected finger of water. She was sitting in the seat, unmindful of the rain or the storm. Her clothes were plastered to her skin.

She didn't seem happy to see him approach.

Dropping the anchor, the boat rocked with the rolling swells. For several seconds he stood watching her. "We need to talk!" Scott yelled over the noise of the storm.

Aleecia stood, stepped into the shallow water, and waded out to where she could swim. Her strokes were smooth and graceful as she swam towards his boat. As she climbed aboard, Scott noticed the distinct outline of her breasts. Nipples, stimulated from the cold, puckered the material leaving nothing to the imagination.

"Come below and get out of the rain. I'll get you a blanket, you must be freezing." He stepped back so she could pass.

"I'm fine. Besides, I'll just get wet again...when I swim back." She opened the door and went down the three steps into the cabin.

Closing the door behind him, Scott waited until she slowly turned around. "Sure you don't want a blanket and to get out of those wet clothes?"

"I'm sure. You said we needed to talk."

She folded her arms under her breasts, which increased his awareness of them and her. They were small but perfectly shaped, like the rest of her. This was a new Aleecia from this morning's sensuous, flirting woman. Weary but watchful with every nerve on alert, she waited for him to begin.

"I want to thank you for saving my life today." Scott noticed the guarded expression sweep across her face.

Aleecia cocked her head and her eyebrows rose.

"Come on, Aleecia, don't look so innocent. You lied to me about your not diving. Only an experienced free-diver could have done what you did."

"What did I supposedly do?"

"Damn it, Aleecia, it's just you and me, there's no one else here. I don't know everything that happened, but if you didn't rescue my stupid ass, then who did? A mermaid?" He opened a cabinet, pulled a bottle of Scotch from the shelf, and took a large swallow. The liquid burned, he gasped and started coughing.

"Okay, so I free-dive, and yes, I brought you the fresh tank. You're welcome. Now let's just forget about it, shall we?" She felt trapped, afraid he would ask more questions than she was willing to answer.

Aleecia started to leave.

His hand darted out to clasp her arm. "Not so fast. You're partially to blame for my stupidity today. If I hadn't seen you below me, I wouldn't have gone so deep or run out of air. I thought something had happened to you."

"I'm sorry."

"Aleecia," his tone was softer, warmer. "Why did you leave? If you needed air, you could have used my spare regulator. When you didn't come back, I thought I had imagined it. Later, when I surfaced, and saw your boat was gone...I felt angry."

Scott's grip on her arm loosened. She could have easily broken the contact, but she didn't. With a gentle tug, he brought her closer.

Run, get away, this is madness. Her mind sent out its warnings but she chose not to heed them. She could only watch as his mouth descended on hers. She placed her hand on his arm and felt the corded muscle through his wetsuit. His lips took hers, and she tasted the bite of the Scotch that still lingered on them. The light pressure of his tongue made known his desire, and she parted her lips allowing him to enter.

Aleecia shut off her mother's warnings and her years of training. Her parents were gone. Somewhere in life there had to be someone she could trust. She didn't want to think of the possibility of killing Scott, not after saving his life. If it came to that, could she do it again?

Shutting the thought from her mind, she allowed the feel of his mouth on hers and his hand on her breast to sweep her, if but for the moment, into the sensuous fog of passion.

The contact of his hand on her bare skin brought her protective senses into full alert. Scott had slipped his other hand under her shirt and was working his way up her back. Breaking the contact, Aleecia reached up and began unzipping his wetsuit top.

Her fingers trembled, and she lowered her eyes. She wanted this, but it had to be on her terms.

"You're nervous." Scott peeled the jacket from his shoulders and pulled his arms free of the tight sleeves.

"A little," she confessed. "It's been a long time since I was involved with anyone."

Squatting down he opened a cupboard door, Scott rummaged around for several seconds before finding what he was looking for. Setting the dusty box on the counter, he looked up smiling. "Me, too."

Picking up the box with shaky fingers, Aleecia lifted the cover. Two of the small foil packages were missing. "All this proves is that you only used two condoms."

"Think what you want." He stood, unfastened the Velcro strap at his shoulder and slid the top of the thin Farmer John's down to his waist. "The question is, do you trust me?"

She looked into his eyes and saw compassion, warmth, and understanding. He was giving her time to back out. The evidence of his wanting her showed plainly against the skintight suit. Her fingers crept to the top button of her blouse and began loosening it.

"Yes." She let the shirt hang open but did not remove it. She resisted the urge to cover herself from his hungry eyes.

"I'm sorry," she felt heat flush her skin. "They aren't very big."

"They're perfect."

Reaching out, Scott cupped her breast in his hand. The touch of his rough palm on her nipple sent out rippling currents of pleasure that emulated her first few seconds in the water, inhaling its life-giving flow.

Drawn to his body by the magnetism of his bare skin, she was again in his arms. Her hands slid down his ribs and gripped the rubber fabric of his wetsuit and the thin liner. Impatiently, Aleecia pushed them lower past his hips, revealing the swollen length of his hardened cock.

With the wetsuit down around his knees, she knew Scott was helpless. Aleecia gave a push on his chest and sent him tumbling backward onto the bed.

"Well, now that you have me at a disadvantage…"

Scott's deep and sensuous laughter further excited her.

What are you going to do about...? She closed the door to her fears.

Forcing herself to go slowly, Aleecia unbuttoned her shorts, letting them fall around her ankles. His voice faded with the last of the sentence formed on his lips.

The white cotton panties she had on were old, thin, and nearly transparent, but Scott didn't seem to notice. His eyes were riveted on the small triangle of russet curls between her legs.

Looking at Scott, she wondered if she was going to be able to do this. Her first and last experience with sex had been with a young sailor. At the time, she had thought he was huge—now, reality stood proudly before her.

"Will it fit?"

He tried to contain the laughter but it spilled out and filled the small cabin of his boat. "Come here," Scott reached out to her. "I'll show you."

Scott took her hand, pulling Aleecia onto the bed. Her shirttail fluttered open, and he glimpsed a wide scar below her ribs. *That must be why she tensed up, why she's leaving her shirt on.* Compassion overflowed his heart. Kissing her forehead, he left butterfly kisses on her eyelids before settling on her lips.

Aleecia's arms crept around his neck pulling him closer. The tip of her tongue hesitantly touched his lips. Scott captured her tongue and drew her deeper into his mouth. With her breasts pressed tight against his chest, a strange feeling of completeness came over him.

The wetsuit locked his legs together, restricting his movement. He kicked and pulled with his feet, trying to work free. Breaking the kiss, Scott growled with pent-up frustration.

Sitting up, he shoved the constricting rubber suit down each leg and pulled his feet free. Scott wadded it up in a ball and tossed it aside. Turning back toward Aleecia, he paused to look at her.

His eyes drank in the sleek power of her well-defined legs. Picking up her foot, Scott kissed her toes. Old scars caused by coral crisscrossed the calloused soles of her feet. His hands slid up her ankle gently massaging her calf. The muscles tensed beneath his fingers before slowly relaxing.

Aleecia closed her eyes and a soft, sensuous smile played across her face. A low moan escaped her slightly parted lips.

"Oh...that feels good." Her mother had given her massages, but nothing like this.

Lying almost nude before him, having his hands explore her body and knowing he was going to make love to her, filled her with nervous excitement and expectations. Heat radiated from his fingers making her body pliant to his erotic touch.

Scott's fingers slipped beneath the fabric and brushed the soft hair covering her pussy. She waited, wanting his intimate touch, only to have his hand slide like hot silk down her other leg. Melting from the slow firm circular motion of his fingers on her skin, liquid fire pooled between her legs. A gentle tug on the last remaining barrier caused her to lift her hips and the material was swept away.

He shifted on the bed and Aleecia heard the crinkle of foil as he paused to put on the condom.

His gentle probing caused her legs to spread. Aleecia opened her eyes to stare into his, only inches away, and she took his lips in a fierce kiss devouring his mouth. A deep moan of surprise and pleasure rushed from her throat as she felt him slip past her inflamed folds and sink his hard shaft deep within her.

"See," he whispered in her ear, "I fit perfectly."

Aleecia felt the smile form and spread across her face. "I like the way you fit inside me."

"Me, too."

Scott licked her neck, the side of her face and took her lips in another searching invading kiss. Ever so slowly, he began to move inside her. With each new thrust into her secret depths, her passion level rose. Driven by a wild need to let go, Aleecia locked her legs around Scott's and twisted. His look of surprise rewarded her as she looked down at him.

Scott's hands found her breasts and his fingers pinched the hardened nipples. Sensitive nerves sent out shock waves that gathered below her waist. Reeling with the force of her release, a large whoosh of air exploded from her lungs in a cry of passion. Aleecia slumped forward on his chest. With her head nestled on his shoulder, her body shook and trembled.

His world exploded, caught up in the hurricane force of his own shattering climax.

"Wow!" Aleecia snuggled against him.

"Yeah," he whispered into her hair. "Wow."

"How did you get this?" Her fingers traced the thin scar below his left eye.

"A barracuda wanted my facemask and was too impatient to wait 'til I took it off. If that wasn't bad enough, the blood drew a shark into the area. If I had been ten feet further from the boat, it would've been over."

"I'm glad you made it," she purred against his cheek.

"Me too." Scott closed his eyes basking in the afterglow of her passion.

Chapter 4

Scott's mind blocked out all but the last few seconds of what was the greatest sex he had experienced since his wife's death, and possibly in his whole life. Did he imagine it? Glancing around the cabin, he checked the windows and the door. They were closed against the storm's pounding rain.

No! It happened!

He closed his eyes against the nagging little voice inside his head. Seldom had his inner perception and constant companion been wrong—when he had taken the time to listen.

Shutting the voice out had almost cost him his life. He wasn't going to make the same mistake twice in the same day. He knew he was right. In that brief moment as she had cried out with the force of her climax, there *had* been a whisper of hot air caress his hand.

Aleecia had been riding his cock with wild abandon. One hand was on her waist while the other had been in firm contact with her breast. Where had the soft kiss across his flesh come from? Scenes of the day flashed across his mind like separate pieces to a picture puzzle.

"Don't move," he kissed the top of her head. "I'll be right back."

"Okay," Aleecia whispered against his damp skin.

Scott slid out of from under her. Aleecia's shirttail crept up revealing several inches of two wide, dark pink scars. He stood looking down at her. *Impossible!* Turning, he stepped towards the head and froze.

Impossible or not, the scars had moved, rippling with each breath she took. In shock, Scott stumbled drunkenly into the small head and closed the door. Splashing cold water over his face, he looked in the small mirror. Nothing had changed, yet it had. Drastically.

The puzzle flew together as separate pieces made an unbelievable picture in his mind. It wasn't complete, and his better judgment wasn't sure if he wanted to see the finished one.

Who...or what was Aleecia? Mermaid? Freak? Mutant? He rested his head against the mirror.

Run, man, just as fast as you can.

Scott sighed and shook his head. "I can't."

The laughter inside his head hurt. *You've been running since your wife died.*

"I know."

A knock on the door brought his mind back to the present and shut out the tormenting voice.

"Scott, are you okay?"

He dried his face and forced a smile. Checking in the mirror one last time, he opened the door.

"Never better."

She stood, fully dressed before him, and all he could think about were her...*gills*. Did they hurt? What did it feel like to breathe underwater?

"The storm has passed. It's time I should be going. Thank you," she leaned forward and placed a kiss on his cheek, "for the wonderful time."

Aleecia opened the door and sprang quickly up the stairs. He felt the boat rock as she dove over the side.

Picking up his glass, Scott drained the contents. The warm amber liquid did nothing to dispel the fog within his mind. He reached for the bottle, filled the tumbler, and with leaden feet turned to the ladder. Up on deck, a fine mist of rain covered his flesh. Dropping onto the bench seat with a groan, he closed his eyes and sipped his drink.

"Now, what do we do?"

Silence descended over the little cove. The wind died, and the clouds parted above him. The afternoon sun warmed his chilled flesh. A rainbow appeared, rising out of the water fading into the sky.

* * * * *

Aleecia sat by the phone, her fingers tapping out the beat of a country song playing on the radio. For the tenth time in as many minutes, she looked at the clock. It was getting late, and Scott hadn't called. Should she try calling him?

He didn't appear to be the kind of man that would walk away after getting what he wanted from a woman. Deep inside, the idea had taken root that their time on the boat was as special for him as it was for her. A gnawing fear crept in. She picked up the phone and dialed.

"Table Rock Inn."

"Room twelve please." She tried to keep the impatience from her voice.

"One moment...I'm sorry, Scott doesn't seem to be in. May I take a message?"

Aleecia dropped the phone and ran out the door.

Bypassing her car, she ran down the hill to the darkened pier. She stepped into the small windowless building at the end of the wooden walkway and began stripping off her clothes. Normally, she didn't wear any gear but tonight, she needed speed. Slipping the booted fins over her feet, Aleecia opened a trap door and disappeared into the water.

Strong, powerful kicks propelled her through the water. Submerged trees and rocks loomed before her. Her extra-sensitive eyes alerted her to the dangers. She twisted her body around and through the debris with the agility of an otter.

Scott's boat rested at anchor in the cove. It was dark and silent as she climbed the ladder. Aleecia stepped onto the boat and saw his nude body on the deck. A gentle swell rocked the boat sending an empty bottle rolling against her feet.

"Damn it!" She had been stood up for a bottle of Scotch. Aleecia swung a leg back over the side. "I hope you catch cold and die." Regretting the harsh words, Aleecia turned from leaving, bent down, grabbed his shoulders and half carried, half dragged him down the three short steps into the cabin.

Reaching underneath his legs, she lifted him onto the bed and covered him with a light blanket. He would have one hell of a headache in the morning. She turned to leave.

"You came back?" His speech was slurred, barely understandable. "You're beautiful."

"And you're drunk. Sleep it off. Things will look better in the morning."

"Wove...who did dis to you?" He fumbled for the light switch.

Aleecia tensed, her body tingled and stood ready to meet the threat. Her heart throbbed with despair.

"Did what, Scott?" Years of training took over. Her hands, hardened against sand bags and used to breaking thick boards, straightened into deadly weapons.

"Tell me, Aleecia," he looked at her blurred double image standing by the bed. "Tell me, and I'll kill him with my bare hands."

Even in his drunken state, his words were menacing.

"Who forced you to have the surgery? Don't try to deny it. I saw your back...what sick *bastard* could do this to you?"

"I didn't have surgery." Aleecia's heart broke. Her muscles tensed, ready to defend her life. "I was born with them."

"I'm sorry." Scott struggled against the booze to sit up. "If you're in trouble or need help," the cabin spun. He spread his hands wide upon the bed waiting for the dizziness to stop. "I'll do whatever I can."

"Why should you care?" The years of bitterness crept into her voice.

"First, tell me why you came back." Scott resisted reaching for her. He wanted her again. At this moment, with Aleecia standing in all her naked beauty before him, it didn't matter what she was.

"I got worried when you didn't show up at the motel." Vivid scenes of her parent's death flashed before her eyes.

"Did you honestly think I would go back into the water today after coming so close to meeting Neptune in person? Besides, I lost the other tank climbing onboard."

"No," she laughed nervously. "I guess I overreacted. I'll find your gear for you."

"I don't think you ever react without reason. Your action this afternoon was quick, decisive, and correct. Swimming out here tonight…exposing yourself completely was an act of desperation and fear, for me. Tell me, Aleecia. Does knowing you…place my life in danger?"

"Yes, I'm sorry. You should leave Table Rock. Find another lake, another woman and forget you ever saw me, deny you ever knew me."

Yeah, man like I said before, run. Get the hell out of Dodge and don't look back.

"It's too late, I'm staying."

Ahh shit! Don't listen to me.

"Why? It's difficult to put into words, but I do care."

"Scott, it's not so simple. Mentioning these," she turned and gave him a full view of her back, "to anyone could get you killed."

Each gill ran from the center of her back along the bottom rib. She exhaled quickly and they fluttered.

He felt her loneliness and heartache. Scott reached out to her.

Hey! Don't I have a say in this?

"Come here."

Aleecia took his hand and allowed him to draw her to the bed. Part of her wanted to be accepted, loved without regard to what she was. The other side of her, the trained warrior, was cautious and on alert.

Scott pulled her onto his lap and slipped his arms around her. "When you're ready you can tell me about it. I'm not going to tell you I understand or I know how you feel, cause I don't. But if you let me, I'm here, and your secret is safe with me."

Tears welled up in her eyes. Aleecia blinked them away, slid her arm around his neck, and gave him a tender kiss. With her breast flattened against his chest, and his hard erection pressed against her leg, the kiss turned heated, explosive, full of passion and need.

Scott! Hello, remember me?

The tension she had been under melted. Pent-up energy pulsated through her body. Her tongue demanded access to his mouth. She pushed Scott back on the bed and straddled his waist. Grabbing his cock, Aleecia placed its swollen tip inside her and thrust her hips against his.

Hey, pal, aren't you forgetting something?

Scott's body matched her driving thrusts. Her fingers entwined in his hair. She swallowed his moans of pleasure. This sex was different. It wasn't the lack of foreplay or even the frenzied pace. He couldn't put his finger on it, and the shudder of her climax evaporated further thought.

Her hot wetness bathed him. His body tensed and stiffened. Pushed over the edge, he felt his own release fill her to overflowing. Looking at the table, Scott groaned in despair.

"Great!" *Yup, ole buddy, you done screwed the pooch this time.*

The box of condoms stood accusingly on the nightstand.

"Yes, it was," she snuggled in the comfort of his arms.

"I didn't have any protection on." Scott held her close. "I'm sorry."

Hey, I tried to warn you, but did you listen? No!

It took a moment for the words to sink in past the euphoria she felt. In shock, she sat up and looked down at his cum-covered cock. "Shit!"

In despair, she sat on the bed. "It's all my fault," she whimpered.

"No, it's not," Scott laid a comforting hand on her arm. "We got carried away with the moment. Besides, what's the chance of getting pregnant the first time?"

"I don't know…but if I am…what kind of life can I give a child? Living like I do, hiding in fear of my life and those around me."

He gathered her close and kissed her lightly on the head. "Whatever happens, we will face it together. If you'll let me." His fingers traveled lightly over her back and along the thick flap of skin covering her gills.

"You want to tell me about it?"

A deep sigh sent her breath stirring across his chest and kissed his fingers. "Not right now, but I will."

Hot scalding tears on his chest surprised him. That she had shared her fears with him and had allowed him this close was sobering.

Had his wife and child found comfort in the arms of a stranger as they plunged to the ground? Amid the chaos and terror, did they find peace? He could only hope.

Aleecia slept, her breathing slow and deep.

* * * * *

In the haze of predawn, amidst a heavy fog, Aleecia slipped over the side. She inhaled, feeling the slight burn as the cool water filled her lungs. Had last night been a mistake? Was her loneliness to blame for her rash decisions?

Scott's air tank lay on the bottom. She marked the location in her mind and began searching for his other tank and vest. She swam across the lake and began searching the west bank.

The shoreline was a mass of stirred-up silt from the storm. She had few limitations under water, but seeing through mud was one of them. Cautiously, she moved forward. Tree stumps and pier pylons sprang up before her face. Aleecia slowly surfaced.

Two piers down, Scott's buoyancy vest and tank bobbed in the water. The bright neon-yellow tank was like a beacon on a dark night. If someone found it an alarm would go out to the lake patrol.

She swam towards it with only her eyes above water. Heavy footsteps on the pier above her alerted her to danger. Aleecia quietly submerged and waited, hoping against all odds the fog would hide Scott's tank from view.

The muffled steps of the person running penetrated the water. Rising from the muddy bottom, she watched the man wade out and pick up Scott's gear. A breeze swirled the fog away. The man looked up, his eyes opened wide and he dropped the vest.

With a startled gasp, Aleecia ducked below the surface and swam. Fear dogged her silent wake. A school of Bluegill scattered around her. Reaching the drop-off, she followed it to the bottom. She had to get back to Scott and warn him.

Retrieving his tank, Aleecia surfaced behind Scott's boat.

He was on deck when she arrived. Handing him the tank, she scampered aboard.

"Thanks for finding the tank." Scott gave her a kiss.

"I found the rest of your gear, but an early morning fisherman got to it first. He also spotted me."

"How did you let that happen? Do you think he recognized you?" He followed her into the cabin.

"I was careless." She spun around. "Do you think I just up and decided to go out and show myself to the world? Hey! Look at me, it's Bass Girl to the rescue."

"I didn't mean it the way it came out." He reached for Aleecia.

She backed up against the bed. "I should hope not. Give me credit for having a higher IQ than my bra size.

"I've got to get home," she started to leave. "I may have to pack and leave in a hurry."

"Just where do you think you would go," Scott blocked her way. "Use that high IQ of yours to stop and think. You start running now and it'll never end. We stay right here and you," he tossed her a towel, "get dried off. Anyone asks, you spent the night here and *haven't* left."

"Okay, Mr. Know-it-all. How did I get out here like this?" She spun around. "Explain the absence of any clothes."

Scott handed her a T-shirt. "Here, put this on. Anyone shows up and finds you dressed in this, isn't going to question where you've been or what you've doing."

Scott grew hard watching her dry her hair. The whine of a high-speed motor and a siren echoed across the lake. "Don't comb your hair. Leave it messed up. Gives you an 'I got laid this morning' look."

He walked up on deck. "Oh, one other thing. Try to act like you enjoyed it."

The damp towel landed across his face.

Scott opened a bottle of water and tipped it to his lips. "You have a coffee pot at home? I could sure use a cup right now."

"Yeah, and I have a big comfortable bed, too."

Scott smiled. "Maybe the coffee can wait."

"Maybe."

He watched the boat approaching, its bow high in the water. The light bar across the top was lit with red and blue flashes.

The guy driving the boat wore of look of relief. He pulled along side. "Mr. Mathis, I'm sure glad to see you. I'm Gary Lawson with the Corps of Engineers. When you didn't show up last night and we got the call this morning that a set of dive gear had been found, we feared the worst." He pointed to the tank and vest lying on the deck of his boat. "I hope these are yours."

"Yes, they're mine. Thanks. I lost the vest yesterday in the storm. I was about ready to look for it."

"I've called in the rescue divers. Seems the guy that found your gear also saw someone in the water. One second the person was there, the next nothing. It was foggy, and he wasn't sure if it was a man or a woman."

"Damn, sorry to hear it. Sure, I'll be glad to pitch in. I'll just get my things together, and I'll be over."

"Oh! When did you last see Aleecia? I tried calling her this morning when she didn't show up for work and didn't get an answer. I hope whoever the guy saw in the water wasn't her."

Scott laughed. "I can promise you, Aleecia is not lying on the bottom of the lake."

Gary looked confused.

"How can you be so sure? She's kind of flaky. I wouldn't put it past her to do something stupid like drowning."

"So, I'm *flaky!*" Aleecia stepped onto the deck.

Gary's eyes got big as he looked at her. Scott grinned at her performance. She looked sexy as hell in his shirt. Her nipples were outlined against the white material. Gary's demeanor changed to anger.

"Where the *hell* have you been?" Gary snarled.

"Not that it's any business of yours, but I've been right here." Aleecia smiled. "We overslept." She walked over and placed her arm around Scott's waist. Her fingers played suggestively with the waistband of his swimsuit.

"Get dressed." Gary ordered. "We have a possible drowning victim across the lake."

"We'll be over there in a little while. This won't be a rescue," Scott said with the voice of experience. "If there is someone on the bottom, it will be a search and recovery operation. I'll run Aleecia home for a fresh change of clothes and meet you at the site."

"If this person drowns, it'll be your fault." Gary fumed.

"My fault?" *What is this guy, the village idiot?* "How," he laughed, "is this possible person all of a sudden my responsibility?"

"There's still time, *if* we hurry."

Gary was fidgeting, anxious to do something even if it was wrong.

"Check your watch, Gary." Scott's patience was wearing thin. "Now, you tell me. Is it possible for a person to survive for over half an hour submerged under water? Add to that the time it would take to get over to the location, set up, and actually find the person in zero visibility." Scott shrugged.

"But we have to do *something*." Gary argued.

"Go mark the area where the person was last seen and keep sightseers away. This will help protect the divers in the water as well as the victim."

Scott started hoisting the anchor. "Go on, it won't take but a few minutes to get dressed and moving. By the time we get there, I'll be ready to enter the water."

Gary pushed the throttle open, and the boat spun in a tight circle headed toward the other side of the lake.

Aleecia doubled over with laughter.

"Pompous ass." Scott set the anchor on the deck. With a last look at Gary's retreating boat, he walked to the control panel and started the engine.

Chapter 5

Aleecia directed Scott to her pier. Before his boat had stopped moving, she hopped onto the wooden walkway. "I'll be right back." She ran up the short flight of steps and disappeared through the door of a small clapboard shack.

Scott tied off the boat and waited. Curiosity got the better of him, and he stepped onto the pier. The little shack was out of place. Although it looked old and weather beaten, the nails weren't. Opening the door, he found her clothes lying on the floor.

"There's a hidden trap door. Unless someone is paying close attention to when I enter and leave the shed, nobody should become suspicious." She stood by his side.

He hadn't heard her approach and her nearness startled him.

"I have a waterproof bag underneath the floor with clothes, new identification and money."

"You like living like this?" He placed his arm around her and kissed her forehead.

"No, but I'm used to it. Are you ready to join the search for the vanishing swimmer?"

Scott laughed, "Sure, let's go."

Aleecia drove while he slipped into his wetsuit and vest. He was ready to slip over the side when they arrived. Several other boats were in the area with divers getting ready. He watched two divers flip backwards over the side, briefly surface, and submerge from sight.

"Confusing as everything is, I have no doubt who is in charge." Gary immediately headed in their direction. "The jackass ran right over two divers in the water."

Gary pulled up close and stopped. "About time you got here. As you can see, I've kept the sightseers back and have divers in the water." His chest puffed up with importance.

"A lot of good it did." Scott's anger continued to smolder. "A boat just passed over the air bubbles of two divers." He glared accusingly at Gary.

Gary whipped his head around. "Where is it? I'll give the bastard a ticket."

"If you didn't see it, better let Aleecia write the ticket."

Gary handed the ticket book across to Aleecia, who began filling it out. The corner of her mouth twitched. She glanced up. Her eyes danced with suppressed pleasure.

He took the ticket book back. "Thanks, I'll make sure it doesn't happen again." Gary glanced down at the piece of paper in his hand, "What the hell? Is this some kind of joke?" He waved his arm around in a wide sweep of the area. "You can't write me a ticket. I'm in charge here."

"Then act like it." Scott's voice shook with suppressed rage. "No one takes a boat into the search area without a safety spotter. Not even *you*. If those divers had been ready to surface, one or both of them could've been killed by your stupidity."

"You can't talk to me like…."

"I just did, and if you don't shut up, I'll do it in front of everyone here. You want to do something, then keep the boats, all of them, out of the search area. You bring this boat inside search parameters again, and I will personally throw your ass over the side."

Gary looked stunned.

"It's obvious to me you know nothing about a search and recovery operation. I do. So do as you're told, and stay the *hell* out of my way." Scott took an air-operated horn from a bracket on the side of the console. Sticking it in the water, he gave two long blasts.

Divers began popping to the surface, and he picked up a bullhorn. "May I have your attention? I'm Scott Mathis. For those of you who don't know me, I'm a Master Diver and instructor. I'll be in charge of the actual search. Those of you in the water already, swim over and relax until everyone has finished getting dressed. Everyone else, when you are ready, would you please join the rest around my boat."

Gary idled off. Scott could tell by the set of his shoulders he didn't like this at all. *Tough.*

Scott turned his attention to the divers assembled around his boat. "Those of you who are rescue diver trained, please raise your hand."

About half the divers raised a hand out of the water.

"We are going to pair off with a non-rescue diver between trained divers. The search will start close to the pier where the swimmer was supposedly seen. Visibility, as you probably already know, sucks. We will be conducting an abreast line search. Ropes will not work due to submerged trees and pylons. It will be a slow methodical sweep down to this point.

"When you hear a blast of the horn, surface and the line will pivot and search a new section. If you should have to surface early, make sure the divers on each side of you know and close the gap. For this to work, you must maintain contact with the man next to you.

"What we don't want to do is lose somebody down there. So, I want you to sound off with a number starting with you," he pointed to the diver nearest him. "You're number one."

When all the searchers had called out, Scott found he had fifteen people, counting himself. "When we surface, we take a count." He scanned the faces of the divers and noticed apprehension in a few faces. "Relax, I don't expect to find anyone down there. Remember to watch your air. Any last questions?"

Scott gave a slight nod to Aleecia, placed the regulator in his mouth, and rolled backward into the water.

Aleecia heard the sound of a motor idling close by. She turned and Gary gave her a spiteful, hate-filled glare.

"After today, you're no longer assigned to working with the high-and-mighty Mr. Mathis. And if you know what's good for you," he snarled, "you won't have anything more to do with him."

She laughed, "Who the *hell* do you think you are? You might reassign my work, but I'll be damned if you're going to tell me who I can or can't see after hours."

A boat with reporters from the local television station arrived and Gary headed off to meet them. Aleecia shook her head in disgust and turned her attention to the line of air-bubbles making its way toward her.

Knowing she was the one responsible for the time and effort spent on the search ate at her conscience. She appreciated Scott's willingness to shield and protect her, but was she asking too much? With Gary's increased hostility toward her, maybe it was time to move on. The thought of leaving Table Rock Lake saddened her.

This section of the lake was relatively free of divers. She could swim without fear of discovery and nobody knew or if they did, they had forgotten about the old mine shaft at the bottom of the lake.

A diver surfaced, called out his number, and headed for one of the Table Rock Marina's dive boats. She marked him off her list of submerged divers. Scott's search plan was working. The line of air-bubbles never showed a gap caused by the absent diver.

Several long minutes later, Aleecia stuck the air-horn under water and sounded the signal for the divers to surface. The line stopped and almost as one unit, the divers appeared on the surface. Thirty minutes had elapsed. She knew they wouldn't have enough air to make another sweep. The divers circled around Scott.

"Way to stay together." Scott looked at each diver's face, searching for signs of fatigue or anxiety. "Okay, head count."

Aleecia listened as the divers called out their number in order. "Number eight, surfaced with low air!" she cried out when he looked in her direction.

"All divers accounted for!" Scott dropped a marker-buoy. "Grab a fresh tank. Soon as everyone is ready, we'll make one more sweep."

Scott swam back to the boat, handed his gear to Aleecia and climbed aboard. "I should have given trash bags to every diver. This place is a mess. Gary been giving you any problems?"

She laughed and pointed towards his boat. "Only until the media showed up. Soon as they arrived, he forgot about me. He did threaten to reassign me to other duties."

"Humph," he snorted.

"And, he ordered me not to spend any time off duty with you."

"*Ordered?* Cock-head actually said that?" Scott finished changing his tank and hoisted the vest over his head.

Aleecia stepped closer and gave Scott a kiss. "Don't worry, I have no intention of obeying."

"Good," he smiled. "I'm glad."

"I'm going down below for a few minutes," she nodded towards the media boat headed in their direction.

Scott winked at her and waited for the sharks.

"Mr. Mathis, before you go back in, may we have a word with you?"

Scott looked at the other divers gathered around the buoy. "I don't have time for a long interview. One or two questions only."

"We understand you took control of the rescue here today. What are the conditions down there? Can you describe what you are seeing?"

"This isn't a rescue, it's a search and recovery operation. I took control because of my qualifications and training. As to the conditions, put a brown paper bag over your head and try walking through a junkyard."

"Any hope of finding the missing person?" another reporter asked.

"I'm not aware of anyone being reported as missing. The fog was thick this morning and the person who reported this could have mistaken trash or a turtle on the surface for a person's head."

"So this search shouldn't have been done?"

"I didn't say that. He was correct in reporting what he thought he saw. Now, if you will excuse me, the rest of the search team is ready." Scott lowered his mask, put the regulator in his mouth and entered the water.

Aleecia waited until the media boat left and came on deck. The hairs on the back of her neck bristled, and she turned her head. Gary was staring at her with a sullen glare. *Up yours,* Scott's description of Gary came back to her. *Cock-head.*

For the next half hour, she watched the line of bubbles slowly make its way across the search area.

* * * * *

Scott unzipped his wetsuit and reached for a bottle of water. Hearing a boat approach, he knew without looking who was on it.

"What the hell are you doing? Grab another tank and get back into the water!" Gary bellowed loud enough for several onlookers to hear.

"I've called off the search until such time as a person has actually been reported missing."

"You can't do that. I'm in charge, and I'm telling you to expand the search."

Scott ignored his ranting and took another long drink of water. "You want to expand the search, go ahead. You can use a set of my gear, but I don't think you'll find anyone to dive with you."

"What do you mean?"

Scott chuckled. "It means we took a vote. Until it's certain someone is missing, the search is over. We've been looking for an hour in an area with no current and found nothing."

"We'll see about that." Gary gunned the motor and sped off after a departing dive boat.

Aleecia watched what appeared to be a heated argument between Gary and the divers on the boat. In the end, the dive boat headed back to the pier leaving him bobbing like a cork in its wake.

"Poor Gary, his moment of fame is over and his captive audience is leaving," Aleecia commented sarcastically.

"Poor Gary? What about poor me? I've been groping in the mud for your dead body for the last hour." He put on a feigned hurt look. "Don't I get any consideration for all my noble efforts?"

"Nope," she teased. "But if you take me home, we can play hide-n-seek, and you can look for me again. I promise you one thing. It won't take an hour to find me."

Scott grinned and sat on the edge of the boat and started removing his gear.

"*Damn!*" Her shoulders slumped.

Scott turned around. "He is starting to annoy me."

"He does have that affect on people." Aleecia shook her head as she watched Gary returning.

Gary pulled along side, tied his boat to Scott's, and jumped aboard.

"I don't remember granting permission to board."

"I didn't ask." Gary stepped in front of Aleecia.

"Get in the boat," he ordered. "We're going back to the office." Gary laid a hand on her arm.

Scott started to stand when Gary, confused and shaken, landed on his back looking up at the sun.

"I told you once, never lay a hand on me again."

She looked relaxed, her arms calmly folded under her breasts. Scott looked into her eyes and swallowed nervously. They were cold, calculating, and *deadly*.

"You stupid *bitch!*" Gary got up and turned on Aleecia, his fingers clenched into tight, white-knuckled fists.

He blinked, and nearly missed the lightning kick that sent Gary reeling backwards over the side of the boat. Scott smiled at him floundering and spitting water.

"I hope you can swim. Next time, ask before jumping onto another boat." He was amazed at the large bruise already forming on the side of Gary's face. "You might want to put some ice on that. It looks painful.

"By the way, don't reassign Aleecia. All I need to do is make one phone call, and you'll be counting polar bears in Alaska." He untied Gary's boat.

He eyed her cautiously. "Is it safe to approach?"

"Yes."

He brushed a lock of hair from her face. Her eyes had lost their sharp edge. "Are you…?"

"Never felt better." Standing on her toes, Aleecia gave him a kiss that lingered on his lips. "God, that felt great."

"What? The kiss or scrambling the few brains Gary had left."

Safe within the circle of his arms, she laid her head on his solid chest. "Both."

He waited until Gary climbed aboard his boat and collapsed on deck. Starting his engines, Scott spun the wheel and pointed the bow back to Aleecia's pier.

* * * * *

Aleecia traced the contours of his shoulder muscles. "Something's troubling you."

He idled back the engine and eased the boat next to the pier. "A little." Scott turned the key, and silence surrounded them.

"Come," she said as the calloused pads of her fingers trailed down the side of his face. "I'll try to relieve your mind and chase the darkness away."

She stepped onto the wooden walkway and tied the boat to a pylon. Aleecia held out her hand. "Come, we'll talk then play."

Scott took her hand, stepped to the pier and walked beside her up the hill.

The house was a one-bedroom bungalow, partially hidden from view by large oak trees. Peeling paint on the siding showed signs of neglect. As he put his foot on the bottom step, the wood splintered.

"Sorry about the place. My landlord doesn't believe in putting any money into it." She held the door open.

Scott entered and froze. The hard wood floors were covered with Oriental rugs. A low coffee table, the only real furniture in the living room, had large pillows scattered about the floor around it. The walls at first glance appeared to be a hodgepodge of eastern décor and medieval weapons. Some he recognized from the movies, while many of the others looked like they belonged in the halls of a torture museum.

He walked over to a pair of magnificent swords. "They're...real?" Their ivory inlaid handles, covered with the scrimshaw of a crouching dragon, were works of art.

"Very much so. They were my grandfather's. He gave them to me when I finished my training."

"As in marital arts?" Scott picked up a metal star from a little bowl filled with the small pointed objects. "You can use these?"

She took the star from his hand. A smile lifted the corners of her lips. In a blur of motion, her wrist snapped. The star sailed across the room and struck a dartboard in the center ring.

"Wow! I'm impressed." He was seeing Aleecia in a new perspective, and he didn't even understand the old. "You must have started your training at an early age."

"I was taken to a remote village in Japan as a baby. For as long as I can remember, everything I was taught involved the martial arts. My grandfather was a master of the old school."

"Meaning?" he interrupted.

"It was not for show or medals. For years, grandfather trained warriors, skilled fighters in the ways of the ancient art of silent death." She grew silent, remembering. "I was his last student."

"I'm sorry for your loss." He lifted his hand, and with the back of his fingers, gently caressed her cheek. Having known the feeling first-hand, he understood only too well the emptiness it brought. "I know you miss him."

"I have him always in my heart. He told me he was ready to go, that he had finally found a warrior worthy of his time. When he left us, my mother left me in the village and came back to visit my father."

Scott's confusion returned. "They lived apart all those years?"

"He was already married. I call him my father, simply because he supported us. His wife was led to believe they had an affair, and I was the result. If only that had been the case, my life would've been different."

"You've lost me." Scott had difficulty putting the pieces of her story together.

"I have no knowledge of my real parents," she confessed. "When it became apparent that my life was in danger, I was stolen away and taken to safety."

He was astounded. Words failed him. Scott drew her close and held her. "This...woman who stole you...she took you to Japan?"

"Yes, she became my mother, changed her name, and adopted me as her own. I owe her my life."

"Where is she now?" He smoothed her hair offering what comfort he could to, in some way, ease the heavy burden she had carried for years.

"Dead." Her softly-spoken word pierced his heart.

"I'm sorry." Scott kissed the top of her head. "How did it happen?"

"It was soon after my mother returned to visit with my father, about my going to college. They were driving down the coast from Portland when his car left the road and plunged over a cliff. The news said they had been traveling at a high rate of speed."

Breaking the contact between them, Aleecia walked over and picked up another throwing star. She flipped it like a coin, snatched it from the air, and in the same fluid motion, flung it across the room. It landed below the other star in the dartboard.

Scott was in a quandary. Should he hold her, or would she resent it? He dropped down onto one of the pillows.

Another star sailed across the room. The soft ring of metal told him, without looking, it had landed next to one she had already thrown.

"What did you do?"

"Soon as I heard about it, I packed what I needed and left Japan. I was afraid I would be next." She walked over and sat down next to Scott. "Who I was ceased to exist."

"What did the police say?"

"I didn't go to the police. I didn't believe the report. He never drove fast on that stretch of road."

"You think...they were murdered?"

"Yes. He had prepared for this. In a safety deposit box was a complete new identity along with enough money hidden away for me to disappear."

"I'm sorry."

The compassion in his voice, the tender touch of his hand was more than Aleecia could fight against. She turned to Scott, laid her head on his shoulder, and for the first time, allowed tears to wash away the agony of her loss.

Chapter 6

This felt so good. Not since she was a little girl in her mother's arms had she been held and comforted. *A warrior must separate oneself from emotion,* the words of her grandfather returned. *A warrior who is ruled by emotions fights with one arm tied behind his back. You want to cry? Cry later, not in front of my enemy, for he shall see your weakness and gain the advantage.*

Aleecia put the heartache back into the dark recesses of her mind and dried her tears. His chest was solid beneath her cheek. She felt the steady rhythmic beat of his heart. Her body responded to the vibrations of its life-giving pulse, and within a few minutes, their two hearts beat as one.

The hard pebbled male nipple, wet with her tears, beckoned to her. Aleecia circled it with her tongue. She felt the instant change in his body.

His chest expanded, and he held his breath. The rhythm of his heart spiked and beat faster against her lips. Scott's body tensed, every muscle taut like a coiled spring.

"Do you...know what you're doing?"

"I have a pretty good idea," she teased. Circling the darkened nub, she sucked on it, gently grating the hard flesh with her teeth.

"I thought," his breathing came in raspy gulps of air, "we were going to play hide-n-seek."

"I told you I wouldn't be hard to find." His muscles rippled beneath her fingers as she slid them slowly down his side. The thin black material of his swimsuit felt like silk. Boldly, she cupped his cock and felt it harden in her hand.

Aleecia left a wet trail of kisses down his chest and across the flat plain of his stomach. The detailed outline of his erection strengthened her desire. She kissed the dark wet spot at the head of his swollen cock. The taste of his desire and need unleashed her growing passion.

Pulling the waistband down, she freed him from the restricting suit. Aleecia lifted her eyes. Scott's breathing was rapid, his eyes closed. A smile of erotic pleasure spread across his face. She circled the tight skin of his ridged shaft with her tongue.

"*Ohaaaah!*" a long, deep moan rolled from his lips.

Aleecia smiled, licked the pearl drop of musky dew and took him in her mouth. She felt his body tremble. A surge of power, a feeling of control swept over her. Her tongue toyed and teased his hardened cock.

A low moan of pleasure rushed from his lips. His fingers clutched at a pillow, bunching the material within his grasp.

The tip of her tongue found a sensitive spot over the large blue vein at the top of his shaft. Each time she touched it, Scott's body trembled. She felt the tension building in his body, felt the rampant pulsating beat of his heart beneath her lips.

With her other hand, she slid her shorts over her hips and wiggled out of them. Aleecia gave him one last teasing kiss and slid up his body.

"Oh…wow!" he managed between deep indrawn breaths.

Planting small suckling kisses up his neck and across his jaw, her lips covered his. His tongue filled her mouth searching, probing, and dancing with hers.

Scott rolled her onto her back. His fingers fluttered lightly over her skin before tracing the curve of her breast in a slow, agonizing circle.

The warmth of his lips closed over her nipple. His teeth grated across the sensitive flesh. She shut her eyes, riding out the wave of sensuous emotion that washed over her pooling between her legs.

"Touch me," Aleecia whimpered.

"I thought I was."

The sound of his gentle sucking on her breast filled her with a longing desire she had shut out of her life years ago. She slammed the door on the unwanted and obtrusive thoughts.

"Not where I need you to touch me." She took his hand and placed his palm between her legs. "Here."

His hand lay unmoving where she had placed it. She opened her eyes. Scott's teasing smile infuriated her.

"Touch me."

"I am. You want something else?"

"Yes." She spread her legs further apart. Begging! She, who had been taught to be self-reliant, had been reduced to begging.

"This is Missouri. 'Show-Me' what you want."

Aleecia placed her hand over his. Using her index finger, she guided his finger inside her. She started to withdraw her finger when she saw the challenging grin on his face, the dare hidden behind the smoldering passion.

"Your pussy is so wet."

Her body had taken over, controlled by hunger and need. She rocked her hips against their fingers buried within her flesh.

"You...you make," her mind struggled to finish the sentence, "me wet." Her back arched, forcing their fingers deeper. The spasms of her climax tightened the flesh of her vagina around their fingers.

"Ahh!" she gasped. Liquid fire bathed their fingers.

Scott was nearing his own climax. His hip was wet from the lubricating fluid dripping from the head of his erection. Not that he needed any. Her pussy was beyond wet. Reaching for the small foil packet she had placed on the table, he tore it open. She took it from his hand and gently rolled it over his hard shaft.

Scott settled between her legs, easing his weight upon her. The head of his cock slid past the wet folds of her flesh. Her legs wrapped around his butt and tightened, forcing him to bury his full length inside her.

In the heat of passion, her eyes had darkened from their normal pale green. Scott ran his fingers through her tangled locks. He had to slow down the hungry frenzy they were in or he would be finished.

He kissed the side of her face and her eyes. His lips touched hers in a fleeting, feather-soft kiss. Her hands captured his head holding him against her. Their kiss turned heated, full of desire and promise.

The grinding of her hips and the pressure of her legs locked behind him drove Scott past thinking or reason. Caught in the undertow of her desire, he rode the crest of the wave higher and higher.

She arched beneath him, lifting them off their bed of pillows. Her muscles tightened around him. Scott followed her over the top and fell beside her into the afterglow of passion's fire. He gathered Aleecia close and held her.

"Scott." The whisper of her breath touched his damp skin like a warm kiss. "I'm glad you came to Table Rock."

He kissed the top of her head. "Me, too. I came here to justify my continued existence in a world where everything had become meaningless and superficial." A long sigh filled the quiet of the room. His fingers traced the thick fold of skin covering her gills.

"Instead, I find a marvelous woman of incredible passion, energy and lust for life, wrapped up in a shroud of mystery."

"My gills...don't bother you?"

"No," Scott chuckled. "Okay, I was shocked at first. But they don't make you a freak or some kind of monster. They're a part of you that cannot be changed. You were born with them and have become stronger because of them. I'm just sorry you've had to live in fear all these years."

She placed a kiss on his chest. Aleecia snuggled deeper into the hollow of his shoulder. Her breathing slowed. Her arm grew heavy across his waist, and the steady rhythm of her heart beat next to his.

"Aleecia?" Scott whispered against her hair. "Rest, my dear."

Who knows what tomorrow may bring. Scott closed his eyes.

* * * * *

He woke to a darkened room. Sometime during the night, she had gotten up and covered them with a sheet. The hollow pit in his stomach reminded him of his lack of food. Aleecia's warm body lay beside him, her arm and leg thrown across his body. He stirred and she woke up.

"What time is it?" Her voice, thick with sleep slurred the words.

He moved his hand and checked. "Almost seven. You hungry?"

"Starved." Her fingers made slow spiraling circles on his side, each one going lower towards his waist. "What did you have in mind?"

"I was thinking, maybe a thick juicy steak."

Her fingers had reached his groin. Using one fingernail, she traced the blue vein from the base of his penis to the tip. "Okay, if you insist."

Aleecia flipped back the cover and scampered from their impromptu bed on the floor. "Give me a few minutes to shower and dress. We can leave the boat here and take my car."

Standing outside the shower, he watched her opaque image through the glass door. His response was automatic to the sensuous picture before him. Steam rose above the door like fog upon the lake, filling the small room.

The sound of the water spraying against the walls quieted. "What did you say? I couldn't hear you over the shower."

"I said, 'I should have waited until you were through'."

"Why…?" she asked as she opened the door. "Oh my!" Her eyes grew large. She licked her lips.

"Have you been out here priming the pump?"

Scott laughed. "No need to do that. Watching you is all the priming I need."

"I'm finished," she stepped out of the shower. "It's all yours."

Looking at his swollen cock, she giggled. "May I recommend a cold shower?"

Scott took the towel, twirled it in his hands, and lightly snapped the cheek of her ass as she walked away.

"Hey! Watch it. Don't start something I'll have to finish." She winked and strolled sassily to her bedroom.

He finished his shower and went down to the boat for a fresh change of clothes. Aleecia waited at the car and tossed him her keys. "Here, you drive."

* * * * *

Scott pulled into the center turn lane and waited for a break in the traffic. A car stopped, breaking the long line of vehicles. He waved his thanks to the driver and pulled into the drive of Ruby Tuesday's parking lot.

"Looks like we'll have a wait," he frowned at the people standing outside.

Aleecia laughed, "Anywhere we eat, we'll have a wait."

"So it would seem," he sighed.

Finding an empty space in the back, Scott parked the truck. "We're here, might as well get in line."

"They have a bar." Walking beside Scott, she took his hand. His fingers curled around hers. The warmth of his touch spread a soft warm cloud of joy around her heart. *So this is what it's like to feel normal, to be going to dinner with someone and not have to worry about what comes after the food.*

Ruby Tuesday's was crowded. He waited, looking around. Posters of local attractions, country music stars, and old advertisements covered the walls. Scott gave their names and followed Aleecia to the bar. "What'll you have?"

"White wine." She sat down and ran her hand over his leg.

He ordered their drinks. A television silently aired a ball game that nobody seemed to be watching. The clang of dishes and raised voices came from the kitchen. Adding to the din were the conversations of a packed restaurant complete with at least two screaming toddlers.

"I hope you weren't expecting a quiet romantic evening." He spoke loud enough for her to hear.

"No, I came here to eat. The romantic evening will be later." Her hand crept higher up his leg.

From the corner of his eye, he caught the movement of another person sitting down at the bar. Scott glanced in his direction. That he was alone in a place crowed with families and couples seemed odd. Scott turned his attention back to Aleecia.

"Mr. Mathis! Party of two!"

Scott and Aleecia picked up their drinks and followed the waitress to their booth. The woodwork had a deep rose-colored finish, polished to a lustrous shine. They sat down on the dark green leather-covered the seats and took the menus.

A decorative divider of beveled glass ran the length of the line of booths. He moved his head and the bottles at the bar appeared to jump and bend. Ceiling fans slowly turned, circulating the air.

They placed their order and went to the salad bar at the front of the restaurant. He gave Aleecia her plate and followed her down the line. Scott glanced up, and the man at the bar dropped his eyes.

He followed Aleecia back to the table. There was something about the lone drinker that was bothering him, but he couldn't put his finger on it.

"Scott, I want to thank you."

"For what?" He took a sip of his drink.

"For treating me like a...woman."

Scott smiled over the rim of his glass. "The last time I checked you were very much a woman."

The food arrived, and Scott cut into the thick juicy steak.

The man was still at the bar. Scott had been known to nurse a drink, but this man was taking longer than seemed normal.

"Are you planning on diving in the morning?" Aleecia asked between bites.

"Yes."

"Mind...if I join you."

"I would love to have you beside me, but after today there could be more media coverage. There's also the probability of other divers showing up to go along now that they know I've arrived."

She tried not to show her disappointment. "Oh."

Scott reached across the table and took her hand. "After all the excitement of the day is over and the media goes on to something else, I look forward to having you beside me. Right now, we'll have to take each new day and adjust accordingly."

"Thank you," she squeezed his hand.

Scott laid his plastic card on the tray and waited until their waiter returned. He glanced over to the bar, a half finished drink sat on the counter. The man was gone.

Aleecia's attention was on a blonde headed toddler in a highchair across the isle. There was a tender expression in her eyes filled with longing and sadness. He recognized the thoughtful expression. How many times had he seen the same desire on his wife's face before their own precious child had been born?

"I think you would make a good mother." Scott voiced his thoughts.

"I...I can't."

He read the regret behind her words and the suddenly tear-filled glassy eyes.

"It would be too dangerous. What if, it turned out...deformed, like me?"

"Deformed?" He gently caressed the back of her hand. "You are different, but you shouldn't let it stop you from living a full and happy life."

"Scott," she looked around and lowered her voice, "you don't know what it was like. Living in fear all the time, afraid one of your trusted friends would say something outside the village. Knowing, if they did, you would be killed or worse." She shook her head adamantly. "I've enough problems of my own without living with the fear of my child being be ripped from my arms and used for some scientific experiment."

"You survived, and I feel confident that you'd ensure your child would, too."

"I can't be certain. The risk is too great."

Scott signed the receipt. "Nothing is ever certain. Shall we go?" He stood and offered his hand to Aleecia.

Scott pulled out of the parking lot into the stop-and-go Branson traffic. The construction of the new monorail hadn't helped. The new theme parks and the opening of a Mall of America had resulted in a transportation nightmare.

"It's early, you want to see a show or go anywhere?"

She looked at the clock. "Most of the shows have already started. It will be an hour before we could get in. We could go out to the mall but you need to get over into other lane and turn left at the light."

He turned the signal on. The light turned green and he edged over into the other lane. "The mall it is."

Several minutes later, Scott turned onto Mall of America drive.

The three-story structure lay sprawled across almost ten acres of land. Even for its size, it was smaller than the original one in Minnesota. They strolled, hands clasped, along the wide corridors amid the shoppers and tourists.

"I haven't been to a mall in years." Scott remarked. "Seeing all the families going about their shopping, kids having a good time looking at everything around them. The hustle-n-bustle of the food courts and the sound of laughter always reminded me of what I had lost."

"I'm sorry, Scott, you should have said something." She placed her other hand on his arm.

"It's okay…really." He turned towards her and lightly touched her cheek. "Tonight…is different."

"How so?" she whispered. Her mouth was inches from his.

"Because…you're here." Scott lowered his head and kissed her lips. "You make the pain bearable. The bad memories less horrifying, the good memories more sweet and precious." He pulled her closer and placed a gentle loving kiss on her forehead. "Thank you."

Aleecia gave him a squeeze. "You're welcome."

Scott looked up and stared at the reflection in the store window. The lone drinker from Ruby Tuesday's stood across the way, apparently engrossed in the merchandise placed on display. Somehow, Scott had trouble picturing him needing anything from Victoria's Secret. He slowly turned around to face the store.

The man was gone.

The hair on the back of his neck lifted. What were the odds of seeing the same person in two different places the same night, when they were miles apart from each other?

His inner voice spoke up. *Slim to none.*

"Come on," he broke the embrace. "Let's go exploring."

They came to *Flashbaxx*, a nightclub that offered dancing to the tunes of the 60's and 70's.

"I haven't danced in years." Scott pointed to the flashing neon sign over the door. "You want to go in?"

"Sure," she raised her voice over the noise rolling out the opened door. "I must warn you. I'm not much of a dancer."

Scott held the door for her. "You said you didn't dive either."

Chapter 7

Scott started to believe he was seeing things and imagining problems where there weren't any. He had kept a watchful eye for the man he thought he had seen, but with no luck. Aleecia's talk of cloak and dagger mystery had seriously affected his own thinking.

They crossed the dam at one-thirty in the morning. There was only one other car on the road, and it was about a half-mile behind him.

"You want to spend the night in my cramped rolling tin can, or shall I take you home?"

"My place is too far away." She slid her hand up his leg. Her fingers brushed his crotch and the bulge of his cock.

Already beginning to stiffen at her touch, Scott shifted in the seat to give himself more room. "I thought you were tired?"

"I said my feet hurt from the dancing. Nothing was said about being tired." She stroked him through the jean material. "If you're not *up* to it tonight, I'll survive."

"Do I feel up to whatever you had in mind?" Scott groaned as her fingers reached the zipper and began to slide it down.

"Oh, yes," she purred seductively. "Very *up* indeed."

"I don't know," he teased. "I'm thinking along the lines of skinny dipping in the pool."

Aleecia grew quiet.

"What's the matter? If you're worried, the hotel is almost empty this week."

She shook her head. "We better go to my place, Scott. It's too dangerous."

"Care to explain?"

"Might as well, seeing you know everything else." She relaxed against his shoulder. "What happens when you take a fish and put it in chlorinated water?"

"It will..." Shock rolled over him like a tidal wave. Scott swerved off the road and slammed on the brakes. "My God," he pulled Aleecia into his arms. "The things you have to live with...I didn't know. I'm sorry."

"Why should you've known? It's my Achilles heel. The only defense I have is avoiding it completely. Can we go now? Please."

He checked the mirror. The road was clear, not another car in sight. Scott eased off the shoulder and accelerated. A few minutes later, lights appeared several hundred yards behind him.

Scott pulled up to Aleecia's house, got out and held the door while she scooted over.

"If you still want to go skinny dipping...last one in cooks breakfast." She took off down the hill towards the pier.

Aleecia ran like a deer through the night. He was halfway to the pier when he heard her hit the water. "Good thing I know how to cook."

Scott walked to the end of the pier and unbuttoned his shirt. "You cheated."

Her laughter filled the air. "Only a little."

He finished undressing and slipped into the water.

Aleecia ducked under the surface.

Holding onto a wooden cross beam, he waited for her to surface. This was her world. His inner voice started humming the tune from *Jaws*.

Knowing she was down there swimming around him, taunting him with her nearness, heightened every nerve. Each wave against his shoulders caressed his skin like a thousand tiny fingers. The pungent odor of wet wood and rotting vegetation assaulted his senses.

He could feel her presence under the water. Something touched his leg, and he flinched. Not being able to see what she was doing, or about to do, seemed erotic.

Her silky wet lips closed around his cock. His fingers tightened on the wet wood, and the air in his lungs burst forth in a loud gasp. This took the meaning of skinny-dipping to a new level. Scott leaned his head back on his shoulders and closed his eyes.

With her gentle sucking and the water massaging his body, he was quickly losing control. His heart pounded savagely in his chest. White-knuckled, he gripped the wood as his body began to tremble.

White lights burst before his eyes like shooting stars. The roar of his own blood filled his head and each heartbeat reverberated in his ears. Uncontrollable spasms traversed his legs and up his back.

Aleecia surfaced, her face inches away. Her pale green eyes held an eerie luminous glow.

Scott gasped for breath. He felt drained, unable to move or even speak.

"You look like you could use some help getting out." She slipped her arm around his waist and helped him up the short ladder. "I'll come back later and get the clothes."

His strength was beginning to return when she stumbled. Her weight took them both to the ground. Her labored breathing alarmed him.

"Aleecia! What's wrong?"

"Get me to the house…quickly."

Scott picked her up and hurried up the hill. "Tell me what to do, dear, don't pass out on me."

"I…need," she fought against the encroaching fog to speak. "Warm salt water."

Running to the kitchen, he turned the tap and waited impatiently. Adjusting the temperature, Scott filled a large glass with warm water and added a generous amount of salt.

"Here." He cradled her head and helped her lift the glass to her lips already tinged blue.

Aleecia filled her mouth and inhaled the whole glass. She grimaced with the sudden burning. Forcibly exhaling the water through her gills, she held the glass up.

"More?" Scott questioned.

Her hair barely shook, as she gave a slight nod.

Returning with two glasses, he held each to her lips as she inhaled both, and spewed the water from her back. She was breathing easier, and her color was turning back to normal.

"What happened?"

Aleecia looked up with a sheepish grin. "Next time I'm giving head, I need to remember a former president's comment when asked if he smoked grass. I need to swallow...not inhale."

"How can you joke about it?" He fidgeted beside her.

"Don't be so alarmed. It wasn't your fault. If I had stayed in the water longer afterward, it wouldn't have bothered me. See," she swiveled around. "I've gotten rid of it."

Her lower back was covered with thick milky white fluid.

"Thanks for your help." She leaned over and kissed his cheek. "In case you're wondering about the water, I have filters installed to remove the chlorine."

Scott glanced over at the clock, "I might as well start fixing breakfast. It'll be daylight soon."

"Go ahead. I'll get dressed and pick up our clothes."

With a quick kiss and a playful slap on the cheek of his ass, Aleecia headed to the bathroom.

* * * * *

Aleecia stood in the doorway watching Scott at the stove. A gentle warm feeling wrapped itself around her heart. *If only this could last,* she silently wished. "That smells so good. I might have to tie you up and keep you around."

"You want to load up the food and take the boat out for a breakfast with a view?" He turned the stove off.

"Sounds like fun." Taking a small hamper from the cupboard, she began filling containers. "We might as well take enough for the day. Save a trip to shore."

They carried the hamper between them down to the boat. Scott started the engine while she cast off the mooring line. "Ready when you are."

Scott idled out of the cove into deeper water and increased speed. Heading towards the dam, he pulled up at a small island off of Indian Point. "This looks like a good spot for watching the sun come up."

"Perfect spot." She poured a cup of coffee and handed it to Scott. "Breakfast is served."

Scott pulled out a couple deck chairs and took a heaping plate from Aleecia. "Is all this for me?"

She smiled and winked, "No."

Aleecia curled up on his lap and took the plate. She took a fork full of food and held it in front of his mouth. "It's for both of us."

"Long time since anyone fed me." He took the food and began chewing. There was something very personal about being fed. In a way, it was more intimate than the wonderful sex they had shared.

The sun peeked over the trees spreading reddish gold shafts of light across the water. Birds lifted from their perchs in the nearby branches, their early morning cries piercing the air.

"This is lovely. I'm glad you suggested it." She fed him another bite.

"Me, too," he drew her head closer and kissed her lips.

The warmth of the early morning sun shining brightly in a cloudless sky and the slow roll of the boat from the swells lulled them to sleep.

* * * * *

The high-pitched whine of a small outboard motor awakened him. The sun had risen high in the sky. Aleecia lay curled up in his arms, her breath warm against his neck.

Easing out of the chair, he settled her on the stiff canvas cover. "Don't get up," he gave her a kiss. "We fell asleep."

"Wake me if you need help," she mumbled, and her eyes drifted closed.

Stretching to work out the kinks, he turned around. The emotional shock of recognizing the fisherman nearby felt like a physical blow in the solar plexus. Even though he wore a large coat, Scott knew the lonely drinker from the restaurant and the man in the boat were the same.

Anger replaced the shock. Being watched by the media, he could deal with, but this...Invasion of his privacy crossed the line.

Scott forced a wide smile. "I don't know who you are," he hissed between clenched teeth, "but you have succeeded in pissing me off."

Walking over to the cabin, he turned the radio on. The twang of a steel guitar playing an old Willie Nelson hit blared from the speaker.

Opening one eye, Aleecia frowned. "I thought you said for me to sleep?"

"Sorry, but I wanted to cover the sound of our voices."

She screwed up her face. "Why?"

"We have company." With a shift of his eyes, he directed her attention to starboard. "Look but don't make it obvious. Do you recognize him?"

"No. Should I?"

"I was hoping maybe a jealous boyfriend." Taking the rope, he began pulling in the anchor. "He was at the restaurant last night and at the mall. I get the impression he's following us."

"Boyfriend!" she laughed. "I've *never* been that hard up."

The engine caught on the first try. Aleecia stepped up beside him.

"What are you going to do?"

"See if he follows us to the dive site." He added power and the boat came to life, skimming through the water and leaving a wide wake fanning out behind.

"Suppose it's me he's watching, not you?"

"The thought has already crossed my mind." His voice, laced with steel, sliced through the noise of the motor.

"Scott...this isn't your problem."

"You're wrong," his eyes glistened with pent-up anger. "I'm making it my problem."

"Scott, listen to me." She placed her hand on his arm.

"No! You listen to me! Five years ago, I stood looking at a smoking hole in a Pennsylvania mountain pasture. I couldn't do anything to save their lives then, but I *damn* well can do something now. I'm not going to stand by and let some son-of-a-bitch terrorize and harm someone I care about. Damn it," he slammed his fist on the fiberglass cowling. "Never again!"

She looked at Scott through eyes wide with shock. His reaction to the man in the other boat was a surprise, to say the least, and a warm feeling crept up into her heart at his concern. Never since she was a little girl had anyone cared so much for her as Scott did now. She only hoped it could last.

Entering the shallow water of the cove, the muscles in Scott's arm flexed. He had slammed the throttle into idle. She half expected to see the metal bend from the sheer force of his grip on the handle.

"I'm not going to let you dive. Not in your present state of mind in zero visibility." She tried to reason with him. "You're upset and tired. It's too dangerous."

Sliding off the seat, Scott stepped around her, released the anchor and raised the dive flag.

"Scott!" Aleecia watched as he picked up the floating dive buoy and threw it several yards from the boat.

"I forbid you to dive." She had hoped it wouldn't come to this.

"Think you're going to stop me?"

"There's no thinking about it Scott. One way or another, I will stop you." She stepped in front of his diving gear.

"It's getting late. Please move." Scott took a step towards her.

She gave the appearance of moving aside. Grabbing his hand, she used his forward motion against him.

His head bounced off the carpeted deck. Scott blinked.

"Give it up, Scott. I can keep this up all day, but I would rather spend it doing some rational thinking about the present problem." She sat on the bench seat.

"You aren't the only one who has lost someone. How do you think I felt when my mother died? I was in Japan. Just like you, there was absolutely nothing I could do." Turning sideways, she drew her knees up under her chin and looked out over the lake.

He sat down on the seat beside her.

"We are a lot alike, Scott. Hiding our lonely lives from others, shutting out the world by living under the surface of it," she sighed. "But that is where the similarity ends. I do it out of necessity."

The faint whine of a small outboard on the lake grew louder as it approached.

"You hide from the guilt of surviving, because, for whatever reason, you weren't on the plane with them."

"You're partially correct," he wrapped his arms around her. "I sold SMtronics as a result of the guilt. What good did surveillance cameras and metal detectors do to protect my family?

"Thinking about the possible danger you face brought the anger back," he paused for several seconds. "I'm sorry."

"Apology accepted." Aleecia snuggled closer to him. His arms around her felt good. Okay, so she was lying to herself. They felt wonderful.

A lone tear rolled down her eyelash, hung suspended, and dropped onto her cheek. Wonderful things in her life never lasted.

"Our uninvited guest has arrived." Aleecia leaned back against his chest, turned her face, and kissed his cheek. "Shall we invite him over for coffee?"

"Don't waste good coffee on him," Scott chuckled. "If he nurses it like that drink at the bar last night, we'll never get rid of him.

"Do I have your permission to dive?"

"I suppose." She turned around to face Scott. "As long as you promise to be careful."

He leaned forward and tenderly kissed her lips. "I promise."

Scott entered the water, submerging into its murky brown depths. At twenty feet, his feet touched the bottom. Adding air to his vest, he adjusted his buoyancy and leveled out horizontally. With less than eighteen inches of water between him and the mud, he was able to see objects lying on the bottom.

Each of the mesh bags he was using would hold ten cans. At the rate he was filling them, he would be out of bags long before he was out of air. Scott found a picnic table complete with umbrella and attached his last marker buoy to it.

Scott reached the surface about forty yards from the boat. A line of buoys bobbed on the surface. He swam back to the boat.

"Hand me more bags, please." He floated beside the hull, holding onto the ladder.

"How are you doing on air?" She handed several empty bags down to Scott.

"Half a tank." He clipped the bags to his belt. "Any activity from our audience?"

"I caught him taking a couple pictures. Otherwise, he sits there with his pole in the water. He still hasn't caught any fish.

"Do you want me to start pulling in the filled bags?"

"Sure, leave the first and the last ones. They can be a reference point." Scott swam over to the first marker, took a compass reading, and submerged. A few minutes later the sound of his boat engine reverberated through the water.

Scott continued to sift through the mud and silt gathering years worth of accumulated trash. With his air pressure down to five hundred pounds, he tied a marker to a lawn chair and headed for the surface.

"Figured it was about time you should be coming up." Aleecia reached down and grabbed his fins.

He dropped the regulator and the hose fell to his side.

"Thanks," he pulled himself aboard. The table and umbrella sat in one corner. Red mesh bags were piled underneath it.

He gave her a kiss. Her hair was damp, as were her clothes. "Have you been in the water?"

Releasing the Velcro strap across his chest, he lowered the tank and vest to the deck. Scott removed his weight belt and picked up a bottle of water.

"I couldn't reach one of the markers, so I went in after it."

"Swing the boat around. We might as well pick up these other bags."

Pulling a small winch from a storage compartment, he attached it to a short boom at the stern.

"Find something heavy?" She started the motor and swung the boat around to the first marker.

"Yeah, a Jon Boat, complete with outboard." Scott hooked up a fresh tank to his vest. "I'll have to tie on a heavier line to get it up."

"You want me to hook it up? Won't take but a minute for me to go down and be right back up."

"Too risky."

"I think our visitor had a rough night. He's sound asleep and won't even know I'm gone. Besides, his boat is off the bow."

"Okay, but be quick about it."

Taking the end of a heavier line, Aleecia entered the water, removed her shirt and disappeared.

The line played out and stopped. Scott felt two solid jerks on the rope, took a couple turns around the winch drum, and began lifting the sunken boat from the bottom.

Aleecia surfaced, slipped her shirt over her head and gave him a bright smile.

"She's coming up stern first."

Within minutes of having the raised boat on the surface, it was floating and tied off at the stern of his boat.

Aleecia climbed aboard. The white shirt, nearly transparent from being wet, clung to her breasts. "Don't worry, it won't take long to dry.

"Are you going to take this load in or do another dive?"

"I figured on putting as much of this load as possible into the Jon Boat, have lunch and then do another dive." Scott pulled his boat along side another marker.

"Sounds good," she reached over and pulled the bag aboard. "If he's still asleep, I'll go with you. Two people working should get things done a lot quicker."

"I don't know," he shook his head, "seems too risky right now. Maybe later if he leaves."

Scott looked over at the man fishing nearby. His head, slumped forward on his chest, bobbed gently with the waves. "He does appear to be sleeping soundly."

When the last of the buoys were aboard, Scott turned the wheel and gunned the engine. The powerful motor roared and swung the boat around in a tight circle. A large wave rolled across the surface catching the fishing boat on the side. He glanced back in time to see the man roll with the wave and hang partially draped over the side, nearly capsizing the boat. The second wave toppled the fisherman into the water.

Scott swung the boat around again and headed towards the swamped boat. "Take the controls! He's fallen overboard!" Scott dove into the water before Aleecia had slowed the boat to a complete stop.

Reaching him, Scott turned him over and felt for a pulse. "Give me a hand getting him aboard."

Aleecia reached over the stern and pulled as Scott muscled him up the ladder.

"Get on the radio and call for help." He began CPR.

Aleecia picked up the microphone, "Lake Patrol, this is Fields on board *Clean Lakes*. We have an emergency, two miles southwest of the Coombs Ferry access. We have a fatality, male, approximately forty-five years of age. Be advised CPR has been initiated."

"Ten-four, *Clean Lakes*. Authorities and paramedics are enroute."

"Give it up, Scott. He's gone."

"I can't quit. Not while there's still a chance." Switching from compressions to breathing, Scott began pumping air into the man's lungs.

"You know CPR, do the compressions. I'll breath."

"Whatever," she knelt on the deck. "Still say it's a waste of time."

She began the chest compression. A fleeting smile lifted her mouth at the feel of bones breaking beneath her palms.

Fifteen minutes later two lake patrol boats pulled up along side. The paramedics came aboard.

The paramedic looked up at the officer and shook his head.

"He's dead."

Chapter 8

Scott walked out of the police station. Aleecia, close by his side, held his hand. The rest of day had been shot, answering questions and waiting for the detective to finish his interviews. The authorities were treating this like a major crime instead of a heart attack.

"Routine procedure," they'd told him. If that were the case, no wonder people were hesitant to get involved.

"I'm glad to be out of there." He opened the passenger door and waited 'until she got in. "I could sure use a drink. This has been one hell of a day."

Scott walked around the front of the vehicle and got in.

"A cold one sounds good. I'm ready for some food." Aleecia scooted over and leaned her head on his shoulder.

Had the cops picked up on her attitude of indifference? Thinking back on the morning, and her reluctance to help him with CPR, doubts and questions began to surface. Could she have swum over to the other boat, and using her skills in martial arts, killed the private investigator?

Yes, she could have, he told himself.

His inner voice whispered. *What are you going to do, if she did?*

He didn't want to think about it, but the possibility of Aleecia's involvement stayed at the forefront of his thoughts.

Scott picked up a cold six-pack and made another stop for food. Popping a tab, he lifted the can to his lips and sighed. "Here's to a better day tomorrow."

Aleecia raised her can and tapped his. "Tomorrow."

Life had been easy, before Table Rock. Unencumbered, he had done what he wanted. In a moment of weakness, he had succumbed to temptation, and life once again started making demands on his time and emotions.

He thought about walking away and realized with a sudden inner reflection, that leaving was not a viable option. Their relationship wasn't practical, but when it came to matters of the heart, a soft breast and a hard cock often silenced the warning bells of reason.

Aleecia felt the noose tightening around her neck. The police had refused to tell her who had hired the private investigator. Common sense told her it couldn't be the Feds, and if it wasn't them, then who?

If they knew about her, Scott's life would be snuffed out like her mother's. The thought of leaving him to survive on his own brought a sharp cry of despair within her soul. Together, they stood a chance. Apart, she could lose him forever.

She had to stay or convince Scott to leave with her. The only trouble with leaving, there was no place to go where he wouldn't be recognized. When he'd sold SMtronics, his picture filled the television screens, even in Japan. Since then, his passion for the 'Project Clean Lakes' had gotten his face in every dive magazine and on the cover of every environmental publication around the world.

"I'm sorry I got you into this mess, Scott." Turning her head, she kissed his shoulder. "I want you to know one thing. I won't leave you to face this alone."

"Well," Scott laughed, "thanks for the comforting words."

"For your information," he placed his arm around her, "I wouldn't leave, even if you asked me to. You're overreacting. The man died of a heart attack. After a couple days, no one will remember you were even there."

She snuggled closer to him. "I hope you're right."

He pulled into her driveway and got out. With her arm around his waist, they headed towards her little cottage.

Curled up on the floor amid the pillows, she matched his silent mood. Taking the last French fry, she held it up to Scott.

She watched his eyes grow warm with desire. One corner of his mouth lifted sensuously into a half-smile. His tongue licked the salt along its long and fragile length.

Her lips became dry, almost parched from the intense heat of his gaze. Licking her lips, she heard the sudden intake of his breath and saw the slight flaring of his nose.

His mouth hovered near the hard burnt tip of the fry. Scott closed his teeth over it and gently nipped it off.

She was damp with need. With each lick and nibble, her wetness grew. Her nipples ached, wanting the attention of his mouth.

With the last of the slim slice of potato gone, his lips captured her finger. Aleecia closed her eyes, savoring the heady feelings created by his soft suckling of her flesh.

"Mmm," she groaned.

Hot lips move over her palm, burning their touch into her skin. His tongue traced the dark blue vein in her arm making her squirm.

Taking his hand, she placed it over her breast. "Feel the hard pounding of my heart and know it's your touch that causes it to race wildly within my chest."

He took her lips in an open mouth frenzy of thrusting tongues and swallowed groans.

Scott's hands worked underneath her shirt. Aleecia reached down, yanked it over her head, and flung it aside. With the feel of his solid hands on her flushed skin, her head rolled back on her shoulders. His mouth closed over the pulsating vein in her neck, sucking and licking until she was limp.

His hot breath, blown across her nipple, sent shivers of delight rippling across her body. The hard pull of his mouth on her breast lifted her off the pillows.

In one fluid motion, Scott removed her shorts and lacy panties. He stood and began removing his clothes.

Her hand went between her legs. She slipped her finger between the soft folds of her flesh and stroked the wet, hard nub of her clit.

Scott started to open a condom, and she stopped him.

"Not yet." She reached up and wrapped her fingers around his erect shaft. With a gentle tug, she brought him to his knees.

Aleecia teased his scrotum with her tongue. The muscles in his stomach quivered. His ragged indrawn breath broke the tension-filled silence of the room. She kissed the base of his ridged shaft and along the extended blood-engorged vein.

Scott fell forward, his hands by her side and arms locked, holding his weight.

Spreading her legs, she invited him to taste her wetness even as her tongue slid over the smooth head of his cock.

Day old stubble on his face scraped across the tender flesh of her inner thigh. His breath, hot on her already fevered flesh, fanned the flames of her desire and need.

Lifting her hips from the cushioned floor in order to bring his mouth into contact with her, brought a chuckle of amusement from Scott.

"Patience, my love. All in due time." He blew a forceful stream of air against her clit.

"Patience," she gasped, "my ass."

"A very lovely little ass it is, too."

His words were muffled, sounding distant and faraway. His tongue touched her and as quickly lifted from her flesh. Again and again, he tormented her with his darting soft touches. Each time a soft whimper escaped her lips.

Unprepared for the full assault of his mouth, Aleecia's body jerked, her hips lifted from the floor, and a scream of ecstasy filled her ears. She surrendered her body. Her world and thoughts centered on his tongue inside her.

Turning her head to the side, she kissed his ridged shaft, licking and stroking him with her tongue.

"Please," she begged. "I want you inside me."

He slid off to her side and reached for the condom.

Aleecia took the packet, removed the contents, and kissing the head of his cock, rolled the thin clear material in place.

He knelt between her legs. She reached between their bodies and guided him past the swollen lips of her pussy.

When he started to withdraw, she stopped him. "No more teasing, Scott. I *need* you to make me feel," she paused.

"Feel what, my little mermaid?"

"Mermaid!" She gave him a shove and rose up on her knees. "Is that how you see me, as some sort of freak? All I am to you is a good story, so you can brag about screwing a *mermaid*," she spat out in disgust.

She started to stand.

"Wait, Aleecia. I..."

Aleecia spun around; her foot lashed out and connected with Scott's jaw. He recoiled against the blow and lay unmoving on the floor. Kneeling beside him, she drew her arm back, fingers held rigid and ready to strike.

Her mind flashed back to another time when the same hurtful words had ripped her heart in two. Tears welled up in her eyes, dimming her vision.

Keep your heart and mind pure, the words of her beloved master, filtered through her rage and feelings of betrayal. *Anger will cloud the mind and make the heart black.*

Her hand shook, and tears flooded over her lashes wetting her cheeks. "Damn you, Scott Mathis."

Leaping to her feet, Aleecia ran out the door and down the hill towards the lake.

She hit the water in a flat dive, submerged, and welcomed the momentary burn of the water filling her lungs. Blindly, she swam through the dark waters, driven towards her private sanctuary at the bottom of the lake.

With a heavy heart, Aleecia entered the jumble of broken timbers and jutting rocks. Deeper into the shaft she went, swimming in a blackness that was confining, almost suffocating. Turning sharply, she ascended through a small narrow airshaft in the ceiling of the abandoned mine.

Her head broke the surface at the floor of a second tunnel. Climbing out of the airshaft, she stood and reached for the old switch on the support timber. The lights flickered and burned bright, lighting the tunnel with an eerie pattern of shadows. The fact that they worked at all still amazed her. She had often wondered where the power came from, and why, after all these years, it was still on.

Cobwebs crisscrossed the openings between the support beams and the rock wall. The air was damp and heavy. Aleecia turned on another switch and the low hum of the old circulation motor broke the deathly silence.

Aleecia walked over to the air mattress she had brought in after first finding the cave, shook out the blanket and lay down. In the lonely isolation of her secret cavern, she let the ache of her broken heart surface.

Curled up in a fetal position, she wept for all the elusive dreams she had thought were within her grasp. Her taste of love had awakened her hopes of marriage, children, and a life of normalcy. Dreams that now lay shattered because she was, after all was said and done, a mutant freak. Scott's hurtful words, unknowingly resurrected from her past, tormented her, and echoed in time with the hum of the motor.

Mermaid…Mermaid…Mermaid…

* * * * *

A dull ache throbbed in his head. Scott moaned as he attempted to move. He opened his eyes. Even that small act caused the pounding to increase. Looking around to get his bearings, he wondered what the hell had happened.

He gingerly touched the side of his head. Had he been attacked, and Aleecia taken against her will? No, that didn't seem right. There was no evidence of a struggle. The blur of a fast moving foot flashed before his eyes.

Aleecia? "Damn!"

"Aleecia, where are you?" Scott carefully rose to his feet, trying not to move his head more than was necessary. He shifted his jaw back and forth. "Next time you change your mind, love, a simple no will suffice."

Her clothes lay scattered where he had tossed them. Scott walked to the bathroom, knocked, "Aleecia?" and opened the door. "Honey, I'm…"

The room was empty.

The bedroom? He tried to smile but decided the increased discomfort wasn't worth the effort.

He eased the door open, prepared to duck should anything come flying towards him.

The room continued the Oriental theme prevalent in the rest of the house. A thin mattress lay on the floor covered with a blue comforter trimmed in gold. A pagoda lit by the setting sun filled the center of the material. He glanced around and backed from the room.

Scott's breathing increased, his mouth felt like cotton. Returning to the bathroom, he checked the shower. The telltale signs of rising panic penetrated his jumbled brain cells. He forced his breathing to slow, and concentrated on trying to figure out where she could be.

Slipping on his pants, Scott walked down to his boat. His footsteps on the wooden pier echoed in the quiet night. Stepping onto the boat, he felt it rock slightly with his weight.

"Aleecia?" he called out. Mocking silence greeted him.

Scott stood on deck, looking out over the lake, its surface, smooth as glass, reflecting the twinkling stars overhead. She was out there, somewhere. Finding her, in her own environment, would be impossible, even in the day. But a compelling desire rose up from deep inside, insisting that he try.

If she didn't return by morning, he would do just that. Try. He had a feeling he knew which area of the lake she would be in, but finding her, if she didn't want to be found, would be impossible.

Scott went below, lay down on the bed and flung his arm over his eyes.

The boat rocked with a sudden gust of wind. Scott woke instantly, waiting for her to appear. With a sorrowful sigh, he closed his eyes and drifted back into a restless slumber.

Pre-dawn gray arrived, slowly driving away the night. Scott heated water on the small gas stove he used when anchored overnight. He fixed a strong cup of instant coffee and went on deck. Impossible or not, he was going to try and find her. Walking up to the house, he found her clothes still on the floor and the house empty.

His knuckles turned white around the insulated steel cup. Closing the door, Scott stomped down the hill. Untying the ropes, he jumped aboard and climbed the short ladder to the bridge. Taking one last look toward her house, he started the engine and headed out to search for Aleecia.

Scott had the area in sight and started to turn into the shallower water when he spotted a familiar boat approaching.

"Son of a," he slammed the throttle to idle, "bitch. What the hell do you want this morning?"

Gary approached and slowed down.

"I need to speak to Aleecia."

"When I see her, I'll be sure to convey your message." Scott's tone was barely civil as he looked with disgust at Aleecia's supervisor.

"What do you mean, when you see her? Isn't she on board?"

"No, she isn't. After her ordeal yesterday, she said she needed some time off. She didn't call you?" Gary could go to hell. He'd be damned if he would tell him the truth.

"Worthless bitch. She knows better than that."

Scott wanted nothing more than to pound the crap out of Gary, but now wasn't the time or place.

"What can I say?" Scott climbed down from the tower and disappeared into the cabin. He heard Gary's engine rev, and his boat rocked with the wave created when he left.

Scott stripped off his clothes and began to suit up. Taking two tanks from the storage rack, he attached the dual manifold. With one last check of his gear, he rolled backward into the water.

At sixty feet, Scott turned on his powerful flashlight. He turned the bright arc in a circle around him. This was futile, but he had to try. To walk away from what they had shared without an explanation didn't sit well with him. No matter how long it took, he hoped sooner rather than later, their paths would cross again.

At a hundred and sixty feet, the pressure was intense. Each time he had to equalize the pressure in his ears, it became more difficult. He hovered about ten feet off the bottom. His light cast contrasting shades of white and gray across the mud.

A catfish, larger than any he had ever seen, lay partially hidden underneath an old tree. It had to be at least fifteen feet long. Its mouth, open to trap food that happened to swim too close, had to be at least two feet wide. A fish that large would do more than scrape a little skin from a man's arm. He would be fortunate to have any flesh left on his bones.

He continued to search the black abyss for any signs of Aleecia. He spotted hewn timbers and swam over to check them out.

Scott searched the debris and spotted the deep, dark hole located behind several of the old beams. The hole was too small for him to go through with his tanks on and this type of dive would require different equipment from what he was wearing.

He felt deep-down this was where she was hiding. Why? The puzzling question desperately needed an answer. Taking his writing board from his vest pocket, Scott began to write her a message.

Please! Come home. We need to talk.

He took a glow stick, broke it and shook the chemicals together. It would last for twelve hours. Hopefully, sometime during that time span, she would come out and see the message.

Scott hung the bright neon yellow light on a beam along with the writing slate. With a sad shake of his head, he expanded his chest, held his arms above his waist and began the slow ascent to the surface.

Five minutes later, he leveled off and hovered at thirty feet. With one eye on his depth gauge and the other on the murky water below him, he watched for any sign of Aleecia.

His decompression stop complete, Scott surfaced.

Chapter 9

Former FBI agent Detective Larry Bates sat at his desk looking over the evidence collected on the death of Perceivel Montgomery, Private Investigator. What had started out as a routine case of heart attack was looking more like murder. Perceivel had been hired by Aleecia Field's boss to spy on Scott and Aleecia. That much Larry knew was true. Gary Tillman's reason for it had seemed a little strange and vague.

There were also some gaps between Scott's testimony and Aleecia's. Scott's mention of a camera and her failure to mention one had raised a warning flag. He picked up the camera the department divers had found and turned it over in his hands. The lab boys had the film. Hopefully the pictures would unravel the mystery.

The coroner's report hadn't been of any help. Drowning had been ruled out, his lungs had been free of water; the broken ribs and sternum had been consistent with CPR. Detective Bates stared at the official finding, Probable Cause of Death, *unknown*.

Everything had come back normal. Mr. Montgomery had been in perfect health. Yet he was dead, laid out on a cold metal table in the morgue.

He knew, deep down in his churning gut, there was a piece of the puzzle missing. And like a dog with an old bone, it gnawed on his consciousness.

Larry logged on to the NCIC network and typed in Aleecia's name. Looking past her present employment, he felt the acid building deep in his gut. He reached for the antacids and swallowed two of the chalky fruit-flavored tablets.

Larry tapped into the IRS files. "Strange." He checked her driving record. "License issued in California in 2002. No speeding tickets, accidents, or even a single parking ticket."

He opened the bank records and stared at the screen, tracking the money flow. "Money stopped coming into your account, on a normal schedule, on this date. The first withdrawal was...for cash, made a week later, at the Los Angeles International Airport."

Other than her bank account, Aleecia Fields had never existed until four years ago.

Arthur Ridgedale had made every deposit. Larry grimaced with the resurrection of his long time adversary and reached for more antacids. He tapped the screen with a pencil. "Why are you involved in Aleecia Field's life?"

A partially burned file had surfaced after the Pentagon had been hit September 11, 2001. Ridgedale's name had been linked to the nurse who had stolen a baby girl from a research laboratory. And he, Larry Bates, had been in charge of its security. The knowledge of his own failure hung like an Albatross around his neck.

He wished now those papers had been destroyed.

"Hey, Larry," a uniformed officer walked past, "here's the pictures you wanted from the lake incident yesterday. The roll of high-tech film we found in his car is there, too."

Larry opened the envelope and began looking at the photos. Glancing around to see if anyone was watching, he took his magnifying lens from the drawer.

He picked up the phone, paused, and with reservations, punched in a number that few people knew even existed.

"Authorization code." The computer generated voice requested.

Larry punched in the sequence of letters and numbers from memory.

"Authorization granted...one moment please."

"Stan, Larry Bates here...I've located Omega Sentry's missing link."

"Are you sure? I don't want to go off on a witch hunt somewhere without proof."

He heard the alarm and excitement level rise in Stan's voice.

Larry's gut churned. He looked at the picture again and closed his eyes.

"Yes. I'm sure." With a heavy sigh, he replaced the phone in its cradle.

Larry closed the file and locked it in the bottom of his desk. He got up and walked to the window. After all these years, and all the man-hours spent looking. "Why me?"

"Hey, Larry! Are you going to join the living or stay lost in space?" a colleague called out.

"What? Oh, sorry."

"You've been staring out the window for five minutes. What gives?"

"I'm tired, getting too old for this shit. By the way, I closed the case file on the heart attack victim yesterday at the lake."

The phone rang and reluctantly, he picked it up. "Detective Bates." He scowled, as he heard the caller's name. There was enough on his mind now, and he didn't need Gary Tillman's whining added to it.

The wooden pencil in his hand snapped.

Chapter 10

Scott checked his dive computer confirming what he already knew. His underwater time limit and depth had been severely diminished for the day. Floating here at anchor, hoping she might see his message and surface was out. If they were still being watched, he didn't want to draw undue attention to this spot.

Pulling the anchor, he headed across the lake to the shallow waters of yesterday's dive. He decreased the power to increase his time on the surface. If he didn't dive again, anyone with knowledge of the sport could correctly surmise his first dive had been very deep.

Checking his watch, he frowned. A mere forty-five minutes had passed, but he had stalled all he could. Scott rolled backwards over the side.

* * * * *

Aleecia woke sweaty and short of breath. Her body, betraying her in sleep, had yearned for Scott's touch. The dream had been so real. She reached between her legs and slid her fingers inside the soft folds of her wet traitorous flesh.

A low moan escaped her lips as her finger contacted the hard nub of her clitoris. "Oh, Scott," she pushed her finger deeper and slowly withdrew.

In her mind, the cavern became a plush bedroom. His hard throbbing cock filled her. Her other hand massaged her breast, twisting and pulling on her nipple. Scott's name, spilled from trembling lips, drifted in the air. Aleecia's muscles tightened, and her hips lifted off the mattress. The hot musky fragrance of her sexual release assaulted her senses.

The hum of the distant motor crept its way past the pounding of her heart.

Mermaid...Mermaid...Mermaid...

"Damn you, Scott." Aggravated at her own weakness and lack of control, she jumped from the bed. For the next hour, Aleecia sparred with her shadow, kicking, punching and attacking her silent companion.

Hunger forced her to open up her supply of emergency rations.

A fine layer of dust-turned-mud covered her body. Aleecia walked over to the flooded shaft, turned out the lights and the fan, and dove head first into the small opening. Reaching the main tunnel of the mine, she turned towards the partially blocked entrance.

The presence of light outside shocked her. With every nerve taut, she cautiously crept to the end of the passage. A glow light hung suspended from a beam. Beside it, a dive slate lay motionless, beckoning her to approach. She hoped Scott had put them there. Even in the midst of his cutting words, she felt he could be trusted. It also meant, much to her dismay, her secret sanctuary had been discovered.

She darted out with an explosive push from the rocks. Grabbing the light and slate, Aleecia swam off, reading his short note.

So, he wants to talk. Whoopee do!

She surfaced under her pier and opened the trap door. Aleecia slipped on a spare set of clothes she had in the shed. Not expecting anyone, she halted at the sight of Gary's vehicle parked in the drive. "Great, the jerk can't wait at the office like a good little boy, but has to show up here," she mumbled walking up the hill.

His lazy ass was parked in her house, sitting on her pillows, like he belonged there. "What the *hell* do you thing you're doing? I don't remember inviting you in."

"What does it look like I'm doing? I'm waiting for you. You are supposed to check into the office occasionally. I was worried."

Aleecia wasn't fooled by his coy concern.

"Scott said you were upset over the incident yesterday, but he didn't seem too concerned for your welfare. He went diving."

His little lift of the eyes and self-gratifying smirk irritated her.

"What's that supposed to imply?" She didn't like his tone.

"Just an observation."

She had had it with Gary. "Well, observe this. You are in my home, uninvited. So, you can leave." She paused, waiting for him to move. "Now," she said a little more forcefully.

Gary smiled indifferently to her demand, irritating her further.

"I don't think so."

Aleecia stepped over to the small corner table and reached into the wooden bowl. With a flip of the wrist, a black disk sailed across the room imbedding one of its deadly points into the table next to Gary's hand.

He jerked his hand back. "My God, Aleecia! You could have killed me with that thing." The color in his face drained away as he stared at the star.

"Gary, I spend more time playing with these stars than you do jerking off." Picking up another star, she flipped it in the air like a coin. "I can give you another demonstration, but I won't be throwing it at the table."

Gary scrambled to his feet. "No, I don't need another demonstration to know you're nuts. Hell, you're crazy, certifiable." He backed towards the door. "Don't bother coming into work. You don't have a job anymore, not after this."

"You can't fire me, Gary. I've already decided to quit." A sense of relief washed over her. She smiled.

"Don't close the door on your way out." Aleecia looked at him pointedly and dramatically sniffed the air. "This place needs some fresh air."

"Listen, bitch, you haven't heard the last of this."

"For your sake, Gary, I hope I have." Feeling tired and emotionally drained, she plopped down on the cushions.

Gary left, but not without one last show of defiance.

The door slammed shut.

"What's done is done." She looked around the room. "Maybe it's time to move on."

Aleecia turned her thoughts inward, seeking strength and serenity from her childhood teachings, cleansing her mind of anger and feelings of despair. Refocusing her Chi through meditation had always worked before. But today, the frayed fabric of her heart resisted her feeble attempts at repairing the rent caused by Scott's words.

With a heavy sigh, her shoulders dropped in defeat. She could hide from the authorities, run from Scott, but not from herself and her feelings.

She loved Scott. There lay the total sum of her fear. If she hadn't placed his life in danger already, she would do so by staying. Her love could destroy both their lives or it could bring fulfillment. Should she take the chance? Or was the risk too great?

* * * * *

Scott pulled up to the marina and tied his boat beside the fuel pump. Gary stepped out of the office and leaned against the building. Scott ignored him and filled his tank, conscious all the while of being watched.

Finished, he hung the hose up, turned, and stared at Gary. Something in his posture and attitude cause Scott to go on the offensive.

"If you've got a bone to pick with me, go ahead and spit it out."

"I just wanted to warn you, watch your back." Gary pushed off from the wall and walked over to the pump.

"Oh," Scott grinned, "and why is that?"

"She tried to kill me today."

Despite Gary's seriousness, or because of it, Scott laughed.

"I don't think it's funny. Aleecia has gone off the deep end. I had to flee for my life."

"Well," he looked Gary over, "I don't see any *new* bruises, and you're not dripping blood anywhere."

"Damn it, Scott. I'm trying to save your life. I stopped by her house, and she showed up. One minute we were talking all nice and cozy and the next, she threw one of those karate star things at me."

"Aleecia is home?"

"Yes! Clean the damn lake water out of your ears, Scott, and listen to me."

"If she threw one at you, it was because you probably deserved it. I've seen her throw those stars. If she had wanted to kill you," he poked Gary in the chest with his finger, "you wouldn't be standing here now."

"I should have known you'd take her side in this. You two deserve each other."

Gary looked at the pump. "I'll write your fuel down."

Scott shook his head as Gary walked back to the office. "Thanks."

At the door, he turned. "Don't say I didn't try to warn you. That girl is nuts. Course, I've always known she was odd."

Scott pulled out of the marina and headed back down the lake. Aleecia had taken off once. He didn't want her to leave again.

* * * * *

Aleecia sat on the floor in front of a half-packed suitcase. *This is for the best.* She tried to convince herself while she added another blouse. *I'll get over it.*

Mechanically, she continued packing her clothes. With her heart screaming at her to stop, she closed the lid and snapped the latches shut.

She went into the living room, gave one last look around, and began taking the weapons from the wall. With loving care, Aleecia slid soft maroon velvet covers trimmed in gold silk over the ancient tools of war.

The door opened. Reaching beneath the folds of her silk kimono, Aleecia spun ready to release her hold on a deadly star.

"Whoa!" Scott held up his hands. "It's me."

He did a quick glance around the room, his eyes pausing on the suitcases before focusing on her.

"You might as well unpack, Aleecia. Running won't solve anything." Scott stood with his legs spread, shoulder-width apart, and arms crossed over his bare chest. A strong look of determination was chiseled across his bronze face.

She picked up two large suitcases and stood in front of Scott. "You think you're going to stop me?"

"One way or the other, I'm going to try."

Her shoulders slumped. "Please try to understand. It's not safe! If I stay, your life will be in constant danger. Why can't you see the truth?"

"Here's the truth as I see it."

Scott's arms lashed out circling her, drawing her towards him even as his mouth descended upon hers in a crushing embrace. Dropping the suitcases, her arms went around his neck.

Opening her lips, she gave his tongue free rein, meeting his probing with her own hungry desires. The kiss became frantic, filled with urgent desperation.

Aleecia lifted her legs, wrapping them around his waist. The kimono rode up to her waist.

Scott walked over the cushions. The swaying motion of his hips ground his hard cock against her flesh. He lowered her to the floor, the silk parted revealing the shining tips of several stars concealed within the fabric. Scott's eyes drank in her nude body. A sultry smile of appreciation spread across his face.

He tugged the tight-fitting black Speedo trunks over his hips. His ridged shaft caught in the material, then sprang up straight and tall when finally freed from its constraints.

Aleecia grabbed a foil packet from the table and ripped it open. In her eagerness, she dropped the condom.

"Here, let me do it," he chuckled. "That's the last one. You tear it and I'll have to go get more from the boat."

He took it from her fingers and slowly rolled it in place.

Taking his hand, she pulled him down to the floor between her legs. Reaching between their bodies, she guided his throbbing shaft past the outer folds of her feminine entrance.

This was the memory she wanted to take with her. Not of the fight they had had, but the feel of his hard cock filling her, pounding deep inside her wet pussy.

In a tangle of arms and legs, she rolled him over. Rising up on her knees, she grabbed his cock and tore the condom free. Before Scott could protest, she thrust her body lower, sending his hot bare flesh deep inside her.

"I don't care," she braced his arms with her hands. "I want to feel you inside me." She ground her thighs against his hips. "Not a damn condom."

Aleecia took his mouth in a savage, wide-open seduction.

Scott's hands caressed her legs and slid up her back. His fingers traced the gill line from the center of her back to the bottom of her ribs, then up, up to her breasts that yearned for his magical touch.

She sat up, giving his fingers access to her nipples.

She rode the cresting wave of her passion, suspended above the turbulent whirlpool that swirled beneath them.

His body erupted, filling her with his heat and sent her crashing over the edge. She felt herself falling, tumbling through the hot misty fog of her own climax. Spent, gasping for breath, Aleecia fell forward into the comfort and warmth of Scott's arms.

In the security of his embrace, she allowed herself the luxury of letting go, putting the vigilant warrior aside, and being a woman. Now — it was time to again take up the shield she had carried for so long.

The words of her beloved master came as a whisper upon her mind. When surrounded by an unknown enemy, it is better to vanish until you know who or what it is you fight against....

The rest was drowned out by a soul-wrenching cry of agony from her heart.

Breaking the intimate contact between them, Aleecia whimpered as his cock slid from between her wet folds. She stood, gathered the kimono around her waist and tied the sash.

"Where are you going?" Scott watched her dress. A puzzled frown etched his brow.

"I'm sorry, Scott." She pulled her kimono over her head. "I told you earlier, but you wouldn't listen. I'm..." she paused, forcing the words past the constricting lump in her throat, "leaving."

"You're what?" He sat up and grabbed her shoulders. "After what we shared?"

"What did we share, Scott?" she allowed herself to be held by his iron grip. "Good sex? Okay, I'll even go as far as admitting it was great sex."

"Damn it, Aleecia!" he gently shook her. "Look me in the eye and tell me this meant nothing more than sex."

She kept her eyes lowered, afraid he would see the truth.

"You can't, can you?"

Scott dropped his hands in frustration. Angrily, he stood and walked over to the window overlooking the lake.

"If you're this damned determined to leave, fine. Where are you going?"

She watched the taut muscles in his back and legs quiver with suppressed anger. "I...I don't know."

He spun around, his face flushed with emotion. "You can't take off without some idea where you are going. I won't let you."

"Scott, darling," she pleaded. "Don't make this any harder than it already is."

"What makes you think you will be any safer alone than with me?" his voice gentled, and he lifted her chin with his finger.

"They'll use you to get to me, Scott. Don't you see? I'm trying to protect you, too."

"Protect me from whom?" He looked around the room. "I don't see anyone waiting in the shadows or lurking behind the bushes outside. I've gone along with this phobia of yours but..."

"Phobia!" she exploded. "My mother wasn't killed by a damn phobia."

"Okay, poor choice of words. I'm sorry." He walked away from the window and stopped in front of her. Scott raised his hand and with the back of his fingers caressed her cheek. "Why now? Why the sudden change and this urgent desire to flee?"

"Scott," she nuzzled his hand, wishing things could be different. "It's better if you don't know. Wait, please. I..."

"What more is there to know? What deep dark secrets are you hiding? If you think for one moment, I'm going to let go of my own special mermaid who swam into my life and stole my heart, you're wrong."

"It won't work, Scott. Not now," she blinked back the tears of regret. "Maybe I was living in a fantasy world to even hope for a normal life," she sighed, "but that's over now."

"Aleecia, my love. Don't cry." He drew her close, his arms locked around her. "We can still grasp those dreams as long as we're together. We'll make it work."

"I can't," she whispered against the hard muscle of his chest.

"Yes, we can, love." His fingers stroked her hair.

"Scott, you have to let me go."

His chest rippled with laugher. "I like you right where you are."

"The man in the boat yesterday didn't die from a heart attack."

Chapter 11

He closed his eyes, and held her tight against him, afraid to let her go. Now, more than ever, he had to convince her to stay.

"I...I won't tell you I understand why you think you had to..."

"Kill him," she finished for him.

Scott dropped his arms, stepped back, and looked into her eyes. "You make it sound like...like a damn trip to the local market. Christ, Aleecia!" He ran his hand through his hair.

"What do you want me to do, fall apart and cry? He was spying on me, taking pictures with a large telephoto lens."

"You can't kill a person for taking pictures." In suppressed anger, he paced the width of the room. "It's against the law here, and I'd assume in Japan as well. After all, there wouldn't be a very big tourist industry if they declared open season on people carrying cameras."

"I don't disregard life. In my teaching, I was taught to value it highly. Especially my own and those closest to me." She walked over and placed her hand gently on his arm. "Try to understand Scott. Because of what I am, we are vulnerable. In order to get to me, the government wouldn't hesitate to use you. Maybe it was unfair getting you involved...but you are." It was time to lay it all on the line. "Scott, I love you. I'll do everything in my power to protect you."

His heart and soul rejoiced at her words. Scott reached for her, his hand stopped inches from her face. Aleecia's misty sea green eyes revealed the turbulence of a brewing storm.

"As much as I want to fit in, it's impossible. You're right, Scott, I'm a mermaid, a freak. Denying the truth of it doesn't change the fact."

Closing the space between them, Scott drew her close. "Others might think you a freak, but I don't." He looked around room, the walls outlined with the shadowed imprint of the weapons now removed.

"I don't want you to leave. Whatever happens, we can work things out. I can make a couple phone calls and get..."

"What you'll do is get us both killed." She wanted to turn away, but didn't have the heart to use force and remove his arms from around her. The security and warmth of his embrace were illusions that clouded her mind with pictures of an unrealistic future.

His chest shook with his soft laughter.

"I don't see anything funny in this."

"Could I finish a sentence without you jumping in?" His breath stirred her hair and warmed her skin.

"Although I sold my company, I'm still on the board. I'll have a couple of packages sent out to give us an idea if someone is watching you." He tipped her head up and took her lips in a soft caressing kiss. "I've never found a priceless treasure at the bottom of a lake. Now that I have, I'm not going to lose it without a fight."

The short bristle of his whiskers scraped along her cheek. "What's this treasure you found?" Aleecia whispered in his ear. "Gold, silver, or is it something mysterious?"

"Nothing so trivial as gold or silver." Scott's hand slid sensuously up her back. His strong fingers teased her hair. The soft touch of his words warmed her ear and sent a lightning burst of heat to ignite the passion deep within her body.

"But...very mysterious." His hand found the sash and with a gentle tug the silk garment parted.

The last word was spoken softly but echoed in the chamber of her heart like a shout from a mountain cliff. His lips touched her earlobe, and she pressed her body tighter against his. The feel of his cock pressed against her, hard and wanting.

Scott's tongue stroked her flesh and drew the wet lobe into his mouth, sucking and nibbling on it. Her legs grew weaker with each tender bite. She was melting from the heat.

All thoughts of leaving evaporated like the early morning fog before a blazing sun.

His lips left a trail of fire down her neck, and she rolled her head to the side. A soft moan escaped her lips.

"Take me, Scott."

Like mermaid's sirens beckoning sailors to the rocky shores, his name floated to him over the turbulent storm of his own desire.

Aleecia's breasts invited his touch. Lifting with each breath, her extended nipples drew his mouth ever closer. His lips closed over the hard nub of sensitive flesh, and she shuddered. A low sensuous sigh ruffled his hair.

Leaving the soft roundness of her breast, Scott's mouth left a trail of wet kisses down her quivering belly as he sank to the floor on his knees. The musky fragrance of her wet pussy inflamed his senses, and he buried his face in her soft curly hair.

Her legs trembled, and her hands gripped his shoulders for support. Soft moans rushed from her open mouth with each ragged breath.

"Take me, don't...make me beg."

Her breasts kissed his cheeks as she slid down his body. His face was assaulted with hot feathery kisses, and her hungry mouth captured his in a tongue-probing frenzy.

Rolling sideways, she turned, landing with her back against the mound of pillows piled on the floor.

Scott felt the hard tips of her breasts crush against his chest. His cock lay nested in a soft bed of hair, its tip poised at the opening of her hot womanly core. With a deliberately slow thrust of his hips, he entered her wet sheath.

Aleecia's legs, strengthened from years of martial arts and swimming, wrapped around him like a vise. Her fingers curled in his hair dragging his mouth to hers. With each thrust of her hips, her tongue emulated the rhythm of his hard cock buried deep within her body.

The pale green of her eyes darkened to a rich emerald. Her body trembled with passion. She met each driving thrust with wild, hungry abandon.

Gasping for breath, a steady stream of deep sensuous moans rose from her throat.

Scott drank in the sweet essence of her mouth. He captured the hot moist air as it rushed from her chest. Her sighs of passion swept through him, echoing within the chambers of his heart and overwhelmed his soul. His legs quivered, his back arched as he filled the inner depths of her pussy with his life giving sperm.

Spent, gasping for air, he collapsed on top of her. "Oh, baby...that was..."

"Intense? Wonderful? Fantastic?" Aleecia whispered in his ear.

"Yes, all those things...and more."

Aleecia's fingers slowly trailed over the sweat-covered expanse of his broad back and crept through his damp hair. "Mmm, definitely more."

"Damn," he rolled to the side leaving a trail of cum across her leg.

"What's the matter?" She watched him flop his arm across his eyes and a frustrated frown crease his brow. "I thought you enjoyed it."

"Oh, I did. Too much so it seems."

Laughter bubbled from her lips. "I didn't know it was possible to enjoy making love too much. Course, I'm not overly qualified in the area of sexology."

"This isn't a laughing matter. Damn it, Aleecia, we're supposed to be responsible adults, and we're jumping into the sack like teenagers with their hormones on overdrive."

"Your point in all this is?" she rose up on her elbow and looked down at Scott's face.

"The *point* is, Aleecia, we didn't use any protection against you getting knocked up."

"Knocked up!" she cocked her head and arched her brow. "You make it sound like a disease. Something to be avoided at all costs. Go ahead and say it, Scott, the word is pregnant. Look at me, Scott."

He lowered his arm and stared at her. Self-disgust written across his face.

"This is the twenty-first century. Women get pregnant and have babies all the time without the *benefit* of a man around to hold their hand. I'm not even sure I can have children, and if I did become, as you so crudely put it, knocked up, I would deal with it."

Shock rolled across his eyes, and he jumped to his feet. "Deal with it! Now who's making it sound like a disease you can cure with a trip to the local doctor? If you're carrying my child, there's no way in *hell* you're having an abortion."

The devastation of losing Lindsey drew his face into a picture of agony, and she felt sorry for his pain and anguish.

"Scott, I wouldn't. Maybe, 'deal with it' was the wrong thing to say." Aleecia rose from the floor and stood next to him. "I would willingly make the adjustments in my life, if and when I ever have a child. And I would want your child."

Aleecia rose up and gave him a soft tender kiss. "I'm going for a swim. Will you join me?"

"In a few minutes. You go ahead, I'll be right down."

Scott watched her slip on a large T-shirt and walk out the door.

She didn't say, my child. Aleecia wants a baby, but preferably not with me. With a heavy sigh and his thoughts in turmoil, Scott slipped on his swimsuit and made his way slowly down the hill. *So much for the love she had professed.*

The sky had clouded up with the promise of rain. The dark ominous clouds obscured the sun hanging low over the Ozark Mountains. A slight north wind dropped the temperature and goosebumps popped out on his arms and legs. A shiver ran through his body. Was it the cold — or a forewarning of events to come?

He had come here to clean the lake, but so far, he had done very little towards that goal. A lot of time, effort, and money had gone into this, and if he was going to receive backing in the future, he needed to start producing results.

Standing on the end of the wooden pier, Scott looked down at Aleecia's smiling upturned face.

"You coming in, or going to stand there?"

"I was thinking of going on a night dive. You want to join me?"

He watched the indecision play across her face. She looked around the cove, now blanketed in shifting shades of gray.

"Sure, why not?" She disappeared under the dock and a minute later stepped through the door of the shack. The T-shirt absorbed the dampness of her skin making it nearly transparent. It clung to her soft curves like a second skin accenting her breasts. The dark areolas around her nipples, visible under the wet material, warmed the blood flowing through his veins.

He had to keep his mind on the job. Somehow, Aleecia had gotten inside his defenses and distracted him. Then she had effectively slammed the door on any hopes of a future with her.

Untying the mooring line from the cleat, he sighed. Better to find out now, before this siren of the lake captured his heart forever.

As they cruised down the lake, Scott donned a jacket against the chilly bite of the wind.

Aleecia studied his ridged stance at the controls. She felt the distance between them like a heavy weight chained to her heart. It pulled at her, dragging her to the dark depths of despair, away from the light of love she had seen in his eyes.

"Maybe, it's for the best." The speed of the boat carried her soft words into the growing darkness of the coming night. He had taught her love and passion. She would carry the memories with her forever, but memories didn't keep you warm or satisfy the longings he had awakened.

Scott idled the boat back, and it drifted to a stop. "We'll dive here."

There was no warmth in his words. Aleecia watched him drop the anchor and raise the dive flag. His movements, although concise and efficient, lacked the customary excitement he normally displayed. His thin smile seemed forced, and she had second thoughts about the wisdom of coming with him.

He was using this dive as a barrier, the water and the darkness creating an efficient buffer zone between them.

Aleecia pulled the shirt over her head and picked up several trash bags. "I'm going in." Without waiting for a reply, she dove over the side and submerged into the darkness.

The momentary burn in her lungs, as her body made the adjustment, was welcome. She was back home where she belonged.

Scott felt the boat wobble and the splash as she hit the water. He paused in getting dressed, his wetsuit around his waist. His shoulders slumped and with a sad shake of his head, he slowly finished pulling the tight neoprene suit over his chest and fastened the Velcro shoulder straps.

His enthusiasm for the dive had ebbed away like the ocean tide. His movements checking his gear were mechanical. Forcing his mind back on the task before him, Scott made the last minute adjustments to his gear before sticking the regulator in his mouth and stepping into the water.

Raising the vent tube over his head, Scott released the air keeping him afloat. Lowering his arm, he began a slow descent. His depth gauge read fifty feet when he touched bottom. The faint greenish glow of his watch faded, leaving him in total darkness.

Taking hold of his flashlight, he turned it on. The brilliant beam shattered the blackness, driving it away and revealing numerous cans and bottles scattered in the mud. Swinging the light around him, Scott searched for any signs of Aleecia.

At the outer fringe of the light, he noticed a light brown fog of sediment hovering about a foot off the bottom. He worked his way toward it, picking up trash as he went. His first trash bag was full when he reached the suspended haze. Attaching the bag to a marker, Scott sensed her presence and looked up. With three full bags in her hands, she swam towards him.

He envied the ease with which she glided through the water. Her agility was beautifully displayed with each graceful movement. The light played off her hair, floating behind her. It accented her breasts and glistened off her skin like shimmering satin.

Scott resisted the strong urge to touch her and caress her face.

Her eyes were squinted almost shut, and he realized his high power light was blinding her. Scott turned it off, plunging him into a silent cold black void. What was she doing? With each passing moment, his excitement increased. He wanted her to touch him. Where was she?

Taking a small backup light from his vest, Scott turned it on and rotated it in a wide arc. It was like she had never been there. *Did I imagine the whole thing?* he asked himself. His only proof of her having been there were four more bags tied to the marker buoy. Aleecia was out there somewhere, watching. He could picture her face in his mind, laughing at him.

Scott checked his gauge and continued picking up the cans and bottles. He tied off the last bag, swung the light around him, and added a burst of air to his vest. The bottom slowly retreated, merging into the encroaching blackness. A stop wasn't required, but he opted on the side of safety and hung suspended at fifteen feet for several minutes.

He tried, in vain, to push thoughts of Aleecia from his mind. Knowing she was still down there in the cold black depths kept bringing her face to his thoughts. On the bottom there were things to do to keep his mind off her; air levels to check, compass headings to remember, watching for trash to pick up and bags to fill. With nothing to do but monitor his air and depth, she tormented his mind.

The wind had increased and the surface chop bobbed him around like a cork, slapping him in the face. The bright beam of his lantern flashed across the surface lighting up his boat. Orange float markers dotted the surface like colored pins on a map. Adding air to his vest, he turned on his back and began gently kicking.

Pulling himself out of the water, Scott noticed the gear seemed heavier. He was tired, worn out physically and emotionally. With a deep grunt he levered himself over the side. Setting the tank on the deck, he looked around amazed at the amount of trash bags already on deck. Aleecia had been busy.

A light rain began falling. He removed his weight belt, letting it fall to the deck with a dull thud. The rest of the bags attached to the marker buoys would have to wait until morning. Sleep was the main element his body needed, and he headed towards the cabin. As he reached for the latch, the boat pitched, and he heard the squeak of the boarding ladder. Scott turned around.

Aleecia stepped aboard. The stern light's dim glow bathed half her body in soft pale shifting shadows. The large mesh bag he had used to store equipment in was slung over her shoulder. It was bulging with bottom trash. Muddy rust-colored water poured from the bag, streaming down her back and legs to pool around her feet.

Her breathing was labored. Aleecia slumped back on the side rail and raised her face to the increasing rain.

"You could have left it on the bottom 'til later." Her strength continually amazed him. There was no way in hell he could have brought the bag up on his own, even dropping his weights and adding all the air his vest would hold.

"Yeah, I could've," she looked across the deck at him, "but I didn't."

"What did you do with all the smaller bags?" Stepping away from the bulkhead, he walked towards her, carefully stepping over trash and gear that cluttered the deck.

"I used them. I found a lot of trash closer to shore. After I filled the smaller bags I put them in this and brought them all back."

Scott laughed softly and ran his hand through his hair. "About the time I think I have you all figured out, you do something I'm not expecting."

With a strained laugh, she leaned back over the water. The arc of the stern light drove away the shadows lighting up her face and breasts. Her hair was matted with black silt and streaks of brown rust covered her shoulders and chest.

"How did you get the crap in your hair?"

"I found a lawn table and tried to dig it out."

Warning bells sounded in his head. "Damn it, Aleecia. You inhaled that shit."

"I got most of it out. I'll be okay." She coughed up thick blackish phlegm.

Scott was already in motion. Grabbing one of the boat's fender guards, he tied it to the anchor rope and dropped it over the side.

"What are you doing?" Each breath was becoming more difficult for her to take.

"Getting you home and flushed out." He took the ladder to the bridge two rungs at a time and started the engine.

"Hold on!" The boat leapt forward as he opened the throttle to full power. "Damn fool woman," he muttered.

The black gumbo under the top layer of silt was difficult to get off a wetsuit. The thought of her having it in her lungs was horrifying. His fingers itched to pick up the handset for the marine radio and call for help. He looked over his shoulder at Aleecia.

She was sitting on the deck with her head back, mouth open. He hoped to God, she was still breathing. Turning his attention back to the darkness in front of him, his worries increased. Suddenly the answer came to him, and he slammed the throttle back to idle.

"What now?" her voice was weak and scratchy.

"Back into the water and breathe through your gills. Now!"

Scott watched her crawl to her feet and fall overboard. Sliding down the ladder, he snatched up a rope and threw it in. "Grab it and hang on."

Aleecia took hold of the rope and wrapped it around her wrist. "I'm ready, but take it slow."

He raced back to the controls and started the boat moving forward in the water. For several anxious minutes, he divided his watchful eyes between the bow and the taut rope behind him.

If the fresh water flowing through her gills didn't revive her and clean out her lungs, he would be left with only one option. The consequences of going to the hospital could be as deadly as doing nothing at all.

Chapter 12

Aleecia held fast to the rope as Scott pulled her through the water. With each passing second, as her gills strained the oxygen from its life-giving flow, strength came back into her body. In her attempt to prove herself to Scott, she had endangered both their lives. What had caused her to act so irrationally?

If she had continued swimming, her lungs wouldn't have filled up with silt. It would have passed right through. Trouble was, she had to keep water moving past her gills and to do that meant expanding her lungs to draw in water.

The boat slowed, and she surfaced. Scott was pulling up to her pier.

"Are you feeling better?"

Concern was written across his face and etched deep in his voice.

"Yes, much. Thank you."

"Go on up to the house and flush your lungs out with clean fresh water." He shut off the motor.

Aleecia reached for the line to tie off the stern.

"I can take care of this. Get your ass up to the house, now."

"I told you I'm fine." His attitude riled her. "I'm not helpless."

"Humor me, and go. If you're not in the shower when I get there, I'll..."

"You'll do what? Carry me to the shower? Turn me over your knee and paddle my ass?" She laughed and started coughing.

"That's an idea I hadn't thought of, yet. Thanks." He pointed towards the house. "Now go, before I do both."

"All right, I'm going." She walked down the pier but couldn't resist one parting shot over his bow. "It would've been fun seeing you try to do either one, much less both."

Aleecia climbed into the shower, took a deep breath to expand her lungs and gasped. She expected it to burn, a little. The pain was excruciating, setting her lungs on fire. The water swirling around her feet was black and the smell of rot and decay assailed her senses.

She braced her mind against the onslaught of the pain, and raised her face to the shower. With each deep breath, she thought her knees would buckle. Sweat poured from her skin. Her arms, leaning against the shower wall, trembled. Drawing on her inner strength, she continued with the grueling torture.

The door opened. Turning her head, she looked at Scott. "I'm better, thanks."

"You don't look any better, cleaner maybe."

"I think...I'll be fine now." She turned her attention to washing the lake grime out of her hair.

"Holler, if you need me." Scott closed the door.

* * * * *

Scott woke in the early morning to moans from Aleecia's bedroom. Still half-asleep, he stumbled into the room and was instantly alarmed. The covers lay on the floor. Aleecia thrashed on the bed, her body covered with a thin sheen of sweat.

Reaching her side, he touched her face. Scooping her up in his arms, he ran for the shower.

Goosebumps popped up on his skin as he held her under the cold spray. Even with the shower on full, heat from her body radiated on to his. Scott glanced down, and he stared with shock at her back. A thick yellowish-green puss oozed from her gills.

Fear lodged in this throat, its bitter acid taste filling his mouth.

"Aleecia, love, talk to me. Come on, damn it...wake up!"

Slowly, her eyes opened, but they had a vacant, confused look.

"Breathe, dear, breathe the water." He held her face up to the shower.

With a gut-wrenching scream, she doubled over on the floor and started coughing.

"That's it. I'm taking you to the hospital."

She looked up, her eyes glazed with pain pleaded with him. "No, Scott. Whatever happens...I can't go." Gasping for breath, she clasped his arm. "My nightstand, next to the bed. Doctor's name is...Terrance Walters."

Scott ran to her room and found the phone number. As he dialed the number, he hoped he wasn't too late.

He listened to the ringing in his ears. "Come on, pick up the damn phone."

"Hello," the voice was groggy from sleep.

"Doctor Walters?" he asked.

"Yes. Who is this, and how did you get my private number?"

"Doctor Walters. I'm Scott Mathis. We have a mutual friend who may die if you don't help me. Aleecia won't go to the hospital."

"Aleecia!" The doctor's voice was no longer sleepy. "What's happened?"

"She has an infection in her lungs and can barely breathe. Her lungs are draining a thick green puss, and she's running a very high temp."

"I'll call in a prescription to the pharmacy. She needs oxygen immediately."

"Doc, I have a small O2 bottle on my boat, but it won't last long."

"Good, go get it and give it to her at five milliliters. I'll stay on the line."

Scott ran out the door and flew down the steps. He grabbed the oxygen bottle and the emergency first-aid kit, and headed back to the house.

Time seemed to stand still as he adjusted the mask over her face and turned on the oxygen. Her body temperature had dropped, but until the infection could be brought under control, it was only temporary.

"Okay, Doc. The oxygen is on, but she's not responding."

"I've cleared my schedule, but it will be several hours before I can get there, so listen carefully. You are going to have to clean her out."

"How?" Scott interrupted him.

"Calm down, Scott. I'm going to tell you. Find a spray bottle and make sure it's clean. Fix a solution of warm salt water and spray it directly onto the folia and into her lungs. If it's as bad as you say, it's going to hurt like hell."

"What else?" he asked.

"When the pharmacy opens, you'll have to go get the medicine and more oxygen. I'll be there as soon as I can get a plane. All I need is directions from the airport."

With a growing feeling of dread, he hung up the phone and went to find something suitable to use. A spray bottle of window cleaner was the only thing he could find. He dumped the contents down the drain.

Scott lost track of how many times he washed the bottle. His fingers were wrinkled and red from the hot water. Mixing a solution of saltwater, he filled the bottle and carried it to the bathroom.

Aleecia was barely conscious. Her pulse was rapid and weak.

"Doctor Walters is on the way." He held the bottle up for her to see. "This is warm salt water. I have to try cleaning your gills and lungs. Do you understand?"

She responded with a weak nod of her head.

Carefully lifting the outer portion of the gill, Scott began to clean the oxygen gathering folia. They were packed almost solid with the infectious pus. The minutes dragged by with little apparent headway. He was on his second bottle when a small portion of the gill was cleared.

With the next spray, Aleecia's body jerked and a muffled gasp escaped her breathing mask.

"I'm sorry, dear. There's no other way to do this." He caressed her cheek. Leaning forward, he kissed her forehead. "You're going to have to be strong."

She looked into his eyes. They were filled with pain, fear, and a determination to see it through. For an instant, he saw inside her soul and was deeply moved. She trusted him.

Aleecia crawled into a cross-legged position on the shower floor and after several minutes, calmly whispered, "Go on."

Beads of sweat popped out on her back as more water made its way past the gills and inside her lung. A mute testimony of the pain she endured.

Scott refilled the bottle again and moved to the other side.

Throughout the time she sat there, only the slightest whimper was heard. The tank was empty. Aleecia was breathing, although with difficulty, on her own.

"I'm afraid the easy part is over." He handed her a large bowl of warm salt water.

For several minutes, she looked at the bowl as though it wasn't there in front of her. She took several deep breaths. Blowing the last one out all the way, she picked up the bowl.

I can do this. Aleecia drew deeper inside herself, down into the dark corner of her mind. Her Master had shown it to her, but it had taken years of practice and patience to reach it. This time she was not alone.

She often found the Master there, waiting to commune with her, show her strength when she thought she was weak, and peace when troubled. There was another spirit with her, besides the Master. Somehow, Scott had gone with her on her journey. He held her close in the darkness. The light of his love covered her like a mantle.

The Master smiled his approval and wrapped his presence around them.

Picking up the bowl, Aleecia lowered her face into in and inhaled the warm liquid.

Pain shot through her. Fire burned in her lungs and spread throughout her body. An uncontrollable gasp sucked in more water, exposing new surface areas of her lungs to its warm cleansing. Lights flashed behind her eyelids as the pain continued to soar higher.

Blackness crept in. She was going down a long tunnel, spinning out of control. With her last remaining strength, she exhaled the water from her lungs.

Scott held her while the violent tremors racked her body. His mind counted off the seconds since she had taken the first of the water into her lungs. Scott's chest burned, he realized he was holding his breath along with Aleecia.

Water gushed from her gills, and she fell limp in his arms. Panic gripped his heart as he realized she wasn't breathing.

Scott pulled her from the small shower and laid her on the floor. Tilting her head back, he began forcing air into her lungs.

Checking her pulse, he found it weak and very rapid.

Don't quit on me now, he silently pleaded. *Come back to me, love.*

Again and again, he breathed for her. Praying she would return, and scared to death, she wouldn't.

Her eyes opened, large and confused. She took her first unassisted breath in what seemed like hours. Scott felt joyous euphoria within his heart. Tears of happiness filled his eyes, blurring her image. Raising her shoulders from the cold wet floor, he cradled her head on his chest and gently rocked her.

"I thought I had lost you," he whispered.

"I heard you calling me back."

"I don't understand how, but I'm glad you did."

Lifting her chin, Scott kissed her lips.

"Me, too." She managed a small smile before settling back against him. Her eyes drifted shut.

Scott took a warm wet towel, cleaned her up, and carried her to bed. She was breathing easy, but he knew they weren't out of the woods yet. He would be glad when the doctor arrived.

"Aleecia," he gently shook her. "Aleecia, honey, wake up."

At first, all he saw was the whites of her eyes. Dazed and disorientated, they focused on his face.

"I don't like leaving you, but I have to go get some medicine from town." He smoothed her hair with his fingers. "I won't be gone long."

"Hurry back." Her lips moved, but little sound emerged.

Her eyes closed, and she was asleep before he could answer. Scott ran to the boat, threw some clothes over his swim trunks and grabbed his billfold. He hesitated only slightly before he decided on taking the boat back to the marina. Untying from the pier, he started the engine. The boat cleared the end of the pier and he jammed it to full throttle.

Scott waited 'until the last possible moment to cut the power. As he pulled up to the pier, Gary came boiling out of the office.

"I'm giving you a ticket for speeding through a no-wake zone." He raised the book in the air and shook it.

"Fine, leave it on the boat." Scott turned to walk off.

"Hey, asshole, come back here. I'm not finished with you."

Scott whirled around. "Look, Gary, write me all the damn tickets you want. Right now, I have a medical emergency to tend to, and neither you, nor anyone else is going to stop me. Far as I'm concerned, you can stick that book up your ass." He didn't wait for a reply but headed for his rental truck.

How he managed to get to the pharmacy and back without being stopped, he didn't know. He had broken about every traffic law on the books in his mad dash for Aleecia's medication.

Sliding to a stop, he jumped out and shouldered the two oxygen bottles. Gary was waiting at the stern of his boat when he arrived.

"I'll give you a hand with those."

"No thanks, Gary. I've got it." Scott stepped aboard and secured the tanks.

Gary followed him onto the boat.

"It's common practice to ask permission before coming aboard someone else's boat." Scott bristled. "What do you think you're doing?"

"I'm going with you to help with this emergency you supposedly have."

The smirk on Gary's face was infuriating.

"Afraid you will only be in the way, Gary. A doctor is on the way, and should be there shortly. Now, please, leave the boat."

"Okay, suit yourself," he laughed. "I'll follow in one of the lake patrol boats."

"Gary," Scott grabbed his arm. His fingers clamped down on soft tissue, grinding it into the bone.

"Let me make one thing clear." Scott got in his face. "You follow me, and I'll make sure the doc has two patients to see, instead of one. Now, get the hell off my boat and stay out of my sight." He gave Gary a shove that sent him stumbling.

Grumbling under his breath, Gary climbed onto the pier. "You haven't heard the last of this."

Scott pulled away with Gary shouting obscenities at him.

* * * * *

Time drags when life hangs in the balance.

Aleecia slept while the fever continued to ravage her body. She had soaked the sheets twice, forcing Scott to jostle her around while changing them. She seemed to be holding her own. At times, she had been out of her head, delirious. As the day began to wane and shadows crept across the wall, Scott's fear of losing her grew.

He heard a vehicle approach and a car door slam.

With his body protesting his every move, Scott climbed to his feet.

At the door, an elderly gentleman, slightly bald with short silver hair stood holding a black bag.

"Doctor Walters?" Scott asked.

"Yes. Sorry I'm late. I got tied up in this awful traffic."

Scott sighed with relief and reached out to shake his hand. "Am I glad to see you. Come right this way."

"How's Aleecia doing, Scott?"

"Still running a high fever at times." Scott led the doctor into Aleecia's room.

Terrance Walters approached the bed and began his examination.

"Give me a hand, Scott, I need to turn her over."

He watched Doctor Walters carefully lift the outer flap of skin over her gills. Using a magnifying scope with an attached light, he inserted a small probe inside her lungs.

Worry lines etched across Walters' face as he examined Aleecia. He removed the probe, and they rolled her onto her back. After attaching an IV to her arm, Walters walked out of the room.

"Well?" Scott asked.

"Any other person would have been dead by now." He leaned against the windowsill and looked out at the lake. "She needs to be in an Intensive Care Unit, but..."

"It's impossible." Scott finished for him. "I know."

Doctor Walters sighed. Scott saw a tear roll down his cheek.

"Isn't there anything we can do?" Scott's voice cracked with emotion.

"Wait...and pray." Doc's hand closed into a fist, and he hit the wall with a solid blow. "Damn, I was afraid this would happen."

"Afraid what would happen?" Scott felt his world once again collapsing around him. A feeling of helplessness washed over him. He had been given a second chance at love, and now it too, was on the verge of being ripped from his heart and soul.

"Aleecia's lungs, as you know, are unique. When exposed to water, they constrict, allowing it to flow almost straight through and over the gills. As long as she keeps moving, everything passes out of her body. When she stops, her lungs expand pulling the water into her lungs just like air.

"She was stationary in the water when she inhaled the sediment. I'll put it in simple layman terms." Doc Walters walked over to the bedroom door and sagged wearily against the jam. "Her lungs are still full of shit, restricting her breathing and filling her system with infection."

"Can't we flush her out again?" He was grasping for straws, anything to keep hope alive.

"Don't get me wrong, Scott. Aleecia would be dead by now if you hadn't done what you did. No question about it. But we don't have the equipment to do enough. I need a sample of the sediment she inhaled to run lab tests. I have to find out exactly what chemicals might be in it. Her lungs have to be expanded and flushed with oxygen enriched fluid to wash out the smallest of the capillary air sacs."

"Doc, we can't sit here and watch her die! I won't allow it."

"Neither will we."

Scott turned around, and Detective Larry Bates stood in the doorway.

"Hello, Larry." Doc Walters had a frown on his face, but his eyes had the gleam of hope. "I thought you had retired to civilian life."

"Semi-retired, Terrance." Larry chuckled, but there was little humor in the sound.

Scott looked from one to the other. "You two, ah, know each other?"

"You might say we are mutually acquainted." Larry walked into the house. "I was assigned to the case when Aleecia was stolen as a baby. The good doctor here was a prime suspect and as time has proven, one of the persons responsible in her disappearance. But as they say, 'that's water under the bridge'."

Scott could hear a helicopter in the distance. "What are you planning on doing now?"

"We are going to take her to a private hospital and try to save her life."

"And then what? Put her in a cage and study her for science?" Scott's anger was near the boiling point. "Aleecia would rather die first."

He started towards Larry, his hands closed in tight fists.

The gun appeared in Larry's hand as if by magic. "Don't, Mathis, I don't want it to come to this, but I'm prepared to kill you if need be. You can either work with us or not. The choice is yours. What's it going to be?"

Scott stopped in his tracks and swallowed. Larry's pistol was pointed unwaveringly at his chest. "I don't like the sound of the other choice.

"What do you want me to do?"

Chapter 13

Scott stood in the driveway watching as the helicopter disappeared from sight. The growing apprehension in his gut had been dampened with the hope of Aleecia receiving the medical attention she needed. But could he trust them?

He sighed. For now, as Detective Bates had so effectively demonstrated, he had no other choice.

"Are you ready?" Scott turned to his newly assigned watchdog, Special Agent Stephanie Brooke. She was a tall, slim black woman in her late twenties. Her no-nonsense attitude didn't hide the wild sensuous gleam in her eye.

"I'm always ready." Her mouth lifted in a wide smile. "I'm waiting on you."

Turning away from her, he strode off with long purposeful steps towards the boat.

"You trying to get rid of me?" She matched his stride easily.

"No," Scott continued down the hill.

"Good, cause it won't work." She followed him across the pier. "Permission to come aboard?"

The situation was so ridiculous, Scott laughed. "And if I said, *no,* would it make any difference?"

"None at all." She stood there waiting.

"In that case, get your ass aboard. We're wasting time."

Scott started the engine and allowed it to warm up. "Untie the stern line."

"Are you always this bossy?" she asked, as she removed the line from around the mooring cleat.

"When I'm on my boat I am." He turned to look down at Stephanie on the deck. "Let's get one thing straight right from the start. You might be a one hell of a kick-ass agent, but when you're on my boat, I'm the Captain."

Scott jammed the throttle open, expecting to see her fall on her ass or better yet, over the side.

She stood there, balanced on perfectly spaced feet, showing a mouth full of shiny white teeth. He turned back to watch the channel, slightly aggravated she was still standing.

"Did I spoil your fun, Scott?" She stood beside him at the controls. "I've been around boats all my life. My daddy was a fisherman. Nice try, though. I'd probably have done the same thing," she laughed. "Better luck next time."

Stephanie moved with the grace of a dancer, or...his mind flashed back to Aleecia gliding across the room, as if floating on air...a person trained in martial arts.

"Ok," Stephanie's voice broke his train of thought. "Why the opossum in the hen house smile and the gleam in your eye? You have something else planned for me?"

"Nope," he chuckled. "Not me."

Scott eased the power back and drifted to the anchor rope. "We're here." Sliding down the ladder, he retrieved the fender buoy and made fast the anchor.

"Do you have an extra set of gear?"

"Do you know how to dive?" He began getting his gear ready. "Cause if you don't, the answer is no."

"I'm certified."

Scott looked her over. Stephanie was about the right size.

He went below and rummaged around in the small closet. "Here, you can wear this one."

"Thank you."

Before Scott could step around her, Stephanie pulled the sweater over her head. She wasn't wearing a bra. It had been a long time since that wetsuit had held a pair of tits. The memory unsettled him.

"If you will excuse me." He stepped around her and went up on deck.

He finished donning his own suit as she came on deck.

"It's a little tight in some areas." She pulled the crotch of the suit down. "But I think I can make due for one dive.

"Scott, what's wrong? You're pale."

"Seeing you in that suit...Well, it brings back bittersweet memories."

"This was your wife's?" She ran her hand down the suit.

"Is there anything about me you don't know?"

"Very little, Scott."

Scott was mildly surprised at the understanding and compassion on her face.

He looked out over the lake. "We had gone diving the weekend before the attack. We anchored out in the bay, sipped chilled wine and made love on the deck under a sky full of stars.

"You remind me of her; full firm breasts, a sexy smile with that same lust-for-life gleam in your eye. In the summer, she would get a beautiful tan, almost as dark as you."

"I'm sorry."

Scott smiled. "Yeah. Me, too."

Stephanie looked out over the wide expanse of water. "Any idea where Aleecia was diving?"

He pointed towards the shore. "Off in that direction, a hundred maybe two hundred yards."

"How will we know for sure?"

"Look for a lawn table, partially buried. She was trying to dig it up."

He helped her into a vest and adjusted the straps. "When we get down on the bottom, there will be a small, clean area free of debris. It won't be easy to find, so keep a sharp look out. We follow that and it will lead us to the table."

They entered the water and descended together. Scott turned on his light at forty feet. Stephanie gave him the standard, finger-thumb touching circle for 'okay'.

He watched her for any signs of stress or disorientation and was thankful there was none. She was breathing easy, relaxed, and her buoyancy was nearly perfect. Any other time, he would have enjoyed a recreational dive with her, but this was anything but a typical dive. Aleecia's life could depend on it.

Checking his compass, Scott pointed in the direction to begin their search.

Stephanie stayed within his view, swimming parallel to him. The arc of her flashlight turned the water into a bright shifting wall of green against the blackness. Suddenly the arc swung towards him and flashed off and on several times. Scott turned and swam towards her.

She pointed to a footprint, clearly visible in the silt. Scott felt elated and held up his thumb. He pointed in the new direction and received an okay.

Twenty minutes later, he spotted the table. The area around it was churned up where Aleecia had dug, trying to remove it from many years of silt and mud. He slammed his hand into the table. Someone's carelessness years before had provided the first link in the chain of disaster.

I'm as much to blame as the person who owned the table. Guilt flooded his thoughts. If he hadn't had the argument with Aleecia, or had chosen another place to dive, she wouldn't be fighting for her life. *If only I hadn't put Melody on that plane. If only...*

Stephanie touched his arm.

He looked up at her. Her eyes behind the mask were large, questioning. With her right hand, she held up her fingers.

Scott returned the okay and pulled a small bottle from his vest pouch. After filling it with the mud from around the table, he signaled to surface.

Back on board the boat, Stephanie picked up a radio and made a call. Several minutes later, he heard the distinct sound of an approaching helicopter.

It hovered overhead while a crewman lowered a rope with a bag attached. As soon as the mud sample was placed in the bag, the craft flew off towards the airport.

Scott watched it until it was out of sight.

"What happened down there?"

"When?"

She unzipped the wetsuit and pulled it down to her waist. "Don't bullshit me, Scott. What happened to you at the table?"

He turned away from her naked breasts.

"Damn you! Look at me when I'm talking."

Scott looked her in the eye.

"You freaked on me down there, and I want to know *why*?" She lowered the wetsuit past her hips.

"Memories." Stepping past her, he went below and began removing his suit.

"You mean guilt, don't you?"

Stephanie removed her suit and followed him into the cabin. "You can't change what happened here, anymore than you can change what happened to your wife and daughter."

Scott reached out, grabbed her by the throat, and jammed her against the wall. "Leave Melody out of this!"

"It was an accident, Scott. It wasn't your fault. You have to let it go."

"*Damn* you, you meddling bitch." Scott released her and stormed out of the cabin.

On deck, he stowed the gear and hauled in the anchor.

"Scott, I was out of line." She walked across the deck. "I'm sorry."

"Yeah, you were." He wondered what her game was. At least she had gotten dressed.

"Anything I can do?"

"Help me gather in these marker buoys. You can drive." Scott picked up a long pole with a hook on it. Stephanie maneuvered his powerful launch with ease. With the last bag on board, he pointed down the lake.

"Head for the Marina!" He marked the area on his map for future reference. This information would be useful to the local people involved in the lake cleanup. Scott had a gut feeling he wouldn't be coming back anytime soon...if at all.

* * * * *

Scott pulled out of Branson with regret. All the hard work in preparation for his arrival had been for naught. Getting the same level of support again would be difficult. It had taken years to develop the reputation, trust and respect necessary to be considered legitimate. He sighed. "I did it once, I can do it again."

"You say something?"

"Talking to myself," he grinned. "I find myself doing it a lot on the open road."

"Well, whatever it takes to stay awake." She slid out of the passenger seat. "I'd hate to be taking a shower and you have a wreck."

"Don't use all the water." Scott watched a semi get extremely close before going around. "I could use one, too."

Stephanie sniffed the air. "Yeah, you do smell a little ripe."

Movement in the rearview mirror drew his eye to it like a magnet. Stephanie stood naked in the short hallway, silhouetted against the rear window. She stretched, like a graceful cat, reaching her hands to the ceiling. Opening the door to his small bathroom, she turned her head and met his eyes in the mirror. "Watch the road."

Having her in his home, and at present naked in the shower, with over twenty hours to go before they reached their destination was going to be difficult. Scott shifted in his seat. She was a beautiful woman, and he was responding naturally to her.

Her voice came from the bathroom, and Scott winced. Reaching over, he turned on the radio and increased the volume. A good agent, probably, or she wouldn't be here. A beautiful woman, hot and sexy, without question, but she couldn't sing for shit.

A short time later, a wet hand snaked across his peripheral vision and turned down the volume. "Isn't that a little loud?"

"It was." He turned his head and encountered a wet, bare tit. Her pert nipple nearly poked him in the eye.

"Don't you think you ought to put some clothes on?" He concentrated on watching the flow of traffic.

"Why?"

A loud blast of an air-horn from a passing semi brought a smile to his face. "Well for one thing, you're putting on one hell of a show. For another, you're taking over the wheel."

He laughed as she spun around and grabbed a fresh set of clothes from a small overnight bag.

"Okay, I'm dressed. Pull over."

"Take the wheel. Cruise control is set and right now, the traffic is light."

"Sheesh, I suppose while in your motor home, you're the boss, too." She reached over and grabbed the wheel.

Scott slid underneath her arm and stopped. He was eyeball level with a multi-colored butterfly tattooed low on her belly. She flexed her muscles and the wings moved as if in flight.

"Come on. I can't stand like this all day long." She derided. "You need a shower worse than I did."

He moved out of the way and Stephanie sat down. "Ok, I got it. No need to play nursemaid."

Her ample breasts were barely concealed by the short halter-top she wore. Scott looked down past her exposed cleavage and swore he could see the butterfly winking at him.

"When you get through looking, I could use something to drink. Preferably something with caffeine."

"I'll put the coffee on."

Stephanie took her eyes off the road for a second, looked up and smiled. "Coffee's fine, black and no sugar."

He put the pot to brewing and stepped into the shower. Turning the water on, Scott leaned his head against the wall. "How in the hell did my life become complicated this fast." A month ago, he had no problems, worries, or hassles. Now there was a woman he cared for, fighting for her life in some unknown hospital, and a horny government agent driving his RV.

"Shit."

Scott left the bathroom and received a wolf-whistle from the driver's seat. "Nice ass. Do I get a view of the front?"

Without turning around, he held up his hand and extended his middle finger. Her laughter followed him to the bedroom.

He dressed and handed her a cup of steaming black coffee. Its fresh aroma teased his senses. Sitting in the passenger seat, Scott sipped from his cup.

"You look beat, go ahead and get some rest. I'll wake you when I need a break."

"Thanks, I didn't realize how tired I was until my shower."

"Scott," her eyes shifted. "Try to relax. Aleecia is in good hands. Probably the best in America, if not the world." She reached her hand out and placed it on his leg. "Go on, we'll talk more about things after you've rested."

He slid out of the seat and set his cup in the sink. "You want a refill first?"

She chuckled. "Scott, I'm fine. Now go."

* * * * *

Mistress of Table Rock

Something was wrong. The lack of motion brought Scott out of a deep sleep and an erotic dream. Pushing the curtain aside, he noticed the neighborhood wasn't the best in the world. Glancing at his watch, he figured they were in East St. Louis.

He rolled out of bed and staggered to the coffee pot. It was strong, hot and blacker than a lake bottom at two hundred feet. Lifting a cup from its hook, he poured a cup. After four hours, it was also bitter.

"Hey baby! What's a fine little piece like you doing driving this piece of shit? You got yourself a rich keeper? Can't be too rich rolling in those whips."

"Yeah, and I bet he's got a little white cock between his legs. All you stuck up bee-autches think you gotta' mix a little cream in your coffee. It ain't too late to cross back over sista'. We'll take you back."

"Yo, bitch! Why don't you try a real playa' on for size? Once you ride this cock, you'll make the switch! I leave my ho's sleeping in a wet spot, and you look like you need a nap!"

The multiple voices and their laughter drifted to his ears. Scott bolted to the door and threw it open. Four black men in their late teens to early twenties circled Stephanie. They were a scruffy lot, sporting T-shirts under oversized jerseys of the St. Louis Cardinals. Another thing about them Scott noticed. They were all wearing brand new tennis shoes.

The one closest to Stephanie appeared to be the leader. He was wearing a rag around his head and had enough jewelry stuck, hung, and pinned to his body to open his own pawnshop.

"Look who showed up to save his bitch? Little punk-ass bitch boy is gonna try and kick our ass for dissin' his ho'. Come on if you think you got skills, bitch! We ain't got nothin' but space an' opportunity!"

Scott looked at them and laughed.

"What you laughing at, mother-fucker? You think we're a joke and shit?"

"You guys picked the wrong bitch to mess with." Scott leaned against the door. "She doesn't need any help."

While they were staring at Scott, Stephanie shifted her weight to the left and lashed out with her right foot, catching the leader with a sidekick that nearly took the kid's head off as it forced him into a neat backwards spiral towards the steps.

Her attention flew back to the rest of the motley crew just as another thug threw a punch at her face. Blocking a blow with her left arm, she gripped it at his wrist and twisted it, putting enough pressure on the delicate tendons and nerves to make him forget about throwing another punch with his free arm. As he screamed and dropped to his knees in front of her, she readjusted his jaw with an open-handed jab to the chin, snapping his head back and sending him tumbling after his fallen leader.

But she had no time to pay attention to him or his fallen brother. Her attention was on punk number three, who had more balls than brains.

Grinning, she bent at the knees, getting her balance just in time to meet his charge. Instead of blocking it or side-stepping it, she reached below him, gripped the crotch of his jeans in one hand, the front of his shirt with the other, and using his own momentum, sent him sailing into the metal frame of the door. He met the immovable side of the motor home and landed partially draped over the steps, inches away from where Scott stood.

Scott shook his head. "Don't say I didn't try to warn you."

The other two were just rising from the ground. With a little shove of his foot, Scott sent her third victim rolling down the steps to meet the other two, who tumbled back onto the asphalt.

Stephanie looked around for the forth punk. Scott saw him clear a chain link fence, running for safer ground.

"You could've helped a little." She stepped around the prone body of a would-be assailant.

"And let my coffee get cold?" He raised his cup and took a sip. "Besides, I never fight on an empty stomach."

Chapter 14

Mile after endless mile passed by as Scott fixed his eyes on the white dotted line. Stephanie kept the coffeepot filled, and they had changing drivers down to a science. Pit stops were for fuel and replenishing their stock of plastic wrapped microwave fast food.

Conversation after the encounter in St. Louis had been kept to driver changes, fuel status and the constant construction on Interstate 70. He chafed at the bit with each single lane slow-down.

"What's she like?" Stephanie sat with her feet on the dashboard, her knees against her chest.

"Who?" Scott wondered why she even bothered wearing a top with so much flesh already exposed.

"Don't play poor dumb white trash, Scott." She spun around with her back against the dash, and her feet propped up on the back of the seat.

"You don't ask easy questions." He thought for a few minutes. "How do you describe a sunset to a blind man, or the sound of a whippoorwill on a still summer's night to a man who can't hear?"

"Do your best, Scott. Take your time, I'm not going anywhere."

He reached above the visor for a new pack of smokes and tapped the case against the steering wheel. He pulled one out and lit it.

"Aleecia is an amazing woman. Intelligent, attractive, passionate and very scared."

"Why?" Stephanie lifted her cup and sipped her coffee.

"She's convinced her step-mother was killed, along with the man who supported them."

She shook her head. "Didn't happen, Scott, I've read the report."

"And you believe everything you read?" he snorted.

"In this case I do. Larry Bates was the agent in charge, he filed the report." She got up. "You want a fresh cup?"

He handed her his mug, "Please."

"There are a lot of things I can't tell you, right now. But I am certain she was never in *any* danger from us." She raised her hand to stop any interruptions. "While it is true there was an initial threat to her life, it was later rescinded."

"Why the hell didn't your people tell Doc Walters?" Scott thought of all those years, living in fear each and every day. "After all, he was under suspicion for being involved."

"They did. I must say one thing about Aleecia. Something you didn't mention."

He cocked is head and gave Stephanie a quick glance as she sat down. "Go on, I'm curious. You said you didn't know her."

Her soft chuckle drifted across his ear. "You're right, I don't know her personally. Only what I've been allowed to read or been told. From those things, few as they may be, I know she instills great loyalty from others. All those who had a part in her abduction as a baby should be given a medal for saving her life. Even though the powers-that-be tried to tell them Aleecia was in no more danger, she never surfaced until the private detective was killed.

"Don't look so shocked. We both know the truth. He didn't die from a heart attack. Ironic, the way things turned out. Twenty-five years after she was taken, the man responsible for her security as a baby was the one who found her."

Scott flipped the butt out the window. "And the fear that kept her away eventually caused her capture."

"Scott, what is so special about Aleecia?"

The coffee went down the wrong pipe. He coughed, spewing what was left across the windshield. "You mean...you don't know?"

"Everything up to this point has been on a need-to-know basis. And I assure you, very few people know." She got up and handed him several paper towels.

"You might as well be included in the growing number of people who do. If they do try to keep this hush-hush, your life will be in just as much danger as mine."

Her eyebrows rose, and her mouth puckered into a slight smirk. "How can you figure?"

His chest burned from the coffee. "The more people who know a secret, the greater the odds someone will talk. Even if I don't say a word, they will assume I did."

She laughed, tears ran down her face, and she doubled over. "You're nuts, absolutely certifiable. What in the hell could she possibly have, or know, to be that great of a threat to national security?"

"She has gills."

She burst out in hysterical laughter. "Like a fish?"

"Exactly like a fish." He smiled.

"I suppose they're behind her ears like the mutant in the movie, *Water World*."

Scott snickered. "Those weren't very practical. Not big enough to filter the air sufficient for a human. Aleecia's gills are on the bottom of her lung, just below the last rib."

Stephanie sobered, her face seemed to pale, and her eyes grew large. "Oh my... Oh shit. They're real, honest to God, working gills. You aren't jiv'en me...That explains the helicopter, the Lear Jet, and the tight security."

"Congratulations!" He beamed. "You just won the grand prize in the game, Truth or Dare. Now you get to choose. Is it behind door number one, door number two, or could it behind door number three?

"*Beep*! Sorry folks we've run out of time. Tune in next week to see which door our winner will choose."

She flipped him the finger, and Scott laughed.

Several miles went by. She sat there, lost deep in thought, digesting everything he had said. He figured her feelings and emotions closely matched his when he had made the big discovery. He sympathized with her. Sometimes the truth was harder to believe than fiction.

"You're in love with her." Her voice was soft, but she spoke with conviction.

"Yes." He looked at her, and then moved his eyes back to the ribbon of highway in front of him. "Does it surprise you?"

"A little."

"A little," he mimicked. "Well, Miss Secret Agent, let me tell you something. It shocked the hell out of me."

* * * * *

"Scott, pull over."

"Here?" They were in Virginia, driving through rich farmland. The next big city wasn't for thirty miles. "Why?"

"I'm asking you to, Scott. I don't want to have to make it an official request."

Apprehension boiled like acid in his stomach. He checked his mirror, lifted the turn signal, and slowed down. The motor home coasted to a stop.

"Ok, what now?" He slid his legs around to the center and faced her. "Were you instructed to shoot me if I revealed her secrets?"

"Nothing so dramatic or drastic. From here on out, I'll drive."

"And I'm guessing I'll be blindfolded in the back. Right?" He sat there, slowly shaking his head and scanning the countryside.

"Whatever." He stepped around her and sat down in the small kitchen booth. "Let's get this over with as quickly as possible."

She took a thick black cloth from her bag and wrapped it around his head. "Give me your hands."

"Is this necessary?" He swiveled his head towards the sound of her voice.

"Unfortunately, yes. Scott, for what it's worth, I wish it didn't have to be this way, but I have my orders."

Scott held his arms out, and felt the cold bite of steel tighten around his wrists.

He tried to keep track of the time between turns, and the direction. For the first half hour it was easy, after that, she made so many stops and turns he had no idea where they were.

The squeaking of a metal gate caught his attention. Stephanie drove through it and proceeded slowly for several minutes before stopping, and turning off the engine.

Tension mounted with each passing second. A motor hummed in the background. An air-conditioning unit kicked in, and somewhere off in the distance a door slammed. He heard the rustle of her shorts as she slid across the drivers' seat.

Heat scorched his lips. He opened his mouth to protest. Her tongue darted out, searching, dueling with his for right of passage. Despite the fact this wasn't Aleecia and he was held captive, or maybe it was because of the latter, his body began to betray his heart.

He jerked his head to the side. "What the hell do you think you are doing?"

Stephanie's hands were roving over his body. "Something I've wanted to do ever since the boat." Her fingers played sensuously in his hair.

"Un-cuff me." He clenched his fists, and pounded them on the table. "Damn it, now!"

"That would ruin the fun. Besides, you might try to hurt me, and you can't handle me. I let you grab me on the boat, otherwise you would be at the bottom of the lake."

Her hand snaked down between his legs, and she grabbed his crotch. "Bitch!" he spat.

Laughter from close by his ear tickled the hair of his neck. "Oh, Scotty, baby. Call me anything you want, but when your cock is in my mouth, you'll be begging me for more."

He jerked his head violently to the side and threw himself out of the seat. His shoulder crashed into the floor and his head bounced off it.

"I don't love you." His breathing quickened, trying to catch up to his racing heart.

"Love," she laughed. "This has nothing to do with love, Scotty, only sex, nothing more, nothing less. Keep your love for fish girl. I'm sure she will appreciate it more."

A large bell began to ring, and Scott felt the motor home begin to move. He would have sworn he was on an elevator.

"Talk about being saved by the bell."

Her voice, laced with sarcasm, told him this wasn't over yet. She reached down and helped him to his feet.

He felt the shift of weight in the frame through his feet. The door opened.

"Agent Brooke, you can remove the cuffs and blindfold now."

Scott blinked against the sudden light. He glared at her with all the disdain he could bring forth, and at the moment, it was considerable.

She took the cuffs off. "I know what you are thinking. Don't try it, now or in the future. When you insisted on being with Aleecia, you entered a whole new ballgame with a different set of rules. It's not too late to change your mind. Say the word now, and you leave the way you came in."

"If I stay?" Scott already knew what he was going to do.

She smiled. "First, you get to see Aleecia."

He rubbed his wrists where the cuffs had been. "What's the second?"

"That's the fun part." She ran her tongue across her upper lip. "You start an extensive, agent training program, and I'm your teacher. First thing we work on is that nasty little temper of yours."

"Let's go see Aleecia." Scott stepped out the door. He got his first good look at the man who had ordered him released. He was short, balding, and wearing glasses. The white lab coat the man wore was plain without any embroidery or unit identification.

"Mr. Mathis, if you will follow me please." The man walked through an open door.

He glanced back around the large cavernous room. His motor home was indeed on a large elevator. They had to be at least forty feet underground.

Scott followed the lab coat with Stephanie at his heels. "So much for friendly introductions," he mumbled.

Stephanie snickered.

They entered a long, wide hallway running parallel to the underground cavern. Everything was white, even the tiled floor, giving it the effect of closing in around you. Solid white doors, with small black numbers, lined the left wall. Their brass-finished knobs appeared strangely out of place in the sterile-looking environment.

Stephanie came up to walk beside him. "Rather overpowering," she whispered.

"Too much white."

"I know." She was silent for a few minutes. The only sound was the clicking of their heels on the tiled floor.

"I feel like one of those numbers on the door," she whispered.

Her tone was serious. He glanced at her. "How so?"

"Simple...Black Power." A wide-toothed smile spread across her face. "If it wasn't for those numbers, think how difficult it would be to find your way around in here."

Scott rolled his eyes towards the ceiling and then joined her in laughter. Lab coat looked over his shoulder with a disapproving scowl.

After turning down another hallway, the mute lab coat opened a door and motioned them in. Against one wall were standard, government issue, gray metal lockers.

Scott turned around and blinked in surprise. Stephanie had removed her clothes and stood naked before him.

"What the hell is going on?" The memory of her aggression in the motor home was still fresh in his mind.

"If you want to see Aleecia, get undressed. Remove any jewelry, and follow me."

Stephanie reminded him of a Marine Drill Instructor with her legs spread apart, chest puffed up, waiting to inspect the troops. She had a hungry, predatory look in her eye.

Removing his clothes, he stored them in one of the lockers.

"Damn, I knew you were hung. Nice cock. Follow me."

Scott followed her into a small shower area. An antibacterial soap dispenser was attached to the wall.

She turned the water on and ducked beneath its spray. Turning the water off, she filled her hand with soap and began washing. "Get a move on, Stud Muffin. We haven't got all day."

He followed her example and applied the soap to his body.

Watching her run her lathered hands over her nipples and breasts, his cock stiffened to a ridged shaft. He nearly lost it when she washed between her legs, deliberately spreading the pink lips of her pussy open for him to see.

"You're supposed to wash all over." Gliding across the wet tile, she grabbed his cock, running her hand up and down the hard length. "Like this."

He couldn't stop the groan escaping past his lips.

"Now, finish and get rinsed off." Her smile was sensuous and her eyes blazed with the heat of lust. She gave his cock one last squeeze, and used his shower to rinse.

"Don't forget to wash behind your ears." She sauntered out of the shower.

Scott turned the shower on cold and shivered beneath the icy spray. "Damn you, Stephanie."

* * * * *

Dressed in sterile gown and mask, Scott entered still another room. Aleecia sat naked in a large stainless steel tub. A mask, fitted over her face, kept a supply of water flowing through her lungs. He saw the horror in her eyes, the pleading for help in her stare.

She tried to move, and he saw the restraints on her arms. Tubes in each arm were attached to bags on steel poles. His fists clenched until he felt the pain of his nails breaking through the skin.

"My God, what have they done to her?" His voice broke with emotion.

Stephanie laid a hand on his arm. "Scott, I'm sorry."

He walked over to one of the people standing around her. "I don't know you, and I don't give a damn who you are. You will release her, now! She is a human being, not one of your lab rats."

"And just who in the hell are you? I don't remember seeing you around here before."

Scott poked him in the chest with a trembling hand. "Your worst fucking nightmare if you don't do as I say and release her immediately."

"But we don't know if she's dangerous," another of the group added.

He spun around and got in the man's face. "She's not the one you have to worry about." Walking over to the tub, he bent down and kissed her forehead.

"You bastards!" he spit out with disgust. "You even tied down her feet."

"Agent Brooke, stop him!" the man ordered.

"Professor, I happen to agree with Mr. Mathis. What you have done is degrading and inhumane. Scott, release the straps. If anyone tries to stop you, they'll have to go through me first."

He sent her a look of gratitude and released the straps holding down her arms and legs.

Aleecia ripped off the mask, threw her arms around him, and sobbed.

"Are you all right, love? Did they hurt you?" He cradled her in his arms as she laid her head on his shoulder.

"It hurts…when I breathe."

He felt the small tremors that racked her body with every breath she took.

"Can she breathe without the water?" Scott looked from one face to another. "Damn it! Somebody answer me.

"We…we don't know," a small weasel-faced man finally spoke.

"Where is Doctor Walters?"

"There is no Doctor Walters here," the weasel spoke again.

"Any of you touch her again…" his head swiveled as he glared at each of the gowned men, "and I will break your damn arm."

He stepped in front of the one Stephanie had addressed as Professor. "You had better find out where Doctor Walters is, and get him in here, immediately. Because when I start breaking arms, yours is going to be the first."

The Professor scrambled away with fear in his eyes.

"You," he pointed to the weasel, "get Aleecia something to wear...now!" he growled.

Weasel scurried off with his tail between his legs and returned a few moments later with a light green hospital gown. Scott took it, draped it over Aleecia's shoulders, and tied it closed.

Scott dipped his finger in the shallow tub of water and tasted it. "Who knew to use warm salt water?"

Weasel spoke up. "We were given instructions by the man who brought her in and told not to use chlorinated water."

Scott breathed a silent prayer of thanks for Doctor Terrance Walters.

Aleecia's breathing grew more harsh and labored. Scott was beginning to worry when the door opened.

Doctor Walters crossed the room and laid his hand on her arm. "I'm here now, dear. Let's see what they did to you."

Scott looked at his face. Somebody had been using it for a punching bag. "Doc, are you okay?"

Walters smiled woefully. "I...tripped and fell getting out of the plane, but enough about me. We must tend to Aleecia."

Scott held Aleecia's hand and watched the Doc's face as he began the examination. His eyes narrowed as he checked her gills, and looked inside her lungs. The chiseled age-lines in his forehead grew pale as his face hardened in anger.

"Imbeciles!" Walters slammed the lighted probe on the table with enough force to bounce the other medical instruments placed on a tray. The light flickered and went out.

"What's the matter Doc?" Scott's mouth was dry, and his heart leapt to his throat in fear.

"Professor Higgins is a brilliant scientist." He ripped off the Latex gloves. "But I've seen him show more compassion to a monkey than he has to Aleecia."

"Terrance, is something wrong?" Aleecia looked up at her old and trusted friend.

"The flow of water they used was too great, dear. Your lung tissue is severely abraded." Doc turned his back to them and began writing on her chart.

"What about my gills?"

Scott winced as her fingers tightened around his.

Doc's shoulders slumped, and his head dropped forward. "Aleecia, your gills are very delicate. I'm afraid they are damaged worse than your lungs."

Scott felt Stephanie's hand on his shoulder. The squeeze of her fingers was comforting and at the same time, a stark reminder of where they were.

"Will they heal?" Aleecia whispered. The repeated warnings of her mother came back to her.

Terrance Walters turned around slowly, tears dampened his cheeks, and his lips trembled. "I'm sorry, dear child. I don't know."

Chapter 15

Scott sat in the small, nondescript waiting room of the facility's hospital. A half-filled cup of cold, bitter coffee sat on the only table next a small stack of magazines. All of which were months old, but looked brand new.

This place is depressing, not just the room, but the whole damn complex. No pictures on the walls. Everything is in the same damn sickening white. If I don't get out of this hole in the ground soon, I'm going to...

The door opened, and Doctor Walters came in and plopped down in the seat next to him. "I'm too old for this." He laid his head back against the wall and sighed.

"I'm not going to lie to you, Scott, and give you a bunch of false hope. The surgeon was great. You couldn't have asked for a better one. The trouble lies in one simple fact. Nobody has ever operated on a person with gills. Over all, the surgery went great. Only time will tell if it was effective."

"How much time?" Scott refused to give up. They had both gone through so much to end up with nothing.

"Right now," he gave a slight shrug of his shoulders and his lips drew tight, "I haven't a clue, a month maybe two. Hell, Scott, it could take a year for them to fully recover, if they ever do. I'm sorry."

Doc laid a hand on his shoulder. "I know you both want, and deserve a more definite answer, but I don't have one."

"Thanks for being honest." Scott sighed. "When can I see her?"

"I'll send someone to get you, soon as she wakes up."

They stood, and Scott took his hand. "Doctor Walters— thanks for being here for her."

"I could say the same to you, Scott. It shouldn't be much longer. Oh!" He glanced around the room and chuckled. "One other thing, try thinking in color. It helps to imagine pictures on the wall."

Scott was on his fourth renovation of the room and was adding a plush burgundy carpet when a nurse opened the door.

"Mr. Mathis, Aleecia is awake now. If you would follow me please?"

Jumping to his feet, he followed her through the door.

"She is quite an amazing woman." She prattled as she led him down a short hall. "Everyone in the place is talking about her."

She stopped at another door, and Scott glanced at the room number.

"Put these on please." She handed him a pair of shoe covers, a shower cap and mask.

Inside, his eyes were drawn instantly to a bed draped with a clear plastic tent. Aleecia appeared to be asleep. Scott started to lift the edge of the tent when the nurse stopped him.

"I'm sorry, we're not taking any chances with infection. If you wish to be in there with her you need to follow me."

The shower room she led him to wasn't a surprise.

"Mr. Mathis, I suggest you hurry. I have to get back, and this place is a maze of crisscrossing halls. It wouldn't do to be lost down here."

Scott got undressed and entered the shower.

His surprise came when he turned around and observed the nurse's slightly large, bare ass stepping beneath the spray of another showerhead.

She smiled at him and continued washing. "This place is murder on me. The one redeeming quality of working here is the food. Unfortunately, as you can see," she lifted a tit and washed underneath it, "I've enjoyed my share of it. Course, if you were willing to help me exercise, I might be willing to skip a few lunches."

Scott felt an unaccustomed heat across his face and he looked away.

"I've embarrassed you, please forget I said anything." She turned her back and began rinsing.

Scott felt sorry for her. "Nurse, it's nothing personal and I'm not offended. If I wasn't in love with Aleecia and you were available," he pointed to his ring finger to remind her of the one she still wore, "I would be more than willing to help you exercise."

"Oh, how stupid of me. I forgot to take it off. I...I wish my husband felt the same way." She fled into the other room.

Scott rinsed and turned off both showerheads.

He found her sitting, quietly crying in the dressing room. He took a dry towel and placed it over her shoulders.

"You must think I'm a...terrible person." Her eyes were red and puffy. She crossed her arms over her breasts.

"No, I don't." Scott leaned over and kissed her cheek. "I think your husband is a fool. Here," Scott opened up her sterile gown and held it for her. "May I have the honor?"

There was a new light shining in her eyes as she stood and accepted his help in dressing. She seemed to lose some of the haggard dry expression worn by so many in the place.

She smiled, "Aleecia is a lucky woman."

Scott followed her out a different exit than the one he and Stephanie had used. The smell of disinfectant in the short hall was overpowering. He entered the door she held open and was standing back in Aleecia's room.

He slipped underneath the plastic hood and stood next to her bed. "Aleecia, I'm right here. Everything is going to be all right, love."

Her eyelids fluttered and slowly opened.

"Hi." She tried to laugh but it hurt. "You look funny."

Her throat was on fire and her mouth was dry. Shifting her eyes, she spotted a water pitcher on a stainless steel bed stand. "Water, please."

"No water, Aleecia," the nurse smiled. "How about some ice chips?"

"Yes...please."

He placed a few of the pieces in her mouth and watched as she sucked on them. Lowering his face, he was stopped short by a gruff, but kind voice.

"Not so fast, lover boy. No kissie-face 'til she's out of danger. You two make any sparks in here, and the whole room will go up in flames."

Aleecia laughed and started coughing. She winced with the pain and looked into Scott's eyes. "Tell me."

He smoothed her hair from the side of her face. "Nobody knows for certain."

She closed her eyes in sleep.

Scott sat beside her, holding her hand, thankful she was alive. Whatever price was required, he would gladly pay the cost.

* * * * *

He struggled to open his eyes. Someone was calling his name. Through sleep-blurred vision, he saw Aleecia was still asleep.

"Scott, over here."

Shifting his stiff body around, Stephanie motioned him to leave the oxygen tent. Slipping from behind the curtain, he stretched.

"Not the most comfortable place to sleep," she whispered. "Let's find someplace to talk."

He followed her through the maze of corridors and into a medium-size room filled with tables and chairs. The sound of pots and pans being banged around came through a large opening in one wall. The rich aroma of coffee assaulted his senses and he gravitated towards it.

"Help yourself," she invited with a short laugh. "This place never closes. It serves four meals a day and isn't half bad."

Four older men sat around a small table. They had stopped talking and were watching them. Scott filled a cup, took a sip, and followed Stephanie over to join the men at the table.

"Mr. Mathis, please have a seat."

He took one of the empty chairs, and Stephanie sat beside him.

"Our names are not important, but for the sake of this meeting, you can call me Bill. Mr. Bates convinced me to allow you to enter our little group of highly selected individuals. I hope his judgment of you is not misplaced. Now we have to figure out what to do with you."

Scott sat drinking his coffee, watching the facial expressions of the men around the table, especially Bill who was the apparent boss. However, in this place, appearances could be deceiving.

"We've examined your credentials and are impressed with your electronic background, as well as your diving abilities. Question is..." Leaning forward in his chair, he placed his fingertips together, interlocked them, and rested his chin on his outstretched thumbs. "Will you fit in?"

"Fit in?" Scott picked up his cup and took a drink of his coffee. Holding it in front of him with both hands, he surveyed the group. Looking over the cup, he met the spokesman's eyes with an unblinking glare. "I guess it would depend on what I'm supposed to fit into."

Bill's eyes fluttered to the man on the other side of Stephanie.

"Don't look at him unless you're not the boss." Scott felt of spark of elation when the man's expression faltered. He turned his head slightly. "Well, *bossman*, is your name Bill, too?"

"Who I am isn't important. If you need a name, Bill is as good as any. It might be less confusing that way."

Bill number two never shifted his gaze. When he smiled, the eyes remained cold and hard like burnished steel. He thought of Aleecia and made his decision.

"If I like what I hear, we'll stay." He was fishing for a reaction. It wasn't long in coming.

"Mr. Mathis, as of right now, you're free to go. Say the word and Agent Brooke will take you and your motor home back out on the road. You can go back to sulking over the death of your wife and child by hiding in murky lakes. Go back to picking up trash for people who don't give a damn about this country other than what they can get out of it, at that moment in time."

Scott seethed inside. *How dare this overstuffed pompous buffoon...*

"As usual, Agent Brooke is correct. You do have a hot temper. I can see it in your eyes. You want to kick the shit out of this old fart. Don't try it. You wouldn't make it out of that chair. As far as our lovely and very unique Aleecia is concerned, I'm afraid her leaving with you is non-negotiable."

For the longest time, Scott stared into fat Bill's eyes. Neither man wavered. Scott knew that, for now, he was beaten. He lowered his eyes and exhaled a long breath.

"I'm in."

Bill number two smiled, "Smart choice.

"May I call you Scott? We are a compact, very secret, and highly sensitive organization of the government known as Omega Sentry. We are at the President's bidding twenty-four hours a day, three hundred and sixty-five days a year. If we can't do it, no one can.

"The name was taken from a secret project abandoned twenty-five years ago. Even though it was abandoned on paper, it's never completely gone away."

He pulled out a folder marked with red and white boarders and the words, 'Top Secret, Authorized Personnel Only', stamped across the front. He tossed it in front of Scott. "Go on, you need to finish putting all the pieces of the puzzle together."

Scott picked up the folder.

"Go on, look at it!" Bill snapped.

Scott opened the folder. Inside were two pieces of paper. Both of them were marked top and bottom with Top Secret in bold red letters. Scott began reading.

November 4, 1979

Delton Research Laboratory

Department of Defense

Special Operations

Pentagon

Washington DC

Subject: Omega Sentry

Dear Sir,

In regards to Omega Sentry, we have exhausted current funds for the project with only one positive result in our attempt to create a more advanced soldier. Our success is somewhat diminished by the fact that the only living specimen is a female. The males were stillborn or died within hours of birth.

We feel strongly that further DNA-altering research should not be carried out at this time until further knowledge in this field is available.

Please advise.

Sincerely,

Arthur Ridgedale, PhD

Special Research Division

Scott glanced around the table. He ground his teeth together until his jaw hurt. *You bunch of pious bastards. Who gave you the fucking right to play God?* He picked up the other letter and began to read.

November 26, 1979
Department of Defense
Special Operations
Pentagon
Washington DC
Delton Research Laboratory
Miami Fl
Subject: Omega Sentry
Dear Mr. Ridgedale,

Further funds for Omega Sentry are unavailable. It is with deep regret, that the program has been canceled. Destroy all evidence of its existence.

Sincerely,
General Joseph Daniels
Special Operations Officer

Scott closed the folder and laid it on the table. The mist cleared in his mind as many of his questions had been answered. None of which changed his feeling towards Aleecia.

"Okay, General, I take it you're retired," Scott paused to watch the effect of his words.

The General's eyes shifted to each person around the table before coming back to settle on his. A slow grin lifted the left corner of his mouth. "You're very perceptive, Scott. What do you think would happen if the world found out about this?"

"With all the stink they raised over Dolly and the cloning of humans." Scott shook his head. "I don't even want to think about," he picked up the folder, "this."

"The secrecy of Omega Sentry is of the highest priority. None of the lives around this table are above sacrifice to maintain it.

"When Aleecia was taken, all her records were destroyed. The letter you read was our only evidence that she ever existed. Until her picture was taken, we had no idea what, if any, special abilities she possessed. We didn't know where she was, or even if she was still alive. I didn't tell those around this table anything until she arrived here the other night."

"What is my role in all this?" Scott had an idea but wanted to hear it straight from the man's mouth.

"Aleecia needs someone she trusts and who, if need be, will protect her with their life. Stephanie will train you and Aleecia in the use of the latest technology, weapons, and the martial arts.

"You've already seen what Stephanie can do. In time, both you and Aleecia will be able to defend yourselves. You will probably never be as good as Stephanie, but we don't expect you to be."

Scott bit back a smile and nodded to Stephanie. He hoped the laughter he was fighting to hide didn't show through his eyes. *Their lack of information may prove useful,* he thought to himself, *especially when playing against a stacked deck.*

"When do I start?" Scott picked up the mug and realized it was cold. "I'm going to freshen my cup. I'll play your spy games, and I'll do your training. But I'm not living down here in this sterile rabbit burrow, and neither is Aleecia."

Getting up from the table, he paused. "No matter what you think of her, she is not an animal you keep in a cage, and then expect her to do tricks when you wave a banana in the air."

Scott strode over to the large coffee pot and filled his cup.

Stephanie rose from her chair and followed. "What you're asking isn't possible. They will never agree to your conditions."

"It was no more her fault she was born with gills than it was yours for being born black. Would you give up your freedom and the right to walk along the street, to stroll through a field and smell the flowers, or feel the ocean breeze blowing across your face? Could you give it all up, Stephanie, to submit again to the chains of slavery?"

Her eyes flashed with passionate anger.

"So, deep down you still feel. I was beginning to wonder." Scott slammed the cup on the table. A stack of cups shifted, teetered, and crashed to the floor. "I'm going back to be with Aleecia."

With angry, purposeful strides which ate up the long hall, he threw open the door to the shower and ripped off the gown.

Aleecia was awake. Her sleepy smile warmed his heart. He put his finger to his lips and ducked behind the curtain. Bending low over her, he kissed her cheek.

"They don't know about your martial arts training," he whispered in her ear. "No matter what, they mustn't suspect how good you are."

"Why are we whispering?" Her eyes sparkled with amusement.

"Mice in the walls." He traced her jaw with the pads of his fingertips. She turned her head and kissed his hand.

"Whatever happens, I want you to know...that I love you." He kissed the tip of her nose.

A tear trickled from her eye, and her smile radiated her joy. "I...never figured I'd hear a man say those words to me. I shall cherish them always for I, too, have fallen in love."

"Okay." The nurse cleared her throat. "I thought I told you two, no intimate contact until after we know she is safe from infection. Doctor Walters is on the way in. He wants to see how the sutures are doing."

Aleecia clasped his hand in apprehension. Scott squeezed it, reassuring her. He wasn't leaving.

Doctor Walters came in and smiled as he slipped underneath the plastic curtain. "You're looking chipper, Aleecia. I want to check the sutures on those torn gills."

Scott saw the worried glance she cast the Doc.

"I'm sure everything is fine. Humor an old man who is concerned for a dear friend." He slipped on a pair of sterile gloves. "Roll over so I can take a peek."

She rolled over on her side facing Scott and Doc carefully removed the bandage covering her gills.

Doc's face took on a puzzled look and Scott wondered why. Was there a problem? He tried to keep the worry from his face and alarming Aleecia.

"Turn all the way over dear, and I'll check the other side." Doc Walters held up his hand to stay any questions. "There you go. Are you comfortable?"

"Yes," with her head half buried in the pillow, she couldn't see Scott or the Doc's face.

"Anything wrong, Doc?" Scott shifted on his feet. Sweat trickled down his back despite the cool room.

"Absolutely nothing that I can see. If it weren't for the sutures, I'd be hard pressed to see the scar tissue." He wiped the probe with an alcohol-soaked pad and placed it back in his bag.

"I see no reason why we can't get you back into the water for a few minutes tomorrow." He closed the case and rested it on the bed. "I'll keep you on oxygen for another day, as an added precaution.

"You've made a remarkable recovery for which I'm very thankful, even though I don't understand it. Aleecia, every time I see you, you continue to amaze me. I've always considered it a privilege to know you."

Aleecia smiled and grasped Doc's hand. "Thank you, Terrance. You have always been a dear and loyal friend." A twinkle lit her eyes. "You're not half bad as a doctor either."

Terrance Walters laughed, then leaned down, and kissed Aleecia on the forehead. "Get some rest dear. I'll see you in the morning.

"Scott, you need to get some sleep, too." Doc placed a hand on his shoulder. "You look worn out." He leaned his head closer. "You are the only friend she has in here. Choose your friends wisely and watch your back."

"Thanks Doc, for...*all*...you've done." Scott gave a half-wink and shook his hand.

Stephanie stuck her head through the door. "Scott, let's go for a walk."

She waited while he changed back into his clothes. They retraced their steps down the long hall.

The warehouse-size cavern seemed empty at first glance. His eyes came to rest on his motor home sitting in the shadows of the furthest corner. Stephanie started walking towards it.

"I've gotten permission for you to sleep in it. You have electricity and water hooked up," she yawned. "How is Aleecia doing?"

"Doc Walters is going to put her in the water tomorrow." He glanced over to see her reaction. "I think he wants to check out her oxygen levels."

"You know, Doc will be leaving as soon as she has fully recovered." Stephanie opened the door of Scott's motor home and waited for him to enter.

"I guess I hadn't really given it much thought, but it doesn't surprise me any." He stepped inside and looked around. "Where did they hide them?"

"Hide what?"

"The microphones, bugs. You can't expect me to believe they didn't put any onboard." He opened the small fridge and pulled out a beer.

"You want one?" Without waiting for a reply, he handed her a can and popped the top on his. "Don't bother answering my question. If they are using the latest technology, my company probably developed them. If I can't find my own toys, I shouldn't be playing in the sandbox."

Stephanie took a large swallow and licked her lips. "Thanks. What makes you so sure they bugged it?"

He smiled. "Because it's exactly what I'd have done." He finished his beer and tossed the empty can in the trash.

"Now, if you will excuse me, I'm going to sleep." He stripped off his shirt and stretched out on the bed.

He was almost asleep when he felt the bed sag.

"Damn, you're one persistent bitch," Scott mumbled. "What the hell do you want now?"

"For now, the use of your bed. For your information, lover boy, I haven't gotten any sleep either. I gave up that luxury talking the General into bringing you into the program. Besides your background in electronics and diving, the punk back in St. Louis was right. On occasions, I like cream in my coffee."

"Fine, there's some Coffee-mate in the cupboard." His eyes drifted closed.

Chapter 16

Detective Larry Bates rubbed the grit from his eyes. This was the reason he had gotten out of the Pentagon rat race. He had outgrown the need for the emotional roller coaster ride that working for them provided.

There had always been some crisis to avoid, an all night surveillance to carry out. He pulled out the file on Perceivel Montgomery. Or as in this case, he had to make a homicide quietly disappear.

His former job had almost cost him his marriage.

When he returned early this morning from his debriefing with the General, he had seen the old hurts resurface in his wife's eyes. He had broken his promise. He had told another lie she could add to an already long list.

The intercom buzzed. "You have a gentleman here to see you. He says it's urgent."

He walked out to the desk and realized his work for the General wasn't over.

"Hello, Mr. Tillman. What brings you downtown?"

"I need to talk to you, in private." Gary's eyes shifted around the room.

"Come back to my office." Bates led the way through the maze of desks, filing cabinets and chairs. He waited for Gary to enter, and closed the door.

He walked around his desk and sat in his chair. "Have a seat, Mr. Tillman. Now, what can I do for you?"

"I think something has happened to Aleecia. She's missing."

"What makes you think so?" Bates picked up his pen and began drawing circles on the pad of paper.

"We had an argument the other day, and I went out to her house this morning to try and patch things up."

"Patch things up?" Bates paused in his doodling.

"Yeah, ever since that worthless diver showed up, she's been acting strange. Well different, you know, weird. That's what our spat was over. I told her it didn't look good, her spending so much time with him on his boat with us being engaged."

Bates looked away to hide his startled reaction. "I didn't know, congratulations."

"Well, we were keeping it quiet cause of working together." Gary winked. "You know how it is. Anyway, like I said, I went out to her place, and she's gone. It looks like she was starting to pack and something happened."

"Any idea why she would be packing, Gary?"

"Sure do. Aleecia was planning on moving in with me before this Mathis fellow showed up."

"You think she was packing to move in with you?" Larry had heard some wild tales in his law enforcement career, and this one ranked up with the best.

"Why else would she be packing? It has to be Mathis. Him and that black bitch he had with him."

He raised his eyes. "Oh! He had a different woman with him. Have you seen her before, then?"

"I just told you, he had this black bitch with him, and no, I haven't seen her before. Mathis pulled into the dock, unloaded a bunch of trash and left. They seemed to be in a hurry. This morning, when I got to work, the slip where he parks his boat was empty."

"What does this have to do with Aleecia?"

"Damn it, Bates! Wake the hell up." Gary threw his hands in the air. "They leave, she's missing, and I think they killed her."

"I'll look into this and get back with you. I'm sure she's off somewhere sorting things out. She's probably trying to figure out how to apologize to you and beg your forgiveness. You know women start getting jitters right before they take the plunge. You go on home. Everything will be fine."

"Thanks, I appreciate it." Gary stood and shook his hand.

He watched Gary leave. "Shit!" He threw his pencil across the room and pulled out the anti-acids.

Chapter 17

Something was crawling on him, tickling the few chest hairs he had. Opening his eyes, Scott stared into a head of thick coarse black hair. Her head was tucked underneath his chin and each exhaled breath fluttered over his skin.

He stared to lift his arm from around her. Stephanie looked up with a grin and snuggled closer. How she managed it, he wasn't sure. Her breasts were already pressed firmly into his stomach.

"I thought you were awake. Your heart is beating much faster." Her grin reached her eyes. Their seductive twinkle promised passionate and erotic fantasies were his for the taking.

She must have felt his muscles tighten or something. One minute he was about ready to roll away from her and the next, she was sitting on top of him. He felt her heat through his denim jeans. Stephanie had striped down to her birthday suit and was taking full advantage of it by grinding her cunt against the rising bulge of his cock.

"Don't try and fight it, Scott," her laugh was soft and sensuous. "I need some fresh cream, and it feels like you're loaded."

She had his arms pinned to the side. To remove his pants, she would have to let go with at least one hand. Scott bided his time and waited.

Stephanie leaned forward and dangled a tit enticingly in front of his mouth.

"Taste them, Scott, suck on my nipples and make'm hard," she purred.

Using his tongue, he licked the dark nub of her breast. Her body arched, a low moan filled the bedroom. Scott bit the nipple.

"Oh! Yes!"

Mistress of Table Rock

Her right hand lifted to her other breast, squeezing it and rolling the nipple between her thumb and finger.

Scott let his fingers tease their way up her side, past the breast he was sucking on and to her neck. With all the strength acquired from carrying hundreds of air tanks, Scott's fingers clamped around her throat. In one smooth motion, he lifted her in the air, rolled and slammed her on the floor.

Scott landed on top of her. "You so much as blink wrong and I'll squeeze. If you try any of your fancy moves on me, make the first one count. I promise you, one is all you'll get."

She looked up with shocked surprise and then smiled. "I like to play rough, it makes my pussy wet. If you aren't in the mood, all you had to do was say so."

Releasing her, he rose up and sprang back onto the bed. Her laughter followed as he rolled to the other side.

"You're going to be fun to tame." She got to her feet. "You mind if I take a shower, lover boy?"

He watched her step into the shower. Scott put his socks on and grabbed his shirt. Slipping into a pair of boots, he left without tying them and put his shirt on as he walked across the concrete floor.

"Damn that woman." Scott mumbled. "Worse than a damn cat in heat." His boots thundered on the floor and echoed in the empty hall. What he needed now was Aleecia.

Before the door was closed to the dressing room, his shirt was off and his pants around his knees. Rolling his clothes up in a ball, he threw them into a locker and barely got wet in the shower. Picking up a towel, he dried his face and tore open the package for the sterile gown.

Pulling it over his head as he backed through the door, he heard two different voices laughing. The nurse he had showered with and Aleecia were giggling like schoolgirls.

"I wondered if you wore anything under those things." Aleecia's giggling turned to laughter. "Now we both know."

He raised the tent flap and ducked underneath. Leaning over to kiss Aleecia's forehead, he was pleasantly surprised to have her pull him down to meet her lips. Her hands roamed over his head, her fingers clutched at his hair.

Her tongue fought with his, each seeking the warmth and taste of the other. After the scene with Stephanie in the motor home, he needed this woman to drive away her ghost.

"*Ahhheemmm,*" the nurse cleared her throat. "I'll be leaving now. Ah...just be careful with the IV's."

Scott broke the kiss," We shouldn't be kissing like this, the..."

"Doctor Walters was already here." She laughed and nuzzled his neck. "The nurse was getting ready to take the tent down before you came through the door with your gown around your waist."

"I suppose the nurse got an eye full." Scott worked his way down her body and sucked on a nipple through her gown.

"Oh, yes, ah, she did. Said, now ah, there is a nice ass. Oh! Scott, don't quit. Oh!"

"I don't intend to." His hand traveled down her side and found the hem of her gown. His fingers teased the skin beneath the edge of the fabric and then slowly edged it up over her hip.

"You make me so wet, touch me, and feel how much I want you." Aleecia purred.

Her skin felt like silk as his fingers slid across it to the soft wet folds of her cunt. "Damn girl, couldn't you wait to get so wet 'til I got inside you?"

"You caused it when you sucked on my nipple." She pulled his head back up to hers. "I want you. I don't care if someone comes in. Please!"

He slipped his finger inside her wet slick flesh even as his tongue invaded her mouth, mirroring the motion of his fingers inside her.

She pulled at him, urging him onto the bed. Aleecia grabbed at his gown, pulling it up his chest and over his head.

"The first time I saw you naked in your motor home, I wanted you. Did you know that? You could've had me right then."

"All you ever have to do is ask." He straddled her hips, lifting her gown over her breasts. In awe, he stared at their perfection. Almost reverently, his fingers skimmed the firm mounds of her breast and teased the ridged flesh of her nipples.

"So very perfect." Scott lowered his mouth and took a nipple between his lips gently sucking on the hard pebble of flesh.

Aleecia reached between their bodies and guided his throbbing cock between the hungry folds of her flesh.

A deep groan of satisfaction rumbled from his chest as he slid deep inside her.

Her nails dug into his skin as her body arched beneath him. He felt the muscles spasm around his shaft and spread, rippling outward from her hot core. Slowly, Scott began to move. Withdrawing until only the sensitive head of his cock remained in her. With a demanding thrust of his hips, he filled her again.

Through the sensuous haze surrounding them, Scott heard the scrape of a chair being moved.

"Don't stop," Aleecia's voice whispered in his ear. "Let her watch. You're mine and it's time she knew it."

Aleecia turned her head. Stephanie sat, watching them. Her hands clutched at her own breast. "He's mine." Aleecia mouthed silently. "He's mine."

Stephanie's left hand slid down to the hem of her short skirt. Her fingers disappeared inside her black lace panties.

Aleecia's excitement grew as Scott buried himself deep inside her again and again. She clung to him, meeting each thrust of his hard flesh with one of her own. Her mouth sought his in a wild war of the tongues. Their breathing became as one, sharing each other's erotic heat, swallowing the animal-like moans welling up from deep within.

With her vision blurred by rising passion, Aleecia turned her head.

Stephanie's skirt was pulled up to the waist, and her panties stretched out of the way. With her fingers buried inside her, she was lost in her own sensuous fog.

Aleecia's eyes became fixed on Stephanie's fingers as they matched the rhythm of Scott's cock inside her.

Her world suddenly exploded in a climax that took her breath away. She felt the scorching heat of Scott's release as his body collapsed, shaking on hers.

Stephanie was smiling. Slowly, as if drugged, she lifted her two wet fingers to her lips, kissed them and blew her a kiss. Adjusting her clothes, she stood and walked out of the room.

Aleecia turned her head and placed a kiss on the side of Scott's neck. "I love you."

Scott looked her in the eye. "I never dreamed one day I might find love again. You are the center of my life. I'm yours, heart, body, and with the very essence of my being, I love you."

Aleecia's heart thrilled with overflowing joy. Her lips met his with tenderness, sealing the commitment of their hearts.

A knock sounded on the door. Scott pulled out of her wetness and climbed off the bed. Aleecia arranged her gown, and he covered her with a sheet.

"Come in." The both called out at once.

The nurse came in with a smile on her face and a twinkle in her eye. "Doctor Walters is ready for your water test, Aleecia." She unhooked the IV from her arm. "Dear," she whispered, "you might want to go freshen up first."

Aleecia felt the heat rising up her neck as she scrambled out of bed. Scott's laughter followed her into the bathroom.

Mistress of Table Rock

"Why don't you run along, Mr. Mathis. I imagine you worked up an appetite this morning. Doc Walters and I will take good care of her."

Aleecia came out of the bathroom and Scott gave her a kiss, "Have fun in the water. I promise, we'll be out of this place soon."

"Don't promise what you might not be able to keep," she returned his kiss. "All I need is your love."

"It's yours forever." Scott knew, no matter what happened, it was one promise he would never break.

* * * * *

Standing in line at the cafeteria, Scott could feel the mingling aroma of the foods on the serving line kick his saliva glands into overdrive. When had he eaten last…? It had to have been somewhere on the road before he reached Virginia. He had been living on caffeine ever since.

As he filled his plate, a low rumbling growl came from the pit of his stomach.

"Been working up an appetite this morning?" Stephanie's whisper brushed across his ear.

Scott ignored her and went in search of an empty table, preferably one with only a single chair. Dozens of eyes followed him as he walked across the floor. Hushed whispers could be heard coming from behind shielded hands and lowered heads. Finding an empty section of table, he pulled out a chair and sat down.

Stephanie took the chair across from him.

"If you don't mind, I'd rather eat alone." Scott stabbed at a sausage link and jammed it in his mouth.

Her lips formed a lovely little pout. "I wouldn't think of letting you eat alone. Some things in life are so much better when shared with another." Stephanie lifted her glass to her lips. "Oh, I forgot to wash my hands. How thoughtless of me." She sniffed the air. "Oh goodness. They smell like pussy juice." Reaching across the table, she held her fingers near his face.

"You want to smell a real woman, lover boy?" Pulling her hand back, she kissed her fingers and blew the kiss across the table.

"No, too bad." First one finger and then the other went into her mouth. Her eyes, twinkling with suppressed laughter, never left his.

Scott washed down a mouth full of biscuit. "What do you want?"

"You, in the gym," she looked at the clock, "fifteen minutes."

"Why?"

"Because, I fucking said so. That's why," she hissed between clenched jaws. "The General's orders, your training starts today."

"I'm looking forward to it." He stood and picked up his empty tray. "Lead the way."

He followed her to a large open room. Basketball hoops hung from the ceiling on each side. Large exercise mats were scattered across the floor. Scott counted six people on the mats, and two runners jogging around a track built into the second floor.

Stephanie walked behind a counter, picked up a set of black pullover sweats and tossed them into his arms. A lone sentry, standing guard, was embroidered in gold on the left breast.

"You can get dressed in there," she pointed to the locker room.

Stephanie was waiting on a mat in the center of the floor. As he walked to her, he was conscious of every eye in the gym following him.

"Better him than me," he heard one man say. "I wouldn't wish her on anybody. That is one tough bitch."

"Yeah, that's no shit," his partner wiped the sweat from his eyes. "I went a couple rounds sparing with her. Man, I was so sore I couldn't get laid for a week."

Scott stepped onto the mat.

He saw it coming, but it was too late. With a quick sweeping motion of her foot and a short jab to his chest, he had a nice view of the ceiling.

"Fun and games are over, Scott." Kneeling on the mat beside him, Stephanie grabbed him by the chin. "You've grabbed my throat twice. Don't make the mistake of thinking you can do it again."

"Then back off, and I won't be tempted."

"I don't giv'a fuck what you want or don't want." She stood and motioned him up.

Scott started to get up, rolled away from her, and came up in a crouch.

"You know, there might be some hope for you yet." A slight smile of approval cracked the stern mask of her face.

"Scott, I'm not training you to go out and take on four bad-ass gang members. I did that to show you it could be done." She grinned. "Okay, yes I was showing off, a little. I'm not going to teach you a bunch of fancy show stuff that you see on television. The key element in this is surprise. Both times you grabbed me I wasn't expecting it or I was distracted."

Scott grinned and chuckled.

"You think that's funny. If one word of it gets out, I'll kick your ass from one end of this gym to the other. You're going to learn what to do in the brief second after the attack to immobilize or even kill that person. Let's face it Scott, you don't stand a chance of becoming the next Bruce Lee. Once you lose the advantage, it'll be over."

For the next four hours, Scott found himself looking at the ceiling more often than not. With every move and counter move, his body screamed in agony. Again and again, he practiced the same technique until he got it right.

Scott lay on the mat trying to recover from the last hip throw. He wished the day was over, but it was only time for lunch.

"That will be all, for now. I don't know about you, but rolling around on the floor all morning makes me hungry."

"Have I got time for a shower?" He wiped the sweat from his face.

"Only if I can join you."

"If you can stand the stench, why should I complain. Let's eat." He headed for the door.

"Run, Scott, run." She laughed. "There's no place to hide."

* * * * *

Dreading the afternoon session, he was puzzled when she walked past the gym and turned the corner. She stopped at a door with a security warning, 'Restricted Area, Authorized Personnel Only' written in bold red letters.

He entered the room and stopped, stunned at the sheer magnitude of it. It wasn't so much a room as it was a tunnel, extending maybe three hundred yards in length. Across the short opening was a bench set up with dividers. Each little cubicle had one small wooden stool.

"Welcome to the firing range."

Stephanie strolled over to the barred door, ran her identification badge through the security monitor and placed her hand on the screen. A buzzer sounded, and the door swung open.

"As your training progresses, you will be given a coded pass. Until then, you're to be escorted in each restricted area." She closed the door behind him.

The room extended about forty-five feet in length and twenty in width. He had never seen so many guns in one place. The long walls sported two racks of rifles, one above the other.

Shelves and cabinets, loaded with still more weapons, filled the room.

Scott walked around the room. "You people planning on starting a war?"

Picking up a handgun, she released the slide. The metallic clank of the slide brought a smile to her face. "We're here to prevent one. This is the M1911; shoots a forty-five-caliber shell and is the preferred handgun because of its stopping power, but carrying two sizes of ammunition can be a drawback."

"What about this one?" Lifting the wicked looking short-barreled weapon, he ran his fingers over the smooth black metal.

"It's an Israeli Negev Commando with a forward assault handle and a two hundred round soft assault drum. The little one next to it is my favorite."

Scott laid the Negev down and picked the weapon up. "Another Israeli?"

She smiled. "It's the Para Micro Uzi, equipped with a sound suppressor, laser pointer, night optics and a thirty-three round magazine. It's a wicked little bitch. Another favorite around here is the next one. It's the MP5, a compact nine millimeter submachine gun."

He started to lay the Uzi down when she stopped him.

"Bring that one and follow me." Stephanie led him out over to a small hole in the wall.

"I heard the Black Dragon was working with a new recruit." The man on the other side of the window smiled. "What are you going to start out on?"

Scott raised an eyebrow in Stephanie's direction.

"I'll have four boxes of nine mil and a case of forty-five's." She signed for the ammo and picked up two pair of sound suppressors and eyeglasses.

"Black Dragon," he questioned as they left the armory and went to the firing line.

"It's my call sign in the field." She laid the boxes and the pistol on the bench. "You can probably guess how I got it."

He chuckled. "I have a pretty good idea."

She loaded a magazine for the forty-five. Picking up the weapon, Stephanie went through the safety, loading and firing. "Scott, this is the standard firing position facing the target with your feet spread and knees slightly bent. Using both hands to steady the grip, wrap the thumb of your non-shooting hand over the other thumb."

He watched her demonstrate the technique.

Placing a silhouette target on a wire, she moved it out thirty feet. Scott followed her lead and donned his hearing protection and glasses.

"Time to lock and load." She handed him the magazine.

She spoke into a microphone on the side of the divider. "Permission for live fire?"

"Permission granted." Red lights started flashing from each end of the line. "The range is hot."

The soft whisper of sliding metal when he inserted the magazine was quickly drowned out by a click *kerr-thunk* as the released slide sent a round into the chamber.

"Okay, safety on...take your firing position." She stepped up behind him and placed her arms next to his.

Her tits were pressed into his back. Turning his head, Scott gave her a questioning look.

"Focus on the target, Mr. Mathis. Let the body stance become natural. You may release the safety and fire when ready. Remember to squeeze the trigger."

The pistol jumped in his hand.

"Am I distracting you?" She pushed her nipples harder against his back. "Learn to shut out everything around you for the split second you fire, then go on to the next target."

His first shots were wide, some even missing the black silhouette. Slowly, his shooting improved. He was getting good at shutting out the feel of Stephanie's tits pressed against him. Drawing imaginary breasts on the target in his mind, the heavy weapon seemed to line up on its own, dead center between them.

With Stephanie ever by his side, he went on to shooting in the kneeling and prone position. The weapon began to feel as if it weighed a hundred pounds. His wrist hurt from the constant shock of the gun recoil. The smell of cordite hung heavy in the air and burned his eyes and nose.

"Looking much better, Scott." She picked up the Uzi. "Now, let's have some fun."

Chapter 18

Tired and stiff from his first day of training, Scott headed for Aleecia's room. Finished with his shower, he dressed making sure nothing was showing and entered her room. Bewildered, he stopped in his tracks. His words of greeting froze on his lips.

The bed was freshly made. All the monitors were stored neatly against the wall. Any evidence of her presence had been removed. An icy hand of fear gripped his heart and began to squeeze it.

Going back out to the hallway leading to the shower, he checked the other rooms. Each was a carbon copy of the first. Empty.

Getting dressed in his regular clothes, Scott went in search of Aleecia. Finally, he saw a friendly face. "Nurse! Where is Aleecia?"

Her smile relaxed the cold fingers. Surely if the nurse was smiling, everything was all right.

"Doctor Walters was so amazed at her recovery, she was released from the hospital. I was there when she was in the tank. It was amazing, seeing her breathing under water. I still can't get over it."

Scott threw his arms around her and gave her a kiss. "Thank you, nurse. That's the best news I've heard in ages. Thank you, and please tell the staff how grateful I am. Do you know where she is?"

"Terrance showed her where your motor home was." Her lips lifted in a conspiratorial smile. "You might check there first."

"You and the Doctor on first name basis now?" He thought it wonderful, despite their age difference.

"We've became good friends. He's kind and gentle, like you. His wife is gone, and he's lonely. I hope you don't think any less of me than you all ready do."

"Where did you get a notion like that?" He skimmed her cheek with the back of his fingers.

Reaching up, she pulled his head down and gently kissed his cheek.

"Thank you, Mr. Mathis. Now, go find that wonderful woman of yours and quit taking up the time of a tired old nurse."

"Old?" He laughed out loud. "You look ten years younger today."

Her warm smile followed him out the door.

Walking down the hall, his steps were brought to an abrupt halt.

"I was wondering where you went in such a hurry." Stephanie blocked his path. "Would you care to have dinner with me and a night out on the town? Look at it as a reward for a day's hard work."

"No thanks," he stepped to the side.

She blocked his path again. "Don't be so quick to turn me down. It might be a long time before you see daylight again."

"If you will excuse me, I'm on my way to find Aleecia." With his arms held loosely at his side, he waited.

She looked him over, and gave a slight nod. "Suit yourself, it's your loss."

"You know, Steph. Besides being a bitch, you're a pain in the ass, too."

"Scotty baby, put it in the right hole." Her lips parted in a seductive grin. "I promise you, I'd be the best piece of ass you ever had."

"No thanks," he walked past her. "I'd rather jack off."

Her laughter followed him to the end of the hall.

Scott opened the door to his home on wheels and stepped in.

"If that's you again, Stephanie, please leave."

Moving into the center of the room, he looked down the hall. Aleecia was lying on his bed. The indirect lighting along the wall cast an alluring glow across her golden skin. She looked up, and Scott put a finger to his lips. Picking up a dive slate, he began writing on it as he headed to the bedroom.

Handing it to Aleecia, he waited.

Big brother may be listening.

Starting in the bedroom, he began a methodical search. Scott found the first bug within minutes. An hour later, he had six of the little transmitters in his hand, all of them produced by his company.

"Is that all?" she whispered.

He picked up his laptop, turned it on and waited. "Probably not."

Opening up a small hidden safe, he pulled out a CD pouch and loaded a disk. The screen turned a light blue. Six solid red dots appeared close together with a flashing red circle near them. Another one flashed near the white arrow in the center.

"Two transmitters left," he whispered. "One in here and the other in the bedroom, both video."

Scott located the tiny video transmitters with their hair-thin antennas. They were better concealed than the voice, and he suspected a different person had hidden them. *Damn, she's good.*

Placing the electronic bugs in a sealed glass jar, he put them in the fridge. "Okay, it's clear." He gave Aleecia a kiss.

"They won't be able to hear anything?" She slid her arms around his waist.

"Only the hum of the motor and gurgle of the coolant in the lines." He chuckled. "It'll drive them batty for a while trying to figure it out."

Aleecia snuggled closer, "I've missed you."

He laid his head against hers. "Was it very difficult?"

"Before Doc Walters showed or after? Before was a nightmare." Her body shook with the memories. "Thank God, you showed up when you did."

"Don't fret, dear." Scott picked her up and carried to the bed. "We'll get some rest and begin fresh in the morning."

"What are we going to do? They'll never let me leave."

"Stephanie may help us. She seems to have some influence with the inner circle." He ran his hand down her back and along her gills.

"That bitch," she sat up in bed. "I hate her."

Her eyes turned a stormy green, like the clouds before a tornado descends to leave a path of destruction.

"I'll be damned if I'm going to sit back and let some sex-starved nymphomaniac bitch come between us."

"Are you done?" He tried to keep a straight face but knew he was failing miserably.

"*Done*, I haven't started yet. Don't patronize me. When I get my hands on her, I'll..."

"Do nothing." He cut her off. "I don't know her game, but for now, we have to play along. Remember what I told you? What they don't know is our leverage, our hole card, and we have to make certain it stays face down on the table until we need it."

Scott slipped his shirt off. Her eyes went to his chest and slowly traveled lower. With a playful shove, she toppled him on his back.

"What are you doing?" he teased.

"You've been around Stephanie all day. I'm going to inspect you for bugs." Her fingers lightly frisked up his left leg.

With each intimate touch, he found it more difficult to breathe. He groaned in frustration when her hand reached his crotch and moved to the other foot.

Aleecia's hand crept up his leg at an agonizingly slow pace. Anticipation mounted as her fingers slid along his inner thigh and up between his legs. "Hmm, seems to be something in there." She traced the outline of his erection with a finger. "I'll have to check this out more thoroughly."

The tips of her fingers barely skimmed the surface of his stomach and circled the hard flesh of his nipples. A shudder racked his body. Her hands were everywhere, playfully searching between the hairs under his arms, behind and in his ears. The softness of his hair sliding through her fingers as she searched his scalp was magically erotic.

Her forefinger glided over the contour of his lips, and he opened them to her. Scott captured her finger and sucked on it.

Aleecia close her eyes. "Mmmm. Ohhh." The light sucking and the stroking of her finger with his tongue sent lightning-charged flashes spiraling downward to strengthen the flame of passion which threatened to burn out of control.

She removed her finger from his mouth and lowered her body until only her nipples rested lightly against his chest. Swaying back and forth, the contact of her nipples dancing through the light sprinkling of hair was overpowering. Moving across his chest, down the rippling plane of his stomach, she left a trail of wet kisses in her wake.

Her fingers trembled as she released the snap of his denim shorts. Lowering his zipper one click at a time slowly revealed the smooth, enlarged head of his penis. Using the pad of her forefinger, she stroked the hard tip.

Scott's body arched off the bed, and his hands clutched at the sheet. A long, broken, passion-filled sigh rumbled from his chest. Aleecia smiled and licked the small pearl-drop of moisture from her finger.

In one frantic movement, he ripped off his shorts, and Aleecia laughed. "I would've removed those...eventually."

She placed her finger on the tip of his cock and using her fingernail slowly drew a line down the underside of his hard shaft. His sudden intake of breath and the jerking of his legs caused the bed to rock from side-to-side.

"Mmm. Amazing what a fingernail in the right place can do."

Aleecia continued her examination. Lifting his balls, she ran her finger down the crack of his butt and circled the tight puckered hole. "You need to learn how to relax dear. You're *so* tense. I can feel your muscles quivering. Maybe this will help." The tip of her tongue touched his flesh, licking up another crystal-clear pearl.

His hips rose from the bed. As though his shaft had been launched from a powerful bow, the tip of his cock parted her lips.

Scott's strong hands pulled at her legs and lifted her on top of his heaving chest. His mouth greedily covered her. His tongue darted inside her and stroked her sensitive clit. Floating tongues of fire danced before her eyes. Wanting to be closer to the source of this wild heat, she ground her pelvis against his face.

Sliding off his chest, she wiggled closer and straddled his waist. Grabbing his shaft, she placed it against her wet flesh and slowly lowered her hips.

"Ahh," she gasped. "I love the way you feel inside of me," she leaned forward to capture his mouth, "your tongue drives me wild." She wiggled her hips, and licked the wet musk of her pussy from his face.

Aleecia took a long deep breath and exhaled through her gills.

Scott's eyes flashed, and his nostrils flared.

She wondered what caused the sudden blaze of heat from his eyes, the tightening of his hands at her waist. *Could it be my love, the heat of my body flowing across your fingers excites you?*

Lifting herself up, she watched his face as she drove his shaft deep inside her body. His neck arched on the pillow and his eyes rolled upward.

*Now, let's see what happens when I...*keeping her airway closed, she forcibly exhaled, *do this.*

Scott's eyes widened, and flashed with the brilliance of a comet burning in the sky.

Yes! Yes! Her head rolled back on her shoulders and joyous laughter threatened to overflow her heart. *Oh, yes!*

Dropping forward to claim his mouth, she stole his expelled air, drew it into her own body, and sent it fluttering across his hands.

They moved as one, breathed as one, as the flames of loves' passion consumed them.

Aleecia's sight began to blur, and her head started to spin. Breaking contact with his mouth, she gasped for breath. With the sudden increase of air sucked into her lungs, wave after climatic wave swept over her. She collapsed, trembling on his chest.

Scott's arms crept around her. A warm, comfortable feeling of belonging flooded her heart. She smiled and kissed the throbbing vein on the side of his neck.

Her eyes drifted closed.

"I love you." Scott's whispered words went unanswered. Aleecia was asleep.

For Scott however, sleep was a long time in coming. Staring at the ceiling, a deeper sense of responsibility crept into an already burdened heart. His thoughts drove him to the brink of despair.

I couldn't keep Melody safe, or my Lindsey. How? How in hell, am I going to protect Aleecia?

* * * * *

Aleecia felt delicious warmth at her breast. Heat flowed like warm honey to pool between her thighs. She didn't want it to end, this dream of erotic luxury invading her mind. It was so real. She could feel his coarse tongue licking at her nipple. His mouth suckled at her breast. Even his flesh was real as she reached out and ran her hand up his leg.

This had to be a dream, and she was touching herself. The absence of hair beneath her hand, jolted her partially awake.

A finger found the parted flesh of her pussy and slid ever so sensuously inside. "Mmm," she moaned.

"*Shhhhh,*" a soft whisper reached her ear, "you'll wake Scott."

Her eyes flew open, and she started to lash out with the calloused edge of her hand. Scott's words of warning flooded her mind '*Do nothing*'.

Stephanie's mouth closed over hers, shocking her into silence. Aleecia glanced down, there was indeed a finger inside her warm wet cunt, and it was Stephanie's.

She lay paralyzed under Stephanie's manipulation of her clit. The revulsion she felt began to give way to an exotic, forbidden heat radiating from between her legs. Stephanie's tongue invaded her mouth, touching hers in a playful duel.

Not wanting this, these feelings, or anything to do with Stephanie, Aleecia's body betrayed her.

The scorching fire of Stephanie's tongue left a trail of heat down her throat and across her breasts. Lower and still lower it went, until it hovered playfully around the fingers now deep inside her.

Placing a kiss on her excited clit, Stephanie stood and smiled. "Better wake Scott. You both have a long day ahead of you." With a deep sensuous laugh, she turned and walked down the short hall.

Aleecia lay seething in anger over Stephanie's actions, over her own response to them, and towards Scott, who lay beside her still softly snoring. She elbowed him sharply in the ribs.

He jolted up in bed. "What the hell!" He rubbed his side looking around. "If I was snoring too loud, all you had to do was give me a little nudge, not break a rib."

"I jabbed you because you were sleeping." She flung her legs off the bed.

"What the devil am I supposed to be doing at..." Scott looked at the lighted numbers on the clock, "...five-thirty in the damn morning?"

"Try getting up. Stephanie was here."

She squinted as the light came on.

"Thanks for warning me." She stomped off to the bathroom.

"I'm sorry about the light. You don't need to be so pissed over it. What did the bitch want?"

She slammed the bathroom door, reopened it, and stuck her head out. "She said something about it being a long day."

Scott winced as the door slammed shut for the second time.

Scott crawled out of bed wondering why his world had been turned upside down. Bewildered at her actions, he headed for the kitchen and his morning caffeine fix. The pungent odor of chlorine assaulted the lining of his nose. Leaping to the door, he barreled through it, breaking a hinge.

Aleecia stood in the shower, vigorously washing away soapsuds from between her legs.

Turning the water off, Scott pulled her from the shower and into the kitchen. "Are you trying to kill yourself?" Alarm for her safety tightened his voice.

"I was holding my breath." She stood with her hand on her hips, water dripping onto the floor, and looked at the broken door. "Give me some credit for reaching puberty without your overbearing hand to guide me."

The door opened, and Stephanie stepped in. "Sorry to bust up the party, but time is wasting." She tossed two sets of running gear on the floor. "Here, put these on."

"Steph!" Scott barked. "Are you aware of Aleecia being allergic to chlorine to the point that it would kill her?"

"Yes, we are," she looked from Scott to Aleecia. "Why? What's the problem?"

Scott thrust the coffeepot under her nose. "Smell this."

She quickly drew her head back. "God, that's strong."

"No shit," he spat. "Now tell me something I don't know. Like, how in the hell did this happen?"

Stephanie looked confused, shaken and at an utter loss. Scott felt sure she hadn't experienced these feelings in a very long time.

"It couldn't have...not by accident." Her face paled. "I personally watched the maintenance crew install a filter to the feed line coming in."

Aleecia felt dazed by this information. Her world was spinning out of control, and she could do nothing about it. She looked at Scott's rigidly set face and took courage in his strength.

"Stephanie, you're telling me someone in this ultra secret, underground vault, is trying to kill Aleecia."

"Yes."

Chapter 19

"Get the General," Scott ordered.

Stephanie leaned her head against the door. With her arms spread over her head, and her hands flat on the wall, she looked out the window. "He won't be in for another hour."

"Call him...now." Scott paced the small space between the door and the kitchen sink. "Tell him there has been an accident and Aleecia is dead. He is come straight to you when he arrives."

"What good will that do? She's not dead." Stephanie stepped in front of him. "Sooner or later whoever tried to kill her will know they didn't succeed."

"Not if she isn't here."

"That's insane Scott," she tried to reason with him. "We can't protect her out in the world."

"You can't protect her here!" He held up the coffee pot.

"I've got some say in this," Aleecia spoke up. "After all, it's my life. I'll go back to Branson. At least there I could take a shower without being poisoned."

"It's out of the question. When the General gets here, we'll get to the bottom of this."

"Before or after she's dead?" He glared at her, demanding she recognize the truth of what he was saying.

"Okay, but we can't leave her in here. There's a doctor on duty now who I trust."

"There's my nurse, Helen," Aleecia added.

"I'll brief them and get the show going. Then I'll call the General." Stephanie opened the door. "The fewer people in on this the better.

"Scott," she smiled, "better get dressed."

He wasted no time in slipping on a pair of pants and tossed the black sweat suit to Aleecia.

The door opened. Nurse Helen and a doctor walked in, both visibly out of breath. "We haven't got much time. Where were you when you found out about the water?"

"In the shower."

"Off with the clothes, hurry. If we are staging your death it must look real."

As Aleecia pulled the top over her head, Scott pulled the pants down around her ankles. Helen poured a bottle of water over her and then wrapped a sheet around her.

"Scott, take her feet. Aleecia, you need to be as limp as possible." The doctor put his arms around Aleecia. "Let's do it."

Scott ran, pushing the ambulance gurney before him. Conscious all the while, her assailant could even now be watching. The doors opened seemingly on their own. Stephanie held one door while a stern faced, heavily armed soldier held the other. With a quick side-ways glance, he noticed the Para Micro Uzi in her hand, complete with laser pointer and thirty round magazine.

"Here!" Stephanie called out as they ran down the hall. "It's loaded."

Scott felt the heavy weight of the forty-five fill his hand. "Thanks."

"Just don't shoot my ass in the process," she looked over at Scott and smiled.

A door opened and they rolled Aleecia into the room. "Carlos, secure the door. No one comes in but the General. I repeat...*No one*."

Stephanie paced the room. "How the *fuck* did this happen?"

Aleecia got dressed for the second time that morning and waited nervously for what ever would come next. One thing she was certain of, she wasn't spending any more time down here than was necessary.

The clock ticked off the minutes. Scott sat on the bed, facing the door, the weapon held ready in his hand. "What do we do if someone else comes in?"

"Shoot the bastard." Stephanie ground out between clenched teeth. "Cause if it's not the General, Carlos is dead."

As if on cue, a knock sounded and the door opened. Concern was written across the General's face like a flashing neon sign.

"Aleecia, you're all right," the General's voice shook with suppressed emotion. "Agent Brooke, what is the meaning of this?"

As Stephanie briefed the General, Scott observed a transformation in his stature. The muscles in his jaw twitched, a vein near his right eye became visible, pulsating with each beat of his heart. His back straightened, and his hands closed in tight, white-knuckled fists.

"Mr. Mathis, Agent Brooke's assessment of your abilities seems to have been well founded." The General reached out and shook his hand. "I'm proud to have you on board. Until whoever did this is caught, both your lives are in grave danger. I agree with you. Down here, it's only a matter of time until another attack is carried out."

The General laid out his plan and turned to Aleecia. "Is there anything you need?"

"I want a dozen throwing stars and a harness." She looked at Stephanie and smiled. "Yes, I know how to use them."

* * * * *

Scott watched the long black hearse pull away from the warehouse. Carlos sat in the passenger seat with his weapons loaded and ready to fire should the need arise. The word of Aleecia's death had spread like wildfire through the underground complex. The last of the onlookers walked away, and he was left standing with the General.

"Sir, may I ask you a question?" The hearse disappeared through the gate.

"I think you've earned the right for more than one, but go ahead."

"You seem to be taking this rather..." he hesitated searching for the right word.

"Personally," the General finished for him.

"Ah, yes, sir," Scott lowered his voice, "but I was thinking along the lines of a fatherly concern."

To Scott's amazement, a tear welled up in the General's eye and trickled slowly down his cheek.

"That's because...I am her father." The General turned his eyes away from the main gate. "You look like you could use a drink. I know I could use one."

Scott followed the General through the maze of passageways deep inside the complex to the General's private quarters. The room surprised him. Paneled in a luxuriant walnut, it was the first color he had seen since his arrival. The furniture was solid oak with black, leather-bound cushions on the couch and chairs. A large built-in bookcase and a gas fireplace filled one wall. Over the mantel, a huge oil painting of a woman holding a baby captured his attention.

The General handed him a glass, and he caught a whiff of expensive Scotch.

"I can't tell you the hours I have stood in this same spot, burning this image into my mind. Trying to imagine what she looked like as a child growing up. What her life was like and never knowing." His voice choked.

The General swirled the liquid in his glass, staring thoughtfully into the rich amber liquor as if were a crystal ball. Slowly, he lifted it to his lips and drank. "Call it vanity, if you want, but when they were taking sperm specimens for the DNA research, I jumped in line. They never told me about the gills. I guess they were trying to shield the program and me from the outrage of any publicity."

"The woman in the picture?" Scott sipped his drink.

"Her birth mother... She was also her nurse."

Scott looked at the General's face. He appeared to have aged within the last hour. There was a weary vacant shadow in his eyes. His cheeks seemed sunken as if the demons and ghosts of his past had come to claim their due.

"Does anyone else know?"

For the longest moment, the General stared at the picture, the drink forgotten in his hand. Abruptly, he turned and walked over to a large oak desk. "No one else knows, and it must always remain a secret."

Scott's mind was in turmoil. "Why, sir, after all these years, are you telling me? You should be telling Aleecia, not me."

"Because you love her.

"Agent Brooke is outside. I have a traitor to catch, and you have to leave." The General reached across the desk. "This is the only time I shall say these words to another living soul. Take care of my...daughter."

He took the outstretched hand and held it, looking deep into the guilt-laden eyes of the General. "I'll do my best, sir."

Scott left the General's private quarters feeling like another huge weight had been placed on his shoulders. Stephanie's questioning look only added to the burden.

"What's going on?" she asked as they made their way through the twisting halls. "Do you realize, in all the time I have worked here, no one as ever gone past that door until now? What did you two talk about?"

They came to a door with an electronic security entrance. "Do I have clearance to go in there?"

"No, it's classified. Need to know only." She walked on down the hall beside him.

"So is the discussion I had with General. Are all the arrangements made for leaving?"

"The advance team has already left and is in position." They came to the double doors of the cavern and paused. "I'm worried about Aleecia being by herself with only a driver. Carlos may be good but…"

"Don't be." He pushed open the door and walked across the hangar.

Scott watched the huge elevator descend and drove the motor home onto the platform. He laid the forty-five within easy reach and waited as the elevator lifted him to the floor of the empty warehouse. The outer doors opened, he dropped the transmission into drive, and drove toward the main gate.

He spotted the service station two blocks down the road and pulled into it. Filling the tank, he looked around for Stephanie. She was supposed to meet him here.

"If I knew where Aleecia was, I'd leave the bitch and never look back." Scott mumbled.

In all fairness, they did owe her. She had gotten them out of immediate danger and for now, Aleecia's safety mattered most.

A door slammed across the street. Stephanie, dressed in tank top, shorts, and tennis shoes walked across the street. Across her shoulders was slung a backpack, and she carried a large duffel bag.

"Yo, mister!" she waved. "Can I get a ride? My asshole boyfriend kicked my ass out of the friggin' house."

"Sure, throw your bag in. I was just leaving." He climbed in after her and pulled onto the street. "Here, you drive."

They changed places, and Scott retrieved the computer disk from the safe. He sat down in the passenger seat, and turned on the laptop.

A late model Ford van pulled in behind them a block from the station.

"I was wondering how in the hell you found all the transmitters. What are you doing with that program, it's classified?" She glanced from the road to the screen and back to the road. "How the fuck did you get a copy of it?"

Scott smiled. "Who said anything about a copy? You should know these can't be copied. They have to come straight from the manufacturer."

"Which makes that...?"

"The original program," Scott laughed at her surprise. "I see you've removed the ones from the refrigerator. Knowing I found the last ones, why did you put a tracker signal onboard?" He watched the flashing red triangle on the screen.

"We didn't." Anger tinged her voice, and her knuckles turned white on the steering wheel.

"Pull into the first truck stop on the interstate. Someone wants to go for a ride, we'll give them a long one, all the way to Florida."

Stephanie had a smile on her face as she took the on ramp to I-95 and headed south. The van followed close behind.

The next exit after the truck stop, Stephanie headed back to the coast. "Take over. When you hit highway one, go south."

Scott slid behind the wheel.

She pulled a radio from her pack. "Black Dragon to Black Knight Two. Sorry about the detour, we had to drop off a package. We're proceeding to destination as planned."

The speaker crackled, "Two copies, all clear."

* * * * *

"Black Dragon to Black Knight One. We are approaching your position." Stephanie sat in the passenger's seat, the Para Micro Uzi snug in her right hand. A nine-millimeter Glock rested in a shoulder harness under her left arm. The weapon's black finish was nearly invisible against the Omega Sentry combat uniform.

The radio crackled with static. "Black Knight One copies. You are cleared for approach."

Scott topped a small hill. The sand dunes stretched for miles to the north and south. Ahead of him, the Atlantic Ocean's waves rolled beneath a cloudless sky and the blazing late afternoon sun. Sea oats swayed in the ocean breeze and gulls floated on the currents searching for food.

Three houses stood near the ocean, partially protected behind the first low dune. He pulled up to the center house and stopped. Carlos stepped out, armed with an M-16 assault rifle and the butt of a pistol hanging from a shoulder harness.

The van, which had been their constant shadow, stopped well behind them. The four passengers rolled out the doors and disappeared into the dunes.

"We're here." Stephanie opened the door and waited until he joined her outside.

They walked up to the house and noticed Carlos looking towards the beach. He turned around as they approached. A bruise already starting to form was visible on his jaw.

"What the hell happened to you and where is Aleecia?" Stephanie demanded.

"She's swimming." Carlos didn't look very pleased at having to tell his boss where Aleecia was at the moment.

Despite his concern for her safety, Scott chuckled.

"I don't think this a laughing matter, Mr. Mathis." Stephanie turned back to Carlos.

"You were supposed to keep her with you. Why didn't you stop her?"

Scott knew where the bruise had come from, and he turned away to keep Stephanie from seeing the laughter on his face.

"She informed me she was going swimming, even if she had to kick my ass to do it." Carlos looked sheepish. "I told her, if she kicked my ass, she could go."

"Explain to me then, if you can, why Aleecia is in the ocean and your sorry ass is on the beach?"

"Sorry, ma'am," Carlos snapped to attention. "That's how I got this bruise. She kicked my ass fair and square."

"Where was the rest of your team while you were getting your ass kicked?"

"Laughing at me spitting sand out of my mouth, ma'am."

"I don't believe this. You let that little snip of a woman get the best of you?"

Scott stepped off the porch and headed for the beach, not bothering to wait around for Stephanie to chew on Carlos, or whoever else got in her way. He pulled an oat stem from the sand and chewed on the end as he searched the surf for signs of Aleecia.

Movement to his left caught his attention. A black clad member of Team One sat almost hidden from view a few feet away. "She's been under for almost an hour, Mr. Mathis."

There was a sense of awe, bordering on reverence in the man's hushed voice. He knew how the squad member felt.

"Seeing as how we're all going to be working together, drop the mister crap. Scott will do just fine." He stepped over and shook the man's hand.

"Tom, Tom Seggers." Tom's eyes darted to the beach.

From the frothy, white foam and rolling breakers, her dark russet hair emerged. He was surprised to find she was wearing a modified black Sentry uniform with the back cut away from around her gills. It was a little big on her but still showed off her curves to perfection.

She came running up the beach, full of life and energy, and threw her arms around his neck. "I couldn't wait," her voice bubbled with joy. "Oh, Scott, the water here is wonderful." She gave him a hot sensuous welcome kiss. "You've got to go with me next time."

"There won't be a next time unless I say so." Stephanie's tight voice came from behind them. "I'm in command here, and I tell you when you can or can't go swimming."

Aleecia headed for the house. Scott had seen that look in her eyes before, but he didn't feel like warning Stephanie.

"I'm talking to you," she jogged after Aleecia. "I said…" Stephanie put her hand on Aleecia's left shoulder.

Aleecia's hand came up and grabbed Stephanie's the moment it touched her. With a sharp pull and a twist of her body, Stephanie flew across Aleecia's outthrust hip, through the air to land with a grunt. Rolling in the sand, she sprang lightly to her feet.

Stephanie dropped the shoulder harness on the ground. "Come on, show me what you got. Kicking my ass won't be as easy as Carlos's."

The women circled, sidestepping in the sand, like cats. Carlos stood on the porch with an amused grin on his face. The radio squealed.

"Black Dragon, you might want to reconsider."

"Shut the fuck up, Carlos!" she yelled, never taking her eyes off Aleecia.

"You want a piece of my ass, Aleecia? Let's get it on, right here. After this is all said and done, I still control when you go in the ocean." She closed in on Aleecia, shifted her weight to the left, and lashed out with a swift sidekick to the center of her chest.

Aleecia blocked the kick with a swipe of her right forearm, spun in a circle while dropping into a low crouch, and swept her foot out at the off balanced Stephanie, striking her low on the calf just above the ankle.

Stephanie landed on her back, rolled to her shoulders and lurched to her feet, pulling her body up into a standing position. She quickly hopped into a guarded stance, knees bent and arms raised to protect her vulnerable points.

"Not bad." She grunted as she leapt forward, using her words to try and unbalance, Aleecia, ready to attack.

Stepping into her body space, Stephanie delivered a straight punch to her face, with her left hand, while moving the right, tensed into a knife fist, towards her body.

Aleecia ducked the fist, throwing up her right arm to block, but missed the knife fist closing in on her side.

It connected, driving the air out of her lungs, tiling her to the side, but she kept to her feet.

Stephanie closed in again and threw a series of rapid-fire blows to Aleecia's upper body. Driving her back, she tried to break Aleecia's protective stance.

With a roar of outrage, Stephanie thrust both hands into Aleecia's chest, forcing her arms outward and leaving her open to a blinding sidekick.

Aleecia grunted and went with the force of the blow, staggering backwards before she righted herself and eased into a low attack stance, a slow smile spreading across her face.

"Was that a love tap?" She breathed, shaking her head as if knocking the pain from the blow aside. "Carlos hits harder than you do."

Her face remained calm, poised, her body balanced ready for the next attack.

Stephanie shifted, gave a small hop and her leg lifted high, nearly into a split and her foot dropped to where Aleecia's head had been.

Ducking under the blow, Aleecia grabbed the ankle on its way down with one hand, and shoved it aside, breaking Stephanie's balance. Then she rapidly delivered a crippling chop to her inner thigh. Spinning around, she drilled her in the right side with the knife-edge of her hand.

Stephanie hobbled out of reach, pain etched across her face as she dropped her right arm to protect her side.

Covered with sand, they began a constant shifting, circling, and positioning, searching for a weak spot. Both were breathing heavily, arms held in front of them in defense, watchful for the next blow.

Scott took a glance at the porch. Several of the two assault teams were gathered, watching the match with keen interest. One of the men grudgingly opened his wallet and handed Carlos a bill.

"There's an easy answer to your problem, Aleecia," Stephanie circled, searching for a moment of weakness. "You get to go in that big ocean anytime you want."

She feinted a move towards Aleecia. "In return, I get to fuck lover boy. You can even watch, if you want to."

The moment Aleecia looked at him with desperate pleading in her eyes, Stephanie struck.

Aleecia caught a flying kick to the side of her face. Her head bounced with the force of the blow. Her air exploded from her chest with the force of Stephanie's quick power jab. She let her body absorb the impact, flowing with it, letting it carry her out of Stephanie's reach.

She landed on her ass, and slowly regained her feet.

There had been several times when she could have ended it. But Scott's words of caution kept holding her back, preventing her from using her full abilities as a master against Stephanie.

With her last taunt, the will to continue the charade had changed to anger. An anger, which cut so deep, and could only result in Stephanie's death if she continued.

She dropped her hands, turned and headed back to the ocean. Aleecia turned her head away from Scott, hiding the tears that flooded her cheeks.

"Where are you going? I didn't give you permission!" Stephanie yelled.

"I...I don't need your permission anymore." She ran towards the water, wishing somehow that she might be able to drown in its dark, cold depths.

Chapter 20

"You won't win," a strong male voice came from behind him. "She's been playing this game longer than you have."

"Game?" He slowly turned around to glare at Carlos. "What's the name of it, Death Wish?"

Carlos snickered then broke out into loud laughter. "Believe me, everyone of us on the team has felt the same thing about Stephanie. But there's not one of us who wouldn't sacrifice our life to protect hers. Aleecia could have taken Stephanie. I know it and the rest of my team knows it. Why did she hold back? Why did she quit and walk away?"

"Did you ever play poker, Carlos?" He glanced around the area.

Stephanie sat on the porch, shaking the sand out of her hair, while the two paramedics, Vic and Paul, were wrapping her ribs. The others had left and gone about whatever it was they had been doing.

"Yeah," Carlos smiled. "I've played a few times."

"Did you ever show the hole card before the betting was done?" Scott looked out over the ocean, knowing even as he did, there would be no sign of Aleecia.

"You are playing a dangerous game, Mr. Mathis," he turned back to the house. "Very dangerous indeed."

* * * * *

The bitch, Aleecia thought as she submerged in the rolling surf. *Why did I make that promise to Scott? I could have taken Stephanie the first time and this would've been avoided. Would it? Probably not for long. I should've seen it coming.*

She rubbed her jaw and moved it from side to side. I lost my focus, and she used my anger against me. I defeated myself.

Aleecia followed the ocean floor to a rock ledge overlooking the sheer face of a drop-off. Sitting on the edge with nothing but blackness for thousands of feet below her, she began to meditate on the lessons of her beloved Master, the wonderful, loving care of her mother, and her love for Scott.

Scott was her life. *If I have to share your body, I will. Your love is mine forever. She can't take that away.*

Aleecia surfaced beyond the breakers. Stars filled the heavens, and a waning moon cast its faded light across the beach. She spotted the darker shadows of the sentries, hiding on the dunes, in the tall sea oats.

She noted a low washout in the beach, submerged, and swam towards it. The surf swirled around her, pounding her with its relentless force. Crawling out of the froth, Aleecia inched her way up the beach, blending with the shadows, and becoming one with them in the night.

"Black Dragon to all posts, any sign of her?" From five feet away, she listened as the sentries gave their negative report. She smiled and blew the guard a silent mocking kiss.

Reaching the clearing around the house, she waited. The guard on the porch turned his back. With the swiftness of a deer, she ran on silent feet to the edge of the porch and ducked down as the guard turned around.

His footsteps grew closer and stopped, inches above her head. The whisper of grating leather told her when he turned away. The guard took a step, then another. Aleecia leaped into the air and over the railing, silently landing on the deck. She slipped through the door as he paused at the far railing.

The surprise on Stephanie's face was priceless as she picked up the radio. "All units. Why wasn't I told she was out of the water?"

Several seconds of pungent silence hovered over the room as Stephanie's eyes drilled into hers.

"I'm waiting."

"Beach One. Never saw her come out."

"Beach Two. Negative here also."

Aleecia walked over to Scott, wrapped her arms around him and lifted her lips to his in a long heated embrace.

"How the hell, did you get past all my men without being spotted?"

Aleecia turned her head and noticed something different in Stephanie's eyes. Was it respect, or cautious admiration? "Maybe they need more training."

"Bullshit," she spat. "My teams are the best trained in the world. They have to be." Stephanie tossed the radio onto the couch, walked to the front door and threw it open. The sentry snapped to attention, as a look of dread spread across his face.

"You didn't see Aleecia walk through this door?" Stephanie barked.

"No, ma'am. I didn't see or hear a thing, ma'am."

Stephanie slammed the door and winced.

"How are the ribs?" Aleecia asked.

"Never mind my damn ribs," she snapped.

"Stephanie, are they broken?"

"Vic thinks one of them is cracked." She crossed the room to where they stood.

"I'm sorry. I didn't intend to break any bones."

"You sound like you mean it." Stephanie rubbed her side.

"I do." Aleecia stretched her hand out. "Please, accept my apologies. It was not my intent to seriously harm you."

Stephanie regarded the offered hand, as if questioning her motive, and then slowly took it with her own.

"Aleecia, will you answer me one question?" she paused. "Where did you receive your martial arts training?"

Aleecia paused in thought. There was no one left in her village who could be punished. The Master was dead, as was her mother. "I grew up in a small fishing village on the northern tip of Japan. My teacher has long since joined his Ancestors."

Stephanie laid her hand carefully against her side. "He taught you well. It's getting late. Tomorrow, you'll take over Scott's training." She walked over to the bedroom door. "Good night."

Scott took a deep breath and let out a sigh of relief. The smell of the ocean breeze was in her hair. Salt crystals clung to her skin, glistening like diamonds in the sand. He was thankful she was back and unharmed. Something had happened during her swim. She appeared calm, at ease with the situation they found themselves in.

The warmth and love radiating from her eyes wrapped around his heart. The taste of her salt-covered lips tightened his loins. Aleecia's kiss ignited his ever-present desire and passion for her body. Scott scooped her up in his arms and carried her to the other bedroom. Inside the small room, he swung Aleecia around, using her feet to close the door.

"I was worried about you." Scott carried her to the bed. "I was afraid you would kill her and then have the lives of two people to haunt you."

"I already have two ghosts who trouble my dreams as reminders of what I have done." She pulled her arms from the top and pushed the material past her hips, dropping it on the floor beside the bed. "I don't wish to add more demons unnecessarily."

"Two?" His fingers paused in removing his own clothes.

"I was young, in my late teens. A young American sailor came to the beach not far from our village. I was getting dressed and didn't see him at first.

"Mother was in the States. I was lonely and had been wondering about love and sex. Afterward, he found out what I was. He started bragging how the guys on his ship would never believe he had broken a...mermaid's cherry."

Scott gathered her in his arms. "I'm sorry."

"I never told anyone. I was scared, ashamed of what I had done. I took his body out to sea and made a stone-covered grave on the ocean floor. It was a long time before I went back into the water."

"You did what you thought you had to, to survive. He probably would've bragged about it to his shipmates. Somewhere along the way, he could've told the wrong person and your life would've been placed in even more danger." He kissed her shoulder and removed the remainder of his clothes.

"The guilt is not yours to bear alone, but those who thought they could play God, and control the destiny of peoples' lives." He thought of the General and those involved in creating the first Omega Sentry experiment. "They're the ones who must live with the shame and consequences of their deeds."

Scott knelt on the floor in front of her, leaned forward, kissed first one breast, and then the other. Her hands lifted to his head, her fingers twisted in his hair, and held his face to her breast.

Her nipple grew, hardening between his lips. Scott drew her tender flesh into his mouth and felt her body tremble. A contented sigh floated from her throat.

With a slight push against her breast, she lay back on the bed. Her inner thighs pressed against his ribs. With the fingers of one hand massaging her breast, his other hand crept low on her waist and a finger slipped inside the moist folds of her cunt. Lowering his head, Scott used the tip of his tongue to draw lazy circles around her belly button. Her stomach rippled, like waves flowing across a pool of water. His tongue dipped into the shallow dimple, and her thighs trembled.

Leaving the smooth plains of her stomach, his mouth traveled lower, probing, sucking, searching for and finding the musk-scented outer folds of her pussy. Aleecia lifted her hips, offering herself to him. His tongue slipped inside her delicate flesh and touched her swollen clit.

Mistress of Table Rock

A deep sensuous moan bubbled from her lips as her back arched from the bed.

Scott smiled against her flesh and softly blew across her swollen clit. His tongue stroked and teased her quivering cunt.

Aleecia's legs locked around him, holding him. Her hips bounced on the bed as cries of passion filled the air.

Her body tightened and with a deep shudder, she bathed his face with the essence of her release. Hot, thick musk flowed across his tongue.

Scott climbed to his feet, lifted her legs onto the bed, and settled between them. His cock pierced her flesh, sinking into her cum-slicked pussy.

Aleecia pulled his head down to hers. Her tongue licked his face and probed his mouth.

"Yes, fill me with your life, Scott. Bury it deep within me." She accented each word with a thrust of her hips.

Their breaths mingled, tongues clashed, and soft groans of ecstasy became swallowed up by each other. Their bodies, oiled by the sweat of passion and fueled by desire, spiraled out of control.

Scott's vision blurred. His body stiffened. Molten fire burned his loins as he filled her silken depths.

He pulled out of her and collapsed on the bed.

Aleecia snuggled into his arms. Grabbing the edge of the blanket, she flipped it over them.

"Scott, if I have to share your body…I will. Just promise me I'll never have to share your love."

"That, my dear, is something I will never share with any but you."

* * * * *

Scott threw his arm across his eyes to shield them from the glare of the overhead light. Aleecia groaned and buried her face in the crook of his arm.

The blanket that had kept them warm through the night disappeared.

Stephanie sniffed the air, "I hope you two saved some energy for today. Be outside in fifteen minutes.

"Aleecia, I watched Carlos install a filter and rig it with an explosive device. Anyone who tampers with this one will die."

"Thank you," she got out of bed and stumbled into the shower.

Stephanie yawned. "Need to get you a new bed. This one's noisy." She walked to the door, stopped and looked at her watch. "Fourteen minutes. Don't be late."

Scott ran through the shower, dressed and hurried outside. Team One was stretching out and loosening up.

"Don't just stand there with cum juice on your face, Scott." With every movement, pain flashed across Stephanie's face. She turned her attention back to the team. "Come on, girls, stretch out those muscles."

All eyes followed Aleecia's graceful movements as she shadow-fought in slow motion.

He stepped down off the porch.

"You two been hustling my ass," Stephanie whispered as he walked past. "Why?"

Scott grinned, "It wasn't very hard to do. You're so full of yourself you can't see anyone else." He stepped closer, standing well within her personal space, and looked her in the eye. "If you felt your position might be threatened by another woman, you would've tried to prove yourself."

"What if I had?" Her hands rested on her hips, feet slightly spread apart. Sweat glistened on her brow and trickled down her neck.

"You'd have more than a cracked rib." Scott started to turn away and stopped. Looking into her pain glazed eyes, he started to speak, shook his head and walked off.

A half-mile into their two-mile jog, Scott watched Stephanie's face. "Hey, Vic." He motioned with a flip of his head.

"Yeah, I know." He shrugged his shoulders. "She's smart and a brilliant strategist. If she had a dick between her legs, she would be a Navy Seal. Because she doesn't…"

"She thinks she has to be better than the others." Scott voiced the unfinished sentence.

"Somebody will end up carrying her," he panted for breath. His lungs were starting to burn.

"Won't be the first time. We'll carry you too, if need be." Vic smiled, "Pace yourself, this isn't about speed, or coming in first, but endurance. It's about the whole team, coming back from a mission and leaving no one behind."

At the end of the two miles, they finished as they had started, a team with everyone taking a turn helping Stephanie. Through the whole ordeal, he hadn't heard one complaint from her thin pressed lips.

Paul handed Stephanie a bottle of water and a couple of pain pills.

Scott leaned on the railing catching his breath. Stephanie looked up, and gave him a wink.

Aleecia strolled over and leaned against the railing post. "How're you doing?"

"I'll live." Stephanie started to get up.

Pain flashed across her face. Beads of sweat appeared on her forehead. Scott heard the hiss of air drawn through clenched teeth. He started to move closer to help her.

Stephanie stopped him with a quick jerk of her head, and dragged herself to her feet. "Carlos, see that everyone gets fed. Afterwards, take these two out to the dunes for some weapons training. Scott, Aleecia, can I see you inside, please?" She limped across the porch and through the door.

Scott entered the house and rushed to catch her as she fell, "Aleecia, go get the one of the paramedics."

"No!" Stephanie snapped. "Don't...get anyone. I'm *not* taking a MEDEVAC outta here."

"Anyone ever tell you, you're hardheaded?" Scott carried her to the bedroom.

"Yeah, my ol' man, and now you." She laughed, which sent another barb of stabbing pain across her eyes. "I'm only letting you get away with it cause I don't feel like kicking your ass."

She reached down to remove her black pullover.

"Here, let me help." Scott gently lifted the material. The Ace bandage stood out in stark contrast to her skin. A black bra supported her ample breasts. He eased the blouse over her head.

"Aleecia, fill the tub with hot water, please." Stephanie gathered a deep breath and stood.

"Scott, would you remove the bandage and my bra? Hell, just strip me bare-ass naked and get it over with."

She limped to the bathroom and stepped into the steaming water. "Thanks, I trust you will both keep this to yourselves. Go ahead and eat. I'll be fine." Stephanie leaned back in the tub and closed her eyes.

* * * * *

A surly compromise was reached. Vic and Paul finally agreed not to ship Stephanie out, provided she promised to let the ribs heal.

Scott's body quickly adjusted to the rigors of training. The pace of the two-mile hike on the beach increased, as did his proficiency on the makeshift weapons range.

Mistress of Table Rock

The teams practiced anti-terrorist drills, using the two end houses for search-and-rescue missions. Every couple of nights a boat, helicopter, or van would come and unload supplies.

Aleecia spent hours in the ocean with different members of the group. She excelled in the training. She quickly became an integral part of the team.

With the increased pace in the training, nights of raw passion, hard cocks and wet cunts were soon reduced to being grateful they could sleep in each others arms.

Days turned into weeks, and Stephanie gradually grew stronger. The men were getting restless, anxious to get away and see their wives and girlfriends. Tempers started to flare and fuses grew short.

One morning after a grueling night-ops training, Stephanie called both teams together. "I've got some good news this morning. The General found the man who sabotaged the water supply. The bad news is, the member of the General's staff who ordered it, is missing. He is presumed to have left the country, and may have ties to North Korea." Stephanie paused and allowed the shock to pass.

"I don't have to tell you the severity of this. I convinced the General to hold off going to full alert until tomorrow morning. We have twenty-four hours of liberty, starting now. Keep your beepers handy. If you're going to get laid gentleman, do it today. For most of us, it may be the last we get for a long time." She went back into the house.

The two teams scattered and within minutes, the two vans pulled out leaving a cloud of dust drifting in the wind.

"What would you like to do?" He slipped his hand around Aleecia's.

"Take a blanket down to the beach, watch the sea gulls for a while, maybe take a nap curled up in your arms." She laid her head against his chest. "It really doesn't matter, as long as I get to spend it with you."

They went inside to get a blanket and Stephanie looked up from the paperwork spread across the table. "You two headed out?"

"No, we're going down to the beach and relax." Scott grabbed a blanket from the couch. "Maybe go for a walk in the surf or lay out in the sun."

"After the hell you two have been through the last few weeks, I'd say you've earned it." Stephanie's eyes went back to the paper in her hand.

"Do you want to join us?" Aleecia bit her tongue.

Scott's dumfounded stare would've been comical in another situation.

"If I thought you meant it, I might be tempted."

"Well," Aleecia smiled. "Suit yourself. You'll know where to find us." She strolled out the door without a backward glance.

Scott jogged to catch her. "What the hell is going on? Why did you invite Stephanie to join us?"

"I don't know." She stomped through the sand.

"You invited her."

She kicked up a spray of sand. "Don't remind me."

Scott dropped the blanket, took Aleecia's hand and they strolled down the beach. The surf broke around their ankles, shifting the sand from under foot. Sea gulls swooped down, hoping for a morsel of food. Crabs scurried sideways to disappear into holes dotting the beach.

The ocean breeze lifted the ends of her hair, blowing it across her face. She picked up a flat stone and sent it skipping across the water. A look of longing brought a wistful smile to her face.

"I love it here." She turned to look up into his face. "I guess you never really appreciate something until you lose it, and then get it back."

"I think it's true of everything in life." His thoughts turned to his wife and child. "Second chances are rare." Scott squeezed her hand. "We shouldn't let them pass us by."

They turned around and headed back.

The beach was empty. Aleecia spread the blanket out and sat down. "I think," she started removing clothes, "I'm going to get some sun."

Scott's response was automatic at the sight of her firm tits and the rounded lips of her pussy. His cock came alive and pressed against the material of his shorts.

She folded her clothes, making a small pillow for her head. Lying down, she stretched her arms over her head. Patting the blanket beside her, she smiled. "You going to join me, or stand there all day."

He dropped his pants.

"I didn't bring any suntan lotion with me." The sound of Aleecia's laughter caused nearby seagulls to leap into the sky. Their shrill cries filled the air.

Scott looked down. The thin band around his waist and his white cock showed in stark contrast to his tan. "I'm sure if I looked hard enough, I could find some cream to put on it."

He sat on the blanket and stretched out beside her. "This is nice. Nobody around for miles, warm sun shining down and the ocean wave's soft rumble as they break on the shore."

Scott leaned over and kissed her.

"There you are. I changed my mind." Stephanie stripped off the black Omega Sentry uniform and tossed it on the sand. She spread her legs and stretched her arms over her head.

Scott received a clear view of not only the beaver, but the beaver den as well.

Chapter 21

"Could you move over please?" Stephanie lay down beside him with her arm touching his hip. "Such a beautiful day, and this is so cozy. Thanks, Aleecia, for inviting me."

He looked over at Aleecia and scowled at her. "Thanks a lot," he silently mouthed at her.

Aleecia covered her mouth and giggled.

"One of the reasons I came down here, I wanted to talk about your training." She turned on her side and propped her head on her hand so she could see both of them.

"You two have fit right into the program. Your progress has been great. All of us, and this comes from each member, are glad to have you aboard."

Aleecia rolled over onto her left side and faced Stephanie. "What's the catch?"

"I don't think you're ready for the real thing. Physically, I don't have a problem. It's emotionally that worries me."

"Why?" They both asked at once.

"Let me explain it this way," she paused. "In combat, emotions get you killed. One of my men gets hit, I haven't got time to sit there and cry. I stop the bleeding if I can, then pat him on the shoulder and keep on, and if no one can get to him, or me, sorry.

"Everyone of us has seen combat. Seen buddies we were drinking with a few days earlier, cut in half by machine gun fire, and we carried back what was left."

Scott thought about it for a minute. "Is anyone…ever ready?"

"No." Stephanie shook her head. "But the first time is always the worst. You never forget it." Her eyes took on a haunted look. "I still have nightmares."

"So," he looked from Aleecia to Stephanie, "we aren't going on whatever is coming up?"

"It all depends…"

"On what?" he demanded.

"Say one of you gets captured. I can rescue you and compromise the mission, or…"

"Sacrifice us, and complete the mission." Scott finished for her.

"You get the picture. What do we do, Scott, if it happens?"

Scott sighed and slowly nodded his head. "The mission."

Stephanie reached out and placed her hand on Scott's chest. "Just have to make sure everyone knows the situation." Her fingers slowly slid down to his waist and reached for his cock.

"The recall has been sent out. If you two are going to fuck, you better get a stiff cock in a hurry."

"I thought we had twenty-four hours?" Aleecia sat up and grasped Scott's arm.

"Not when we're at Def-Con Two," Stephanie looked out over the breaking waves with a sorrowful expression. "North Korea shot down one of our planes an hour ago."

Scott sat up and hugged Aleecia. Her look of horror matched his inner fear. He reached out and touched Stephanie's arm.

"We're going?" His mouth was dry, his throat scratchy as he looked into her face. She was reliving the nightmares of missions past. He could almost see the ghosts dancing behind her eyes.

Stephanie slowly nodded.

Aleecia licked her lips. "Stephanie, which team?"

"All of us. Orders from the President."

Scott gave a tug on her arm and Stephanie leaned up against him, her breast pressing his flesh. Aleecia and Stephanie wrapped their arms around each other.

"Whatever happens, we're in this together," Aleecia turned her head to kiss Stephanie's cheek but instead their lips met, timidly at first, as though not real sure what to do next. They touched again, growing bolder, their tongues meeting, tasting each other.

Aleecia's hand wrapped around his cock and pulled on it, sliding her fingers over its hardening length. She turned her head and took his mouth, her tongue gliding past his lips.

Aleecia broke off the kiss, and Stephanie's lips sealed over his. Capturing his tongue, she sucked on it, drawing it into her mouth.

Scott couldn't think, only react as his hands came around their bodies and captured a breast of each woman. Both nipples were extended, and he rolled them between his fingers. Stephanie groaned against his mouth. Aleecia, with her mouth over Stephanie's other breast, moaned.

Stephanie broke the kiss. With her eyes closed, she leaned her head back and pushed his head to her breast.

Scott sucked on the distended nipple. His tongue laved the hard pebble of flesh.

A hot, wet tongue invaded his ear. Turning his head, he took Aleecia's mouth. Her eyes were inflamed with passion. The tips of their tongues touched, dancing to a song only their hearts could hear.

Stephanie lifted their heads and began kissing, first one and then the other. She worked her way down Aleecia's throat and closed her mouth over a breast while her hand busily stroked his cock.

Aleecia lay back on the blanket, taking Stephanie with her. Her hands and fingers twisted and pulled at Stephanie's black, coarse locks.

Scott reached between the writhing bodies and found Aleecia's pussy. His fingers stroked her wet clit.

Aleecia's eyes, glazed over with lust, seemed to stare through him.

Stephanie slid sensuously down her body, leaving a trail of kisses in her wake. Reaching Aleecia's russet curls, she then leaned over and took the sensitive head of his cock between her lips.

Scott's fingers sank into Aleecia's wetness.

Her lips stroked the length of his shaft in a motion that matched the movement of his fingers inside Aleecia's cunt.

Aleecia reached out and pulled at Stephanie's legs, turning her around. Lifting a leg over her body, she covered Stephanie's cunt with her lips as her tongue delved between its wet folds.

Stephanie pulled Scott's fingers from inside Aleecia and replaced them with her mouth.

He watched the two women, their faces buried in the other's wet cunts. Their moans and the soft sucking of flesh mingled with the sound of the waves breaking ever closer to them.

Shifting his body around, he knelt behind Stephanie's wiggling ass. Aleecia reached up and grabbed his cock. Pulling it down to her mouth, she kissed it and placed in at the entrance of Stephanie's wet hole. Scott slid his shaft in, grinding his thighs against the cheeks of her ass.

His body strained, his legs shook. The pounding of the breaking waves seem to be a constant roar in his ears. With a hard punishing thrust of his hips, Scott felt the hot wave of release as he collapsed, arms outstretched on top of Stephanie.

The waves of the incoming tide broke, and washed over their heated bodies. With a shriek of surprise, they grabbed their clothes before they were carried away. They sank to the wet blanket, holding on to one another in laughter.

As the next wave came rolling in at them, they snatched up the rest of their belongs and the blanket, and ran for the house.

They were pulling on dry clothes as the first van returned with Team Two. Team One came rolling to a stop beside the house ten minutes later.

"Sorry to drag you back." Stephanie stood on the porch, slightly elevated above the others. "We are in Def-Con Two, the shit has hit the fan, and we're going in to clean up the mess. The President has called us in because the military's hands are tied, and he wants to keep the country out of war. Get the gear packed and on the beach. Our ride will be here at fifteen hundred hours. Let's do it."

The next twenty minutes were a flurry of activity, as backpacks were loaded with all their gear, weapons and ammunition. The last ten minutes stretched out with nervous anticipation, waiting for the mission to begin.

Stephanie sat off to the side, separating herself from the rest, looking over equipment lists and making notes.

Aleecia got up and stared towards her when Carlos stopped her. "Have a seat. She doesn't want to be bothered now."

From a distance, they heard the low rumbling *whop-whop* of an approaching helicopter. Scott saw the black smoke of its exhaust. The noise became almost deafening as it passed overhead, swung into the wind, and hovered.

They shouldered their packs and picked up their weapons.

With its rear tires inches above the water, the rotor blades kicked up a hailstorm of sand and salt spray. A large ramp lowered to the ground, and a crewman motioned them to board.

"Okay, guys!" Stephanie yelled. "Move out!"

They ran in a double file across fifty feet of sand and up the ramp. Scott and Aleecia ran at the back through a breaking wave and into the waiting arms of the team.

Stephanie took one last look around and followed, giving the crewman a thumbs up as she came aboard.

As the ramp was being closed, Scott felt the power increase and the helicopter begin to rise.

Stephanie went to the front and took a headset from a crewman. Adjusting the mike, she started reading from the list that she had been working on.

Talking over the noise and vibration was impossible, unless you wanted to yell. Scott took Aleecia's hand in his and gave it a squeeze for reassurance. She turned her head.

"I love you." Though he couldn't hear the words, he read her lips and leaned over to kiss her. The taste of Stephanie's pussy was still on her lips.

Carlos tapped her on the shoulder, and she leaned close to hear. Her face turned a brilliant scarlet, and Carlos laughed.

"What did he say?" Scott yelled against her ear.

"He said not to wash my face. It might be the only taste of pussy you would get for awhile."

Scott leaned his head back against the vibrating skin of the helicopter and laughed until the tears ran down his face and his sides hurt. For which, he received a sharp jab of Aleecia's elbow in his side.

The inside of the helicopter was hot. After nearly an hour, the pungent odor of hydraulic oil and jet fuel created a tightening of the gut and a foul taste in the mouth.

They circled a little-used runway and landed near a large hangar. The runway had grass growing through cracks in the asphalt. A small out-building had a door hanging on one hinge. The window was broken, and a tree grew through the roof.

They stood on the cracked pavement as their taxi lifted in the air and roared out of sight.

The hangar doors began sliding open. The whine of jet engines grew in intensity as their speed increased. Inside the hangar sat a large bluish-gray Learjet and a non-descriptive Chevy with government plates.

Stephanie waited at the bottom of the boarding ladder until everyone was on board.

In the back of the plane, a man, dressed in a black three-piece suit, white shirt, and black tie, sat going over some papers. The grave expression on his face didn't ease any of the tension Scott was already feeling.

The door closed behind Stephanie and the plane began to taxi out of the hangar. Within minutes, they were airborne, climbing high above the clouds.

Aleecia's hand crept into his. He smiled trying to reassure her, but deep down he was worried to death.

The suit stood up without introducing himself. "Roughly three hours ago the North Koreans shot down an Air Force Hercules cargo plane. We have every reason to believe they were intentionally drawn into North Korean airspace. The President immediately set Def-Con Two and called an emergency session of Congress.

"As the aircraft went down outside the international three-mile limit but inside the twelve miles North Korea claims, the military is prohibited from doing anything more than watching at this time. The President of the United States is prepared to set Def-Con One.

"You are being tasked to prevent that from happening by recovering this." He turned the overhead television on. "This is the newest of our tactical nuclear weapons. Designed to explode at five thousand feet, it deploys a dozen smaller nuclear weapons in an umbrella over the intended target. It provides maximum killing power within the circle with little-to-no damage five miles outside the blast zone."

Stephanie spoke up, "Sir, you said recover. Why can't we destroy it and come home?"

"We wish it were that simple Agent Brooke. The main explosion triggers the individual devices. If we blow it up, they go off. If you destroy the firing mechanism or the central core charge, the individual nukes can be set off with as little as eight ounces of TNT.

"We have worked for too many years to keep the North Koreans free of nuclear weapons. This weapon," he pointed to the screen, "cannot fall into their hands."

Scott voiced his thoughts. "How do you expect us to bring up the whole missile?"

"We don't. You'll separate the warhead from the rocket using a magnesium cord. When placed in the correct position, it will burn through without damage to the warhead or blowing the rocket up in your face."

"What are the fucking bastards doing to get their hands on it?" Carlos asked through clenched teeth.

"At this time, a ring of North Korean gunboats surrounds the crash site. They are moving a salvage ship in, and we expect it to be in place within eight hours. It appears they were expecting it to go down over land and were not prepared for a water recovery.

"Only the bravery of the pilot kept that from happening. He kept the plane in the air for as long as possible."

"What about the pilot?" Stephanie was taking notes.

"He's dead. He flew it as far from land as he could..."

A map came up on the screen showing the Bay of Korea. "The plane went down here, in approximately twelve hundred feet of water."

Several low mummers and whistles were heard in the cabin. Scott gripped Aleecia's hand. There was only one person in the world who could dive that deep.

"We don't think they can get to the missile any time soon. Right now, they are effectively blocking any and all attempts by us to recover it. The General has convinced the President your team can do the job. All of our resources are at your disposal. Talk it over and let me know what you need in light of the situation."

"Aleecia," Stephanie's eyes drilled into hers. "Can you do it?"

"Maybe. The problem isn't the depth..."

"It's the oxygen level in the water and the temperature." Scott injected to the conversation. "If the temperature doesn't kill her, the lack of air will."

"What are some of the other problems we might face?" Stephanie was looking frazzled around the edges.

He wasn't feeling much better. The idea of Aleecia, all alone at that depth, dealing with a nuclear warhead sent a warning of dread up his spine.

"Divers in the water to protect from an underwater attack." Carlos got up headed to the back of the plane. He paused at Aleecia's seat and placed his hand on her shoulder.

She didn't look up. Aleecia raised her hand and touched his before lowering it back to the armrest.

"If I use a modified wetsuit cut out so I can breathe..." She frowned. "I still have the problem of oxygen levels being too low."

Scott stood up, aware of every eye being on him as he paced up and down the aisle. "We have to be able to add oxygen to the water before it flows through her gills."

The man in the suit jerked his head up and looked at Scott. "Gills?"

Scott walked down the aisle and leaned over in front of the man's face. "What you hear on this plane is classified. You breathe a word to anyone..." he placed his hand on the butt of the forty-five.

"And if he doesn't, I will." Carlos added.

"Carlos, you're in line behind me," Stephanie's cold eyes bore into the suit.

"Ah, I think I'll go check with the pilot on our arrival time." He got up and hurried forward.

"Now, back to the problem at hand." Stephanie stood up. "Vic, Paul, somebody, there has to be a solution."

There was silence for several minutes, then Paul jumped out of his seat. "I've got it!" He ran to the back of the plane and rummaged through the backpacks.

Everybody was looking at him as if he had lost his mind. After dumping half his pack on a back seat, he proudly held up a coil of plastic tubing.

"We can use a nose cannula." Paul wide smile faded. "Okay, maybe it's a crazy idea. Anyone got something better?"

"Not crazy at all." Scott walked back and took the tubing from his hand. "We make one of these out of stainless steel, attach it to a tank and Aleecia puts the open end in her mouth. With the water and oxygen mixing in her airway, her gills can pickup the air she needs."

Scott grabbed Paul and hugged him.

"Paul, write down her measurements for a wetsuit." Stephanie started writing notes of her own.

The remainder of the flight to the west coast was filled with equipment options, possible problems, and how to complete the mission.

The plane landed and taxied to the far end of the runway where a Boeing 777 sat waiting fifty yards away.

Slinging the heavy pack over his shoulder, Scott double-timed it to the larger plane.

He took a seat in the spacious first class section. Aleecia plopped down next to him with a groan. A somber hush settled over the cabin. There was nothing to do now but wait. A movie playing on the overhead screen went unwatched.

Vic stared out the windows, looking at the late afternoon clouds thousands of feet below. Four of the men staked out a claim to the floor in the second galley and were playing cards, their strained laughter an indication of taut nerves.

Carlos broke out his cleaning kit and began field stripping his M1911, a Glock 9mil, and his Israeli Para Micro Uzi. As he put them back together, the *kerr-thunk* of the M1911's slide moving into place had an eerie note of finality in the quiet cabin.

Stephanie sat isolated, emotionally removed from the team.

Scott compared it to the jitters just before a dive that some divers never seem to shake. Once they're in and submerged, everything became fine. The fear of the unknown often seemed worse than reality. Somehow — he didn't think this was going to be the case.

Aleecia sat beside him, eyes closed with a blank expression on her face. He gently squeezed her hand. She managed a slight smile and a tear trickled from under her lids.

Carlos stood, and stretched before stepping across the aisle and kneeling on the floor beside Aleecia.

"I'm not going to feed you some bullshit about not being scared. This is one mission that I wish we could walk away from." Carlos paused and rubbed his hand across his growing shadow of whiskers. "But we can't."

"I know, Carlos." Aleecia opened her eyes, and her lips lifted in a shaky smile.

"You are one hell of a woman, Aleecia. I'm proud to have you on the team."

"Thank you." She leaned over and kissed him on the cheek. "That means a lot."

"Enough of this sentimental crap," he winked. "Why don't you two go on back and get some rest. After we leave Tokyo, you won't be getting much of anything until this is over."

Chapter 22

Aleecia turned her head to Scott, pleading with her eyes to be alone, even for a few minutes, away from the rest of the team.

What would I have done different if I thought Melody might not be coming home? Scott asked himself. *Lots…*

His mind went spinning backward, whirling through time. *An extra kiss at the terminal, a less hurried hug to Lindsey. I'd have spent less time at work, especially the night before, and tucked my daughter under the covers with her teddy bear. There'd have been candlelight, with wine and roses, on the table beside our bed.*

He stood, bent over, under the overhead luggage rack. Carlos's image blurred.

The smile of gratitude flashed across her face as she stood and scooted into the aisle.

Scott whispered into Carlos's ear, and followed Aleecia down the aisle. If she had expected to make a hasty retreat, she was mistaken. Several of the team members sat in the aisle seats. Each one stopped her, and silently held her hand.

Stephanie reached out and pulled her down. Wrapping her arms around Aleecia, she gave her a kiss on the cheek.

Aleecia continued on through the curtain separating first class from coach. Scott glanced down at Stephanie. A tear peeked out from under her eyelid and hung suspended on a lash before dropping to her breast.

Scott placed his fingers lightly on her arm and followed Aleecia.

She stood in the aisle, looking around as if she wasn't sure of her surroundings. Her eyes focused on him, she reached out with both arms as he came near. He held her close, his arms locked around her waist.

"Mr. Mathis." Their one and only flight attendant, a young woman dressed in an Air Force Lieutenant's uniform, stood with a serving tray.

"Thank you. Set it down here, please."

She lowered a seat tray, sat a bottle of wine and bag of nuts down. "Sorry, sir, we didn't have any roses." She raised the armrests in the center aisle, and fixed a makeshift bed on the seats.

Aleecia giggled and hid her face against his chest.

The Lieutenant left as quietly as she had arrived.

Scott lifted Aleecia's chin, her face flushed with embarrassment. Placing a tender kiss on her forehead, he took her lips in a slow compassionate embrace.

"I've never made love on an airplane before," she whispered against his lips.

"Neither have I." His tongue teased her lips open and dipped inside her sweet luscious mouth.

"Would you like some wine?" He kissed her nose and rested his forehead against hers.

"Yes, please."

She sat as he poured two glasses of wine. Handing her one, he lifted his. "To you. The most wonderful woman alive. No matter how far away or how deep you go, I pray my love will always bring you back to me."

"It will, Scott, now and forever." She touched her glass to his and lifted it to her lips.

She snuggled up in his arms sipping the wine as he fed her the salted nuts.

He found it increasingly difficult to concentrate. With the second small morsel, she held his hand to her lips and licked the salt from his fingers. By the fourth one, he was uncomfortable and shifted in the seat.

Aleecia lifted her glass to his lips, "You're not drinking."

A rivulet of wine ran down his chin. She stretched her neck, and her tongue traced the sweet red line to his mouth. "I don't think I could do this without you beside me."

He dipped his head and took her mouth, ravaging it with his tongue. His fingers traced the curve of her breast and teased the nipple.

"I love it when you touch me." Sitting the glass on the tray, she lifted the blouse over her head.

It didn't matter how many times he saw her, she managed to take his breath away with the perfection of her body. No other woman compared. Reaching out he drew the backs of his fingers down her face, neck and across her breasts.

Aleecia gave a soft gasp when he touched her nipple. "Oh…that feels so good."

He fed her another nut, leaving his fingers near her mouth. Like a feeding hummingbird, her tongue darted out, tasting and feeding on the salt.

Her fingers found the bottom of his pullover and wormed their way underneath. Scott laid his head back, a soft broken sigh drifted from his lips. Her hands pulled at the material, tugging it up his body. He arched his back and the cool air of the cabin flowed across his heated skin.

Aleecia's fingers drove away the chill. With a deft twist of her body, she sat in his lap with her back to the aisle. The movement caused the fold down tray to tip, and she grabbed the wine as the remainder of the nuts scattered across the floor.

The glasses wobbled in her hand, the contents swirled, spilling over the edge and splashed across her chest. Her slight gasp of surprise turned to a moan of delight, as Scott lowered his mouth and licked the wine from her skin.

She leaned back against his arm, her head, hanging in the aisle, swaying from side to side. With each lick, her body trembled.

Scott flicked a drop of wine from her nipple and smiled. Her body jerked, a loud gasp spilled from her throat. She raised her head, and he looked into eyes ablaze with wild passion.

His mouth closed over her distended nipple, sucking on it. The rapid pounding of her heart, beat against his lips.

His fingers fumbled with the snap of her black uniform pants. The grating of the zipper seemed loud to his ears. Aleecia lifted her hips, and he tugged the material to her knees.

Settling back into his lap, she wiggled her ass against his cock. "Now it's your turn." She scooted over in the makeshift bed and reached to undo his pants. The zipper started sliding down from the pressure of his erection against it.

She finished unzipping him, letting the back of her fingers slide against the material of his shorts.

Scott rose up in the seat, removed his trousers and shorts in one quick tug and sat back against the cushion.

Aleecia's fingers drifted across his leg, tickling the hair and sending darts of pleasure to his groin. Using the pad of one finger, she slowly traced the vein at the base of his cock to its tip and back down again. His head went back against the seat, his eyes closed. Scott's fingers dug into the armrest near the aisle, while the other hand closed in a fist filled with her hair.

The death grip on her hair loosened. Scott's fingers slid down her neck and back. With a disturbing slowness, he traced the rough flap of skin covering her gills. Leaning back, she took his hand, brought his fingers to her lips and kissed them. Tugging at his arm, Aleecia drew him to lie beside her on the narrow seats.

Her hand gravitated to his head where her fingers played in the light brown locks. The strands were heavy, encrusted with the ocean salt. She twirled a finger, wrapping a lock around it. *Was it only this morning we indulged ourselves on the beach. It seems so…different, as if it happened in another world so far away.*

She looked into his eyes and their thoughtful gaze, darkened with the heat of passion, drew her like a magnet to him.

Their lips touched, the heady sweet flavor of the lingering wine intoxicated her. Tracing them with her tongue, she delved inside his mouth for more. The wet warmth of his mouth, the bouquet of the wine on his breath, and the touch of his skin along the length of hers, sent her desire spiraling out of control.

Her kiss became more demanding as passion's flame grew higher. She pulled him on top of her to free her other arm. The hardness of his cock pressed against her leg. Aleecia's hands played across his back and grasped the cheeks of his ass.

She broke the kiss, and he lowered his head to the cushion.

"I need you, Scott," she breathed. "I need to feel you deep inside me."

He rose up, and she pulled at his body. The tip of his cock teased the moist folds of flesh between her legs. She shifted and squirmed pushing with her hips until he parted her flesh and his hard length slipped inside.

She closed her eyes and a sigh of satisfaction lifted from her throat to whisper in the air.

Turning her head, Aleecia touched her lips to the pulsating vein in his neck. Teasing his flesh with her tongue, she followed his heartbeat up to his ear and playfully nibbled on the lobe.

Scott shifted, "You're a witch." The soft-spoken words caressed her ear. "You've cast a spell over me and enslaved me with the chains of your love."

The tip of her tongue grazed the under-side of his jaw, crept over his chin, and traced his lips. Scott's tongue touched hers, retreated and touched again. His lips settled against hers, and his tongue filled her mouth.

He began to move inside her. The slow withdrawal of his cock sent a shiver of delight rippling through her flesh. The brief emptiness and loss, which followed in its wake, vanished in a dazzling flash as his hard shaft filled her again.

The cheeks of his ass quivered beneath her fingers. His body vibrated with passion. With each slow deliberate movement inside her, the tension of his body increased.

His tongue moving in her mouth, and the motion of his cock inside her, became as one, thrusting, retreating, and plunging into the fevered depths of her flesh. Lost within the rising fog, she rode the crest of the towering wave.

Aleecia's fingers locked with his as she followed Scott into passions' bliss. With one mighty thrust of his cock, Scott's body rose above her, his eyes rolled, unseeing to the top of his head.

The fingers of her other hand clawed at his back, digging into his skin, as the liquid fire of his climax filled her.

A loud raspy groan rumbled from his chest. The weight of his trembling body collapsed on hers.

The cool air from the cabin began to invade their flesh as the flames of passion ebbed away. Scott began to stir, pulling his cock from within her.

"No," she whimpered. "Stay, my love, inside me a while longer." She reached to the floor, grabbed the fallen blanket, and flung it over them.

"Let me hold you in my arms, for as long as I can."

* * * * *

A light touch on his shoulder brought Scott from a blissful slumber.

"Scott, we're about to land." Stephanie stood, leaning over the seat. A look of tender compassion fluttered across her eyes and then was gone. "Time to get dressed." She turned and walked down the aisle.

He woke Aleecia with a kiss on the cheek. "It's time."

Her fingers softly caressed his face. She reached for her clothes, never taking her eyes off of him.

Mistress of Table Rock

They dressed in silence and sat side by side in the empty cabin. His hand sought hers and she clasped it tightly, her fingers intertwined with his.

The wheels touched down on the concrete with a soft thud and a scream of rubber. The loud roar of the engine thrust being reversed filled the cabin. Their bodies strained against the seatbelts. With the plane still barreling down the runway, Stephanie stuck her head between the curtains.

"Get a move on. We have another taxi waiting."

With their backpacks in place, weapons slung over their shoulders or held snug in their hands, they stood waiting as the passenger jet rolled to a stop.

Carlos handed them foil wrapped trays. "You two slept through supper. Stephanie had them kept hot for you."

"Thanks," they both answered at the same time.

"We," Aleecia blushed, "appreciate it."

The door of the Boeing 777 opened. The team jogged down the boarding ladder, across fifty feet of concrete, and into the waiting belly of another large CH-47 Chinook marine transport helicopter.

Scott and Aleecia edged their way around two large crates lashed down in the center and took their seats. They were airborne within seconds.

Aleecia tore into her food, devouring it, and looked with longing at her empty plate. Scott handed her the rest of his. "Take it!" his gut rumbled in protest. "You need it worse than I do!"

Their eyes met in a tender moment of understanding. She reached out and took the tray.

With the noise of the Chinook, conversation was near impossible and no further attempt was made. The mood of the whole team was solemn as they flew through the darkened sky over the Sea of Japan. Grave faces stared back at him through the red interior lighting of the helicopter. A couple of the men gave him a raised thumb or a clenched fist across their chest.

Several sat with their eyes closed, heads cushioned against the webbed backing of their seats.

He held Aleecia's hand and waited.

* * * * *

The noise inside the CH-47 rose, the whine of the engines increased, and the vibration shook awake those who were sleeping. Landing hard, the helicopter bounced, throwing the team against each other in the seats. The engines died down and the loud rotor noise subsided into a low swishing noise as it stopped turning.

Scott looked out the window at the darkened deck of a ship. Dim shadows of the ground crew as they scurried around the aircraft flickered across his vision. The loading ramp lowered, letting in the fresh clean salt breeze of the ocean. The gentle rolling of the ship told Scott whatever they were on was big and probably had a flat bottom.

They hurried out of the helicopter, across the flight deck, and down a long wide ramp. The hangar bay was full of Harrier jump jets and helicopters, chained down against the rolling of the ship as it plowed through the waves.

Scott felt the ship turning and a rumble came, vibrating up through the steel from the bowels of the ship, as its speed increased.

They followed an officer, wearing a white jacket and helmet, around a corner and down the hall. He stopped in the Mess Deck and took off his protective headgear.

"I'm Commander Nelson, ship's Executive Officer. Welcome aboard the USS *Belleau-Wood*. I wish it could be under better conditions. The Captain is a bit curious as to why we were directed to break away from the crash site and steam over the horizon to pick you up."

Stephanie removed her hat. "Commander, I'm sorry for the inconvenience but it was necessary. He will be briefed as soon as possible."

His double-take at finding out a woman was in command was comical.

He glanced across the group and spotted Aleecia's shoulder length tresses. "Just who the hell are you people? Who's in charge and which branch of service? I'm not aware of females being allowed in the Special Forces."

"I'm in charge, sir." Stephanie stepped forward. "We're not military, sir."

"Not military, then you must be Merc's." He spat out the name as if were a dirty word.

"No, sir," Stephanie's eyes blazed. "Who we are is not your concern, sir, but we are *not* mercenaries."

A First Class Petty Officer walked in and spoke quietly with the Commander.

"Is there a Mr. Mathis, here?" the Commander asked.

Scott stepped forward. "I'm Mathis."

"If you will follow this Petty Officer, you are wanted in the Captain's quarters." The Commander was looking even more perplexed as Scott followed the First Class out of the Mess Deck.

He dogged the enlisted man's heels up three decks and forward through several hatches to a door marked, Commanding Officer, LHA-3. A knock on the door brought a command to enter. The Petty Officer opened the door, and Scott stepped through.

The middle-aged man standing in the center of the paneled room looked anything but friendly. He held a paper in his hands that Scott could see was marked 'Top Secret, Eyes Only.'

"Mr. Mathis, I don't know who you people are but when I get orders to move out of position while in Def-Con Two and receive messages that I'm not even authorized to read, I begin to wonder what the *hell* is going on." The Commander held out the message.

Scott opened it and began to read it. One word in it caused his blood to boil, his fist closed, crumpling the message. He walked over to the Commander's desk and wrote out a phone number.

"Captain, if you would get me a secure line to this number, I would greatly appreciate it."

The Skipper of the *Belleau-Wood* looked at the number. "May I ask where I am calling? Or is that classified also?"

"No, sir," Scott smiled. "It's the White House."

Going by the exasperated look on the Captain's face, Scott knew he didn't believe a word of it. He picked up the phone, punched in some numbers, and spoke into the phone. Several long moments of silence permeated the room. The ship's noises filtered through the steel.

He heard the loud clanging of chains being dragged across the steel. A diesel engine started, revved up, and a heavy vehicle drove across the fight deck. The ship's movement was again noticeable, as a heavy swell rolled it to port. A shudder shook the boat as the propellers lifted out of the water.

The Commander of the *Belleau-Wood* snapped to attention. "Yes, sir... Thank you for your trust in this operation, sir... Yes, Mr. Mathis is here." He held out the phone.

Scott took it from his hand and winked. "Thank you, Captain."

He put the phone to his ear, and turned his back to the Commanding Officer of the *Belleau-Wood*.

"Mr. President..." *Some threats were made to be carried out,* Scott thought to himself with immense satisfaction.

Chapter 23

They sat in the Mess Deck listening as the Skipper of the *Belleau-Wood* and its Executive Officer gave them the latest details of the situation in Korea Bay.

"The North Koreans are expecting us to do something and are determined we don't succeed." He pointed to a chart. "We believe the salvage ship is directly over the crash site. As you can see, it is completely surrounded by gunboats. Everything they have has been brought out to prevent us from entering this area.

"They have deployed high intensity lights underwater plus there are divers inside the perimeter, waiting in case we try approaching from below.

"Between us and this line of ships are seven miles of ocean. Five high-speed, anti-submarine patrol boats are crisscrossing the area. Their sonar is active and they are standing by with depth charges and torpedoes to ward off our subs.

"Their shipboard guns are manned, making a surface approach suicidal. So if you have a plan we haven't come up with, I would like to hear it. Otherwise, I'm afraid you've wasted our time and a lot of taxpayer's money."

Stephanie looked at the Skipper. "Captain, we appreciate your help and cooperation. We wouldn't be here if we didn't think we could do this. We plan on cutting the warhead from the missile and using air bags to bring it up. Once it reaches a depth of one hundred and fifty feet, we'll tow it to your ship and bring it to the surface."

"That's impossible," the Captain stammered. "You don't have anything to go that deep."

"Captain," Scott spoke up, and got a warning glance from Stephanie. "You didn't believe me about the phone call I made.

Believe me, we do have the capabilities of retrieving your bomb."

"We stand at the door of World War III if the North Koreans get their hands on that weapon." The Skipper grew red in the face. "Before I allow you to attempt this hair-brained scheme and possibly start another World War, I think I should at least be given the courtesy of knowing how you plan to do it."

"Sir," Aleecia stood up, ignoring the protest of the team. "I plan on diving down to the missile."

"At over twelve hundred feet," he scoffed. "How?"

"With these, sir." She turned around, grasped the bottom of her blouse, and pulled it over her head. Taking a deep breath, she exhaled forcefully through her gills. Aleecia turned around giving the Captain, and his Executive Officer, a full view of her breasts before slipping the blouse over her head.

"Any more questions, sir? If not, we have a job to do." Aleecia took her seat and waited.

Scott had to laugh at the stunned expressions on their faces. He wasn't sure if it was the gills or the fact that a woman had bared her tits on the Mess Deck of their ship.

"Captain," Stephanie stood, "now you understand the secrecy of our mission. If we could be taken to our gear so we can get ready, we would appreciate it."

"Ah, yes...of course. My Executive Officer will escort you to the Welldeck. I'll make sure you are not hindered in any way." He gave Aleecia one last bewildered stare.

"Good luck." The Skipper of the *Belleau-Wood* turned and headed back down the passageway.

"If you will follow me, please. I'll take you to your gear."

They followed the Commander down the passageway to the Hangar Deck, took a sharp left, and descended down another ramp. They passed Jeeps, trucks, and tanks chained to the deck.

"We were told to have one side of the Welldeck clear." The Commander yelled over the noise. "We launched two boats before we came and got you. They're moored along side a destroyer now."

At the bottom of still another ramp, their gear sat on a wet wooden deck. Overhead, rails were built into the ceiling for some type of monorail system. Walkways on port and starboard overlooked the Welldeck.

Their arrival had created an excited tension and the walkways were filled with sailors and marines.

"Commander," Stephanie pointed up, "those sailors will have to clear out."

He spoke into a portable radio and a loud speaker sounded.

"This is the Captain speaking. The Welldeck is secured until further notice. All personnel remain clear of the area."

The team started unpacking their crates. Carlos handed Scott a long flexible stainless steel tube with a plastic lining. "I hope this will work."

Scott took the hose, looked at it, and turned it over in his hand. "It has to, or Aleecia…"

Carlos patted him on the shoulder. "Yeah, we know."

One crate held their dive gear while the other, larger crate revealed six, two-man underwater sleds.

Aleecia dug out her heavy-duty wetsuit and peeled out of her clothes.

The Commander's jaw dropped open, and he spun around.

She had her back turned, but Scott knew her face was bright red. He was proud of her for having the guts to be the first one to strip. Stephanie, not bothering to turn around, was the next to strip, and quickly pulled on her suit.

"Scott!" Aleecia yelled. "We need to cut this suit." She pointed to the back.

He made the necessary slits in the material so she could breathe, knowing full well that the efficiency of the suit would be drastically reduced. His hands trembled as he helped her get the suit back over her head.

At the bottom of the container, a long green cylinder stuck its nose out from under the flotation bags. Scott dug it out and slipped the straps of a regular dive vest over it. He took the steel-clad hose, attached it and a regulator to the tank. After checking to make sure it worked, he said a silent prayer that it wouldn't fail. They didn't have time for a test dive.

"Okay, gather round!" Stephanie waited until everyone was in a tight circle around her. "Just to make sure we all understand. Team One...with three sleds and Aleecia will proceed to the containment ships, stay spread out and shallow to avoid the pickets' on sonar. Prior to reaching the lighted perimeter, Aleecia and three divers will swim under the lights ahead of the sleds. Keep a look out for their divers. We don't want to be surprised and have them drop in our laps.

"We have a chance if we come from underneath them. Team Two will tow the rest of the gear behind Team One. Remember to keep the buoyancy of the gear in check. We don't want it to pop to the surface or have it drag us to the bottom.

"Scott, that's your job." Stephanie turned to look him in the eye. "You stay with the gear until we get inside their perimeter.

"Once we are in and have the area secure, proceed to the salvage ship. Two divers will assist Aleecia down to two hundred feet. From there," Stephanie looked at Aleecia with sad resolve, "you're on your own."

The *whop-whop* of an approaching helicopter caused Stephanie to look up.

"When Aleecia starts down to the crash site, the two of you will come back to the ship and get the wave runners, which just arrived, and stand by to assist."

A runner, gasping for breath, approached with a small package.

Stephanie opened it and handed each member of the team a wristband. "These are new, so pay attention. If you find yourself on the surface, these will activate a detector on the *Belleau-Wood* and one on the console of each wave runner. Don't expect to be picked up before our mission is complete."

The faces of the men said it all. They were as ready as they were ever going to be.

"Commander," Stephanie turned to the Executive Officer, "could you say the magic words, and open the gate."

The lights on the Welldeck went off, and the stern gate began its slow rise. As soon as it was high enough, they pushed their underwater sleds into the water. Scott added air to one of the floatation bags and pushed the gear overboard.

Lined up across the open stern of the USS *Belleau-Wood,* Stephanie gave the signal and they went into the water. Scott's heart rate pounded like a snare drum in his chest. Not so much for his own safety but for Aleecia's. He wanted to scream at her not to do this, and yet…he knew she was the only one who could.

They rode through the blackness, guided only by their compasses and the small red light on the back of each sled. The first part of the trip was shallow, barely under the hulls of the watchful anti-submarine patrol boats. Filing through one at a time, they pointed the nose of their sleds into deeper water. At one hundred feet, they leveled out.

Scott held on to the cargo net and watched the three sleds as they towed it and him through the cold black depths.

* * * * *

The glow of the containment ship's underwater lights lay ahead. Aleecia signaled the team to stop, let go of the lead sled, and dove. She knew the members of the advance team would be behind her. The sleds would follow several yards behind.

Clearing the lights, she began a slow ascent, searching the water above for the Korean divers. There was one directly above her, fifty feet away, making it easy to spot him. In their attempt to locate them, the North Koreans were using powerful handheld lights.

She tapped the team member on her left to begin his attack. Twenty yards further she spotted two more divers close together. The greenish glow of their lights swung from side to side, never checking the water below. She tapped the diver to her right twice on the arm and began to rise.

With only a few yards separating them, they kicked hard with their fins. Drawing her knife, she reached her intended target and drove the blade under his lower rib. Another quick jab and his buoyancy vest was rendered useless. He began to sink.

Carlos hadn't been as lucky in surprising his victim and was locked in a deadly struggle. She started to assist when an arm wrapped around her neck and a bright light blinded her. The sharp edge of steel was pressed against her throat when she heard the release of a spear gun.

The impact of the short steel spear sent her attacker spinning off into deeper water. Scott, with an empty gun in his hand, grappled with another diver. Aleecia kicked, launching towards him. With her knife held in front of her, she grabbed the Korean's air hose and sliced it in two.

Scott used the diver's surprise at losing his air to get his knife into the man's chest.

She spun around and saw Stephanie being attacked by two divers. She started to assist when Scott pointed below. Two divers were headed towards their gear floating below them.

Aleecia flipped and headed down as fast as her fins would take her. She hit the first diver without slowing down, ripping his mask off, and pulling his regulator out of his mouth. Leaving him for Scott to finish, she raced off to the other diver.

Approaching him from above, Aleecia grabbed his head with one hand while her other arm snaked around his neck. With one strong pull of her knife, she slit the man's throat.

Two Korean divers had already reached their gear. The ropes used to tow it had been cut and the drivers of the sleds were slumped lifelessly over the controls. She watched as they released air from the floatation bag and it began an uncontrolled plummet to the bottom. Leaving the Koreans for the rest of the team to take care off, she kicked harder, trying to reach the gear.

Her fingers grasped the webbing of the net. Working her way around it, she found the valve for the floatation bag and closed it. The rate of descent slowed. Aleecia looked at the illuminated dial of her depth gauge. She was at six hundred feet.

The crash site was still over a half mile away. Adding air, she began the slow ascent back to the sleds.

Reaching the sleds, she saw that Scott was nowhere around. She retied the cargo net to one sled. Removing the dead team member from it, she placed him in the other sled. Aleecia checked the water around her and headed in the direction of the crash site.

Half an hour later, she was hovering a hundred feet below the salvage vessel.

Swimming clear of the sled, she turned around. Scott's smiling eyes greeted her as she rounded the bulky net.

Gladness washed over her heart. She went to him and kissed his cheek. Aleecia untied the rope and for the second time, followed it down into the depths.

At two hundred feet, Scott took the regulator from his mouth, kissed Aleecia goodbye and watched her until long after darkness swallowed her up.

Aleecia was becoming light-headed, finding it difficult to think. She turned on the air valve, slipped the special harness over her head, and placed the section of tubing with the two small air holes in her mouth.

The blackness became a tangible substance around her. It pressed against her from all sides, wrapped around her mind, and invaded her soul. With a jolt, the gear crashed onto the floor of Korea Bay. The massive Hercules lay a couple yards from her position. She had almost landed on top of it.

Her arms were slow and sluggish as she reached for a light. Aleecia saw the depth gauge as it passed before her eyes. There had to be some mistake. The ocean floor was supposed to be at twelve hundred feet. Yet her gauge indicated she was two thousand feet below the surface. The pressure forced her to take small shallow breaths, and even then, it took most of her strength to expand her lungs.

She fought with the netting, finally freeing the gear inside.

This was worse than swimming in Table Rock during the winter. The cold gnawed at her lungs. Her fingers and toes were numb.

The wings and tail section of the plane were broken off from the force of the crash. Aleecia, hampered by the need to carry her oxygen tank, made her way inside the huge plane. The missile nearly filled the cargo bay. Thankfully, it had been loaded with the warhead to the rear of the aircraft.

Taking the nose anchor the Air Force had provided, and using every ounce of strength she possessed, Aleecia lifted the heavy eyebolt into place. She sank to the floor of the plane, dizzy from lack of oxygen in her system. The fog slowly cleared as she took deep breaths. She returned to the eyebolt and began to turn it, screwing it all the way in.

Aleecia took several more deep breaths. Leaving the cumbersome tank in the plane she swam back to the gear. Grabbing the end of a long rope and the magnesium cord, she headed back to the warhead.

Her vision blurred as she grasped the airline and sucked greedily at the air bubbles trickling from the small holes. She lay there for several minutes fighting against the pressure, straining to breathe. Her chest hurt and muscles screamed in protest with every movement.

With a slow determined effort, she concentrated on completing one task at a time. Aleecia attached the large hook on

Mistress of Table Rock

the rope to the eyebolt. She didn't have the strength to carry the oxygen tank over to the missile.

Removing the small air bottle from the vest around the large oxygen tank, Aleecia carried it and the burn cord to the top of the missile. Finding the attachment point, aft of the actual warhead, she laid the cord in place.

Taking a few breaths of air, Aleecia placed another cord further back on the missile, over the solid fuel core.

Aleecia set the timers, latched onto the air tank, and pulled it from inside the fuselage.

The burn cord ignited, lighting up the ocean floor. Aleecia turned her head and closed her eyes against the brightness. She kept moving. Time was running out.

Reaching the air bags, she found the cylinder and turned the knob. At first, nothing happened, but then they began to move, shifting, as the air expanded the bags.

Aleecia attached her oxygen tank to one of the floatation bags and waited. She was growing weaker. Knowing Scott was somewhere above waiting for her gave her a burst of strength to tie herself to the rising bags.

The glow from the burning magnesium died down. The rope pulled tight, but she wasn't moving. She raised her arm. Her movements appeared slow as she forced her muscles to obey. Her frozen fingers fumbled with the control valve as she struggled to add more lift to the bags.

Aleecia lost track of time. She lost all feeling in her limbs, and her vision dimmed. She didn't have the strength left. Leaning her head back, she opened her mouth, hoping the rising bags would create enough flow to force water past her gills.

* * * * *

Scott and Carlos hovered at a hundred and fifty feet and waited. Scott searched the depths, straining to see any sign of

Aleecia, while Carlos watched the waters above for any sign of Korean divers.

They had taken their wounded and dead back to the *Belleau-Wood*. Rearmed, they had come back to wait. They had three confirmed dead, two wounded, and one missing — Stephanie. And the length of time Aleecia had been down there caused Scott's insides to twist and knot with fear.

Daylight had come, turning the water into a green opaque canopy over their heads. Any diver coming after them from above would be silhouetted and easily seen.

The rising air bags burst out of the darkness and caught the side of the sled, rolling it over. He scrambled from the sled and kick towards it. Aleecia hung lifelessly from one of the bags.

Scott reached the control valve, turned it off, and started releasing air. They passed ninety feet and were still rising. At sixty feet, the floatation bags were starting to slow their rapid ascent. He dumped more air. Realizing as he did so, an observant watch on the salvage boat could easily mark their position from the rising bubbles.

Twenty feet from the North Korean hull, he achieved neutral buoyancy with the bags. His heart pounded in his chest as he let out more air, this time in a slow trickle. His depth gauge began to show a slow, controlled descent. Carlos appeared beside him holding the limp body of Aleecia.

Scott took the bottle of spare air from the harness of the re-breather he was wearing and placed it in her mouth. He hit the release and air bubbles escaped from her gills.

He looked through the mask into Carlos's eyes, begging him to do what he could with the woman he loved as he turned his attention back to the nuclear warhead, now hanging fifty feet below them.

At one hundred feet, Scott added air to the bags stopping their descent. Taking Aleecia from Carlos's arms, he motioned for him to retrieve the sleds while he continued sending air through her gills. *Come on, love. Don't quit on me now, not after all we've been through.*

Tears welled up in his eyes.

Carlos touched his arm. Only one sled was tied to the bags. Carlos motioned for Scott to go on ahead. He strapped Aleecia into the passenger seat behind him, and sped off for the *Belleau-Wood*.

Chapter 24

Scott sat beside Aleecia's bed holding her hand. The doctors had done all they could for her. She was alive and that, in itself, was a miracle.

Warm air was being pumped into her, and she was covered with an electric blanket, trying to restore circulation to her system. An IV hung on each side of the bed, dripping warm fluids into her arms and legs.

In the beds next to Aleecia, two wounded team members lay recovering from their injuries. One after another, the remaining team members filed through, patting him on the shoulder or giving his arm a squeeze.

"Scott," Aleecia's scratchy, whispered voice reached his ears.

He jumped up from the chair and looked into her eyes. "Thank God. You're alive. I thought I'd lost you, too."

"The warhead, did we get it?"

"Yes, dear. You did it. It's on the Welldeck and creating quite a stir among the crew."

She glanced to the other beds and the smiling faces of the injured men. "How many did we lose?"

Scott hesitated. "Three dead, one missing."

Her eyes closed as the pain flashed across them. A tear ran down her cheek to fall on the pillow. "Who's missing?"

"Stephanie, she's presumed dead."

"No!" Aleecia pushed herself up on her elbows. "She's not dead. They captured her. I had to save the gear and couldn't get to her."

"You did the right thing." Scott smoothed her hair with his fingers. "If you'd been captured, we wouldn't have succeeded."

"We have to go get her." Aleecia pulled herself up into a sitting position.

"Damn it, lie down." He put his hand on her arm to help her back down. She grabbed his hand and twisted. Pain shot up his arm and his face hit her pillow.

"I'm going to go get Stephanie." She let the pressure release on his arm.

"What's going on?" Vic came into the ward.

"I need to get up," she informed him.

"There's no need to get up, Aleecia. You have a catheter in you."

Aleecia reached between her legs. "Not any more I don't. Now, please, remove the IVs'. Or do I have to remove them, too?"

"Aleecia, let me call the Doctor first." He started into the office.

"Screw the Doctor." She ripped the IV out of her left arm and held pressure against the bleeding vein.

A Navy Corpsman came running over. "Here's some tape." He looked at Scott. "Is she always this difficult to get along with?"

Scott shook his head, "Nope, you happened to catch her on one of her better days."

The Corpsman quickly removed the remaining tubes.

"My clothes, please." She swung her legs out of the bed. "Or so help me, I'll walk down to the Welldeck with my ass showing out the back of this gown."

Scott returned with her black Sentry uniform. He also had Carlos in tow, hoping he could help argue against her plan.

"Aleecia," Carlos begged, "This is suicide. They're expecting a rescue attempt. The skipper has already said no to any further searches."

She took her blouse and slipped it over her head. "I'm going. You want to help, fine. If not, then stay the fuck out of my way."

Aleecia hopped out of bed and grabbed a chair as her legs buckled.

"You can't even walk," Scott berated her. "How the hell do you think you can rescue Stephanie?"

She flexed her legs and got the muscles limbered up. "Carlos, are you ready to go get the boss?"

"Yes, ma'am." Carlos sighed.

"You're both crazy." Scott shook his head. "Let's get started."

Aleecia dressed, ignoring the protests of Vic and the Navy Corpsman.

The exit from Medical brought them out on the long ramp between the Flight Deck and the Hangar. Scott held her arm on one side and Vic held the other as she wobbled down the steep incline.

Scott took one look at the determination in her face, the deadly glare in her eyes and knew the only way to keep her from going was to hogtie her. He wasn't volunteering for the job.

At the top of the ramp, leading down to the Welldeck, Carlos stopped. "Aleecia, this is your show. You lead the way, and we'll follow."

"Thanks, Carlos." She looked into the eyes of a battle-hardened soldier with his square cut jaw, a scar running across his rugged face, and saw compassion, understanding, and trust. "It means a lot."

Aleecia walked down the ramp. The rest of the team stood and began clapping.

"Okay, team. Job well done," she stood on the Welldeck with the remaining team around her, "but it isn't finished." Confusion showed on their faces.

"Stephanie isn't dead, or at least she wasn't when I saw her last. I've every reason to believe she's on the salvage boat, and I intend to go get her."

"The skipper won't authorize a search. Too big a chance of creating an international incident." One of them replied.

"I'm going," she walked over to the gear, dug out her throwing stars and picked up a Micro Uzi. "If anyone is going with me, start packing the gear over to that starboard hatch."

Aleecia wore a light jacket over her shoulders to hide her gills. They sat making final preparations to leave.

"Our numbers are smaller so we have to make the first time count." She heard the noise of several pairs of boots on the steel deck overhead.

Five men, dressed in black combat fatigues, came down the ramp and opened a large shipping container. One of them walked over. He was young, with an almost too pretty face, but there was nothing effeminate about the specially modified M-60 machine gun in his hands.

"Ma'am, we'd consider it an honor, if you'd allow us to join you."

Aleecia stood and walked over to him. "We appreciate it, but this may be a one way trip. Besides, you could be court-martialed for going."

"Yes, ma'am," the corner of his mouth lifted into a half smile. "It wouldn't be the first time we've butted heads with the skipper. After all, ma'am, we're Navy SEALs."

* * * * *

The sun was hanging low in the sky when they pushed the sleds out the starboard hatch and followed feet first into the water of Korea Bay. Aleecia was the last one to depart the ship.

They followed the same procedure as before. Single file through the slow moving picket ships, deep under the circle of containment ships.

The six sleds broke off, heading full speed to the ships scattered around the perimeter.

Thirty minutes later, Aleecia approached the hull of the salvage ship. All the members of the combined Omega Sentry and Navy SEALs were waiting. On her signal, they scattered out along the length of the hull, ready for the rescue to begin.

Aleecia crept like a shadow up over the low side. As an armed guard turned toward her, her wrist snapped. The man went down with a strangled gurgle as he attempted to pull the five-pointed steel star from his throat.

A Korean sailor across the deck slumped down as Carlos pulled his knife from the man's ribs. The soft *putt putt* of a silenced weapon sounded in her ear. High up on the superstructure another North Korean died.

Aleecia ran across the deck and into a soldier with a weapon pointed at one of the SEALs. She knocked the gun aside with a sharp blow of her forearm, brought her right leg up to her side, and lashed out with a kick to his chin.

With a heavy grunt, the man staggered backward into the steel bulkhead. She stepped to the side, spun, and delivered a kick to the side of his head.

The man died on his feet with a broken neck.

Aleecia ducked through a hatch and proceeded into the ship's superstructure. She looked at her watch and smiled. Five minutes remained before the North Korean Navy started having fewer ships.

In those five minutes, they had to find Stephanie.

An officer came down the passageway. She ducked out of sight and waited. As he passed her, she stepped out.

"You can live," she spoke in perfect Japanese, "if you tell me where the American is." The laser dot of the silenced Micro Uzi steadied in at the base of the officer's head.

"Go ahead," he laughed. "I will not tell you. Your people cannot ..."

Aleecia didn't have time to listen to his empty prattle. *putt, putt* Blood splattered on the bulkhead, and he fell lifeless on the deck.

A young seaman stepped out of a door, and Aleecia stuck the Uzi in his face. "You can join your officer, or live. Tell me where the American is."

He glanced down to the floor and his eyes opened wide. "She's in the engine room. Down there." The Korean sailor looked at a closed door.

"Thank you." Aleecia spun the man around and the knife-edge of her hand came down across the back of his neck. He dropped soundlessly to the deck. "I wouldn't sleep too long. You're liable to drown."

The outside hatch behind her opened, and she spun around. The laser dot lined up on Scott's chest.

"She's below deck. We have to hurry." Aleecia grabbed the long handle across the door and pulled. The steel clamps holding the heavy hatch moved out of the way, and it swung open. Aleecia stepped through the open hatchway.

The heat boiling up out of the hole in the deck was stifling. Descending into it was even worse. Breathing the super heated air was difficult, and beads of sweat formed, running into her eyes. On the first landing, a North Korean officer was coming up the ladder. Aleecia's wrist blurred as she released another star. He grabbed at his face as the deadly disk of steel sliced deep into his eye. Aleecia slid down the railing and her foot connected with the man's throat.

On the last landing, she ducked down, hoping Scott wouldn't move or make any sudden noises. The scene before her was sickening.

Stephanie lay stretched across a steel table. Her arms and legs were tied at the four corners. Blood covered the table from dozens of cuts crisscrossing her body.

"Tell me Stephanie, how do you intend to take the warhead from North Korean waters?" The interrogator slapped her across the face. Stephanie's head rolled to the side with the blow.

"You will talk, eventually. Why not make it easier on yourself? You don't have Fish Girl anymore. I took care of her. How's the General planning to get their precious nuke back?"

"Fuck you." Stephanie raised her bruised face, and spit on the man's shirt.

"Oh, you want to fuck again?" His sadistic laughter filled the room. "Why didn't you say so?" he motioned to one of the nearby men.

Aleecia watched in horror as an officer walked over, dropped his pants, and started to climb on the table.

Her hand reached inside her blouse and in a blur extended. The officer screamed in pain and looked at his cock lying on the table. She grabbed the magnesium strip from a side pouch, hit the detonator, and threw it across the engine room. It started burning before it hit the steel deck.

She heard Scott's Uzi firing to the right of her, and she went over the left side. Aleecia landed eighteen feet below in a crouch on the steel deck.

The bright light of the magnesium disappeared almost as fast as it started. Within seconds, seawater started gushing through the hole burned through the ship's outer hull. The room filled with steam, the sound of gunfire, screams of men dying, and the ever-rising water.

A crewmember grabbed Aleecia as she made her way towards Stephanie. Aleecia kicked back and up with her foot, connecting with a knee, and her elbow slammed to his ribs. He let go of his hold.

Spinning around, she jumped up, stretched out her leg, and delivered a deadly axe kick to the back of his neck.

Rotating backwards, she landed on the balls of her feet, and lashed out as another face appeared in the thickening steam. The heel of her hand caught the man in the nose.

The man's yell of pain ended as she shoved the broken bone into the man's brain.

She reached the table as the interrogator stood poised, ready to plunge a knife into Stephanie's breast. Aleecia's finger tightened on the trigger sending six bullets into his torso.

The water was up to her knees and rising quickly. Grabbing the knife from the dead man's hand, Aleecia cut the restraints holding Stephanie's arms and legs.

"What took you so long?" Stephanie's voice was weak.

"The mission came first." Aleecia threw Stephanie over her left shoulder and waded through the water. A Korean soldier came down another ladder and opened fire. Bullets slashed through the water inches from her legs.

She reached into her harness and turned. Closing her eyes, she visualized in her mind where the man stood. With a flick of her wrist, a star whirled through the thick mist. She heard the man's scream and the clank of his weapon hitting steel.

Scott was standing at the foot of the ladder. The laser sights of the Uzi swept through the steam-laden air above her head. He reached out and took Stephanie from her shoulders.

"I've got her. Let's get the hell out of here." He followed Aleecia up to the main deck.

Two SEALs stood guarding the door. The passageway was littered with dead bodies.

Alarms were starting to sound throughout the ship. On deck she took a whistle from her pocket, blew it three times, and ran for the side.

As she jumped over the side, the water around several of the perimeter ships glowed with burning magnesium.

* * * * *

Upon their arrival back at the *Belleau-Wood*, Stephanie was taken straight to Medical, while armed marines confiscated their weapons and escorted them under guard to the Captain.

The Executive Officer stood off to the side, out of the way of the red-faced Skipper. The Captain stopped his pacing in front of Aleecia. "I don't know who the *hell* you think you are, but this is *my* ship. Do you understand? My fucking ship!"

He stepped in front of pretty boy, "And *you!* You, I can court-martial. I hope you fucking like small cages and bars, 'cause when I get through with you, that's all you'll ever see. Do you understand me, Lieutenant?"

"Sir. Yes, sir!"

"If the rescue attempt itself wasn't hair-brained enough, whose bright idea was it to try and sink half their damn Navy?"

"Mine, sir." Aleecia snapped.

"Yours?" The Skipper stepped back in front of Aleecia.

The muscles in his neck bulged. His nostrils flared, and a nerve twitched in his right eye.

"Yes, sir. Diversionary tactic to cover our escape, sir."

He turned and paced in front of them finally stopping in front of the Navy Lieutenant SEAL. "Why did you go along with this?"

"Sir. She's an American, serving her country, sir." He paused, "And for the Pueblo, sir. For what the North Koreans did to our men. We couldn't sit back doing nothing and allow anyone else to go through what they did, especially a woman."

The phone rang and the Executive Officer picked it up, listened and hung up. "Skipper, you are wanted in Communications. An Urgent Flash message arrived for you."

The Skipper stomped out of the Wardroom and slammed the door.

The Exec walked over to Aleecia. A smile played at his lips as he stuck his hand out. "Personally, and off the record, I want to say you did one hell of a job kicking ass today."

She took his hand. "Thank you, sir."

"At ease. You may be seated." The Commander walked over to a pot and poured a cup of steaming black coffee. "Help yourselves. I wish I had something stronger to offer."

Aleecia got up, poured a cup, took a sip, and gasped, "Commander, if this was any stronger, we wouldn't need cups."

A shrill whistle split the air. "This is your Captain speaking." His voice boomed from a speaker on the bulkhead. "All ships have been ordered to leave Korea Bay immediately and proceed to normal stations. Secure from General Quarters. That is all."

Spontaneous cheering broke out in the Wardroom as members of Omega Sentry and the Navy SEALs shouted and hugged each other. The ship rumbled as the giant propellers bit into the water. The Wardroom door opened and slammed shut.

"Attention on Deck!"

Everyone froze and snapped to attention as the Skipper walked to the front of the room and stopped in front of the Lieutenant. "You step foot in this Wardroom again with so much as a shoe-lace untied, and I'll have your ass in the galley scrubbing pots and pans.

"At ease." The Captain sat on the edge of the desk, one foot swinging in the air. "I have a message here which states: To the Omega Sentry personnel. Deeply grateful for the successful completion of your mission and I share in the loss of those whose lives were lost. This country owes you a debt of gratitude for your courage and sacrifice in the midst of grave danger. To the Commanding Officer, USS *Belleau-Wood*, LHA-3: Ensure your guests stay on the *Belleau-Wood* is as comfortable as possible until arrangements are made for their return to Tokyo." He looked out over the group. "Signed, Commander-in-Chief, President of the United States."

"Putting my own personal feelings aside, in relation to this message from the President…congratulations on a job well done.

I'll turn you over to the Executive Officer. He'll make sure you get fed and a room assigned."

The Skipper left, and the Executive Officer smiled. "It may take a couple hours to get you a bed for the night. The cooks will have a meal ready in half that time. Until then, feel free to move about the ship."

Scott took Aleecia by the hand and led her down the passageway, through a watertight steel hatch, and out onto the port catwalk. The pounding roar of the waves crashing against the ship filled the wind as it tore at their clothes.

They went on deck and walked back to the stern. A wide wake, frothy white in the moonlight, stretched out behind them and became lost in the night, out where the stars touched the sea.

"I love you," Scott yelled against the wind.

"I love you, too," she wrapped her arms around his waist.

"Will you marry me?"

Aleecia leaned back in his arms. "What did you say?"

"I asked you if you would be my wife."

Aleecia smiled and kissed him. "That's what I thought you said. It sounded so wonderful I wanted to hear it again."

"So, is that a yes?"

"Yes! Oh, yes." On the flight deck of the USS *Belleau-Wood*, under the light of a pale moon, Aleecia danced to a symphony of love, playing in her heart. "Yes!"

Epilogue

The fire crackled in the fireplace sending sparks up the chimney. A chilly wind blew off of Table Rock Lake, and whistled through the trees. A year had passed and it was time for another Project Aware lake clean-up. It felt good to be home.

Aleecia lay naked under a blanket with Scott's warm body pressed against her back. So many things had happened to her since this loving man had come into her life. And although many of them had been difficult, she wouldn't trade a single one.

Her eyes rested fondly on the picture of the Commanding Officer of the USS *Belleau-Wood*. It was taken with Scott and her, right after he had pronounced them man and wife.

The tiny gold Dolphins over her breast had been a wedding present from the SEALs. The Lieutenant had presented them to her as an honorary SEAL, for bravery and courage under fire.

A moment of sadness crept in as she looked upon the kind face of her mother. The General had died of a heart attack shortly after their return from Korea Bay, and he had left it to her in his will. It wasn't until she read the accompanying letter that she understood the significance of the painting. She regretted never knowing her father.

Scott murmured in his sleep as he snuggled closer and covered her swollen belly with his hand. This was probably the greatest gift of all. She prayed her daughter would always have them around to love and guide her, but the future was never certain with Omega Sentry. Life for their little girl would be difficult enough growing up with gills, but she couldn't worry about it.

Omega Sentry would watch over her if something should ever happen to them.

Aleecia pulled a letter from under the pillow. She had almost thrown it away but her curiosity had prevented her from tossing it in the trash. She wasn't sure why she had hidden it from Scott, or why she had waited so long to open it.

Tearing the envelope open, she pulled out the letter.

Dearest Aleecia,

I was heartbroken when you ran off with Scott to get married. I felt that you at least owed me an explanation for breaking things off.

It's cold here in Alaska — lonely, too. There's not much to do except count the bears. Anyway, I shall always think fondly of you and hope you don't regret your hasty decision.

Love always,

Gary.

She started giggling, and covered her mouth with her hand. As her laughter grew, Scott woke and rose up on his elbow.

"What's so funny?"

Stuffing the letter back under the pillow, she turned to him. "I love you."

"So...you're laughing because you love me?" He had a puzzled look on his face.

"Yes, ah, no. I'm laughing because your love makes me happy."

Scott lowered his head, and her heart soared as he reaffirmed his love with a kiss.

The End

About the author:

R. Casteel welcomes mail from readers. You can write c/o Ellora's Cave Publishing at P.O. Box 787, Hudson, Ohio 44236-0787.

Also by R. CASTEEL:

- The Crimson Rose
- Taneika: Daughter of the Wolf
- Texas Thunder

Why an electronic book?

We live in the Information Age—an exciting time in the history of human civilization in which technology rules supreme and continues to progress in leaps and bounds every minute of every hour of every day. For a multitude of reasons, more and more avid literary fans are opting to purchase e-books instead of paperbacks. The question to those not yet initiated to the world of electronic reading is simply: *why?*

1. *Price.* An electronic title at Ellora's Cave Publishing runs anywhere from 40-75% less than the cover price of the <u>exact same title</u> in paperback format. Why? Cold mathematics. It is less expensive to publish an e-book than it is to publish a paperback, so the savings are passed along to the consumer.
2. *Space.* Running out of room to house your paperback books? That is one worry you will never have with electronic novels. For a low one-time cost, you can purchase a handheld computer designed specifically for e-reading purposes. Many e-readers are larger than the average handheld, giving you plenty of screen room. Better yet, hundreds of titles can be stored within your new library—a single microchip. (Please note that Ellora's Cave does not endorse any specific brands. You can check our website at www.ellorascave.com for customer recommendations we make available to new consumers.)

3. *Mobility.* Because your new library now consists of only a microchip, your entire cache of books can be taken with you wherever you go.
4. *Personal preferences are accounted for.* Are the words you are currently reading too small? Too large? Too...**ANNOYING**? Paperback books cannot be modified according to personal preferences, but e-books can.
5. *Innovation.* The way you read a book is not the only advancement the Information Age has gifted the literary community with. There is also the factor of what you can read. Ellora's Cave Publishing will be introducing a new line of interactive titles that are available in e-book format only.
6. *Instant gratification.* Is it the middle of the night and all the bookstores are closed? Are you tired of waiting days—sometimes weeks—for online and offline bookstores to ship the novels you bought? Ellora's Cave Publishing sells instantaneous downloads 24 hours a day, 7 days a week, 365 days a year. Our e-book delivery system is 100% automated, meaning your order is filled as soon as you pay for it.

Those are a few of the top reasons why electronic novels are displacing paperbacks for many an avid reader. As always, Ellora's Cave Publishing welcomes your questions and comments. We invite you to email us at service@ellorascave.com or write to us directly at: P.O. Box 787, Hudson, Ohio 44236-0787.

Printed in the United States
22879LVS00008B/58-66

9 781843 605713